Leslie Connor

a Home for Goddesses and Dogs

KATHERINE TEGEN BOOKS
An Imprint of HarperCollins Publishers

Katherine Tegen Books is an imprint of HarperCollins Publishers.

A Home for Goddesses and Dogs
Copyright © 2020 by Leslie Connor

Library of Congress Cataloging-in-Publication Data
Names: Connor, Leslie, author.
Title: A home for goddesses and dogs / Leslie Connor.
Description: First edition. | New York : Katherine Tegen Books, [2020] |
    Audience: Ages 10 up. | Audience: Grades 4–6. | Summary: "After the
    death of her mother, Lydia moves in with her aunts and learns to find a
    new family of inspiring women and loving dogs."— Provided by
publisher.
Identifiers: LCCN 2019033128 | ISBN 978-0-06-279679-0 (paperback)
Subjects: CYAC: Grief—Fiction. | Aunts—Fiction. | Lesbians—Fiction. |
    Dogs—Fiction. | Family life—Connecticut—Fiction. |
    Connecticut—Fiction.
Classification: LCC PZ7.C7644 Hom 2020 | DDC [Fic]—dc23
LC record available at https://lccn.loc.gov/2019033128

Interior illustrations © 2020 by Julie McLaughlin
Typography by Laura Mock
21 22 23 24 25   PC/BRR   10 9 8 7 6 5 4 3 2 1
❖
First trade paperback edition, 2022

I looked across the lot to where Aunt Brat was standing. A large yellow dog sat beside her, upright and alert. The hairs on his thick coat lifted in the wind while he surveyed the yard in a nervous, not-sure-what-to-do sort of way. He pushed out a bark now and then. But he also looked up at Aunt Brat every so often and dipped his pointy ears and licked his lips. That looked like a happy thing somehow. I wondered if he liked plain or suede shoe leather best. Would canvas be just as satisfying?

"What say we go check him out?" Eileen said. "Huh-haw!"

Also by Leslie Connor

For Jan & Elly
and Sandi & Nancy—
so much love

a Home for Goddesses and Dogs

all Things Boxy

"*You'll be all* right. You come from strong."

That had been my mother's refrain. (One of them.) I would've given anything to hear her say it again, right then, in her voice. But that wasn't going to happen. All I could do was think those words. Not the same.

Lydia Bratches-Kemp, don't feel lonely for her . . . not right now . . . don't feel anything . . . tuck it away.

I buckled myself into the front seat of Aunt Brat's boxy car. Funny. Boxy car, a box on my lap, and outside the window was the little box of a house that I was leaving behind. We could never name the color of that siding. It wasn't white enough to be white, not yellow enough to be cream. The grayish stains the house wore down its front could not be named either, though Mom and I had once tried.

"Look, it's changing color," she'd said. "It must be bored! What do you think we have there, Lydia? Dove-feather gray? Maybe iris mist?"

Today, the thin line of aluminum that framed the windows picked up a dull bluish light from somewhere in the winter sky. The outside of the house was nothing like the inside. Mom had spent the two years since my grandmother had died "personalizing the place," as she'd called it. She'd made little stone-and-mosaic altars to the seasons on the windowsills—with a glue gun. She'd painted moon art on top of Grandma's worn-out wallpaper, and we'd lettered lyrics and poems across the jambs and around the light switches. Mom called it our "happy retaliation after the fact."

We'd loved Grandma the way one loves a family's most difficult member. But she'd made that house feel like a trap. No wonder Mom had wanted us to let loose on the place once Grandma was gone.

Now Mom was gone too. It may sound impossible, but I was prepared—as much as one can be. When it came to death, Mom had been everything from mad to matter-of-fact, to jokey and irreverent, *and*—I'd always thought—forgiving. Her bluntness had made some people uncomfortable. But I'd grown up with it.

We had talked about the day I'd be "finally fully

orphaned." We'd talked about Aunt Brat too. She was my last of kin. I'd go live with her one day. And here that day was; it just happened to be New Year's Eve.

I cupped my hands on the sides of the box on my lap. The driver's-side door opened and I watched my aunt let herself into the car. She swept the fabric of her long boot skirt in with her. She slammed the door shut against a gust of Rochester's winter breath.

I had watched my aunt in recent days. She was tall, and even inside the tiny rooms of the little house, she'd managed to take long strides. I could *hear* that skirt swishing. When she'd reached up to empty the kitchen cupboards her arms seemed to sweep up there, almost like she was performing a solo stadium wave. It seemed familiar, though she'd only ever visited a handful of times.

Grandma and Aunt Brat had never gotten along. Mom had always said she longed to see her older sister more. They'd stayed telephone close. Well, less so in recent years. After Grandma died, I figured Aunt Brat would visit. Maybe even a lot. But then I'd overhear Mom lying to my aunt on the phone. We were fine. Her health was good. (It wasn't.)

"You've got your job and a busy life, Brat," Mom would say. "I'll let you know when things get dicey with this cruddy heart of mine."

I'd felt bad for my aunt these past few days. She wasn't as well prepared for this as I was. I had cried. Plenty. But if death was a dog of a thing—and my mother had said it would be—Aunt Brat seemed harder bitten. She had lost it more than once, convulsing into tears, as we'd cleared out the little house.

"I'm sorry," she'd said when she'd broken down in front of me. "I just wish I had known Holly was failing. I wish she'd called. I would have come."

Now, she smoothed herself into the driver's seat and pulled the belt across her body. She pressed the key into the ignition and shot me a small smile—one a lot like my mother's—as the car started up. She shook back her gray hair, cut blunt as broom straw to meet her shoulders.

"Are you buckled, Lydia?"

"Yes," I said.

"Perfect," she said. "At least it's not snowing." She checked her mirrors and dialed up some heat. Off we rolled, away from the little house of unnameable color— away from my home for the last seven years. It'd be put up for sale now. Aunt Brat planned to use the money to pay the last of our Rochester bills. She hoped there'd be a little "college nest egg" left for me.

"Don't worry," Aunt Brat said. She pulled onto the highway. "You're not trapped. I promise I won't talk at you for the whole trip."

"And I won't do that to you either," I said. We smiled.

"However, it is a long ride. We might want to cover a few things." She looked away from the road for a second to glance at me. "You can ask me anything. Hope you know that."

"Thanks," I said. But I couldn't make her the same offer. I hugged the box I was holding on my lap. I probably sighed a little.

"Are you sure you want to hold that? There's still plenty of room in the back," Aunt Brat said.

"This is fine," I said. I knew it seemed like a weird choice. The box was not heavy, but it was tall enough that it came up to my chest.

I glanced over my shoulder toward the back of the car. I knew what was there: two suitcases of clothes (neither very big), one box of books, and a very cool old wooden art chest, with stacking trays inside.

I drummed my fingers lightly on the box I held. This one was full of, well, paper stuff. Most important, a thick stack of collages: the goddesses.

2

The Goddess of the Third Heart

Mom and I had made the goddesses over the past several years. They'd started out as black-and-white photographs in an old folio. Gold letters on the cover read: "Wasserman Studios, Cleveland, Ohio. 1946." How that folio made its way from Cleveland to a flea market in Rochester is anybody's guess, but that's where we'd found it.

Leave it to Mom: she'd dug the folio out of a steamer trunk full of "paper treasures from the past," as she'd called them. The vendor had dragged a lawn chair over so Mom could sit while she'd leafed through the photographs—and not just because she'd wanted the twelve dollars and fifty cents Mom had eventually paid. No. That vendor had not been afraid to notice the person who'd carted her oxygen into the booth. (You'd be surprised how often we were ignored, how often people looked away.)

The Wasserman photos were all of women. There were brides and debutantes, sunbathers and gardeners. Some were head-and-shoulder portraits, others showed the women standing full height or reclined on summer lawns. All seemed dull eyed.

"Look at them, Lyddie," Mom had said. She'd run her fingers along the edges of the thick, sturdy papers.

I'd shrugged. "They're kind of boring," I'd said.

"Yes, so posed, so staid and obedient. Yuck!" With a devilish grin she'd added, "I think we must get them home and begin to release them to their greater purpose."

She'd gotten the price down by half, and they were ours.

A few days later, I'd found her with one of the portraits— a bride cradling a bouquet—only Mom had collaged a heart over the tops of the flowers. It was not a valentine heart. No, she had cut out an illustration from an old anatomy book; the heart had ventricles, valves, and an aorta. Mom had painted red and blue spaghetti strands from the heart to a little door she'd made in the bride's chest.

"Mom, what is it?" I'd asked. She'd sat looking at it and not minding at all that her paintbrush was leaving drips.

"Hmm . . . I'm going to call her the Goddess of the Third Heart."

I'd felt my own heart sink. All we'd ever wanted was for Mom to get the heart transplant she'd needed. But when she'd been passed up for a third time she'd taken herself off the list.

"It's all good," she'd said. "This is my way of wishing that third heart along on whatever journey it took without me. Here," she'd said, and she'd handed me the paintbrush. "Practice positivity, Lyddie." Then she'd squeezed a fresh dollop of paint onto her palette—plum purple.

The Goddess of the Third Heart was the first of many goddesses, and they were tops on my list of things to bring with me. Well, equal to Mom's long seafoam-green sweater. But that didn't need to be packed because I wore it every day. Indoors. Outdoors. To bed. My second skin. Aunt Brat had left me alone to pack and I'd liked that. For the most part, it'd been clear to me what to leave and what to take. As for the goddesses, I knew that I needed them. But I also needed to keep them to myself.

The holiday and birthday cards, also with my paper stuff, were from my totally off-duty father. (When we spoke of him we called him Kemp.) I probably didn't need the cards at all—seven years' worth of store-bought sentiments, most of them never opened. The few that were opened still had cash folded inside. That's what he did: he sent cards and money. Money I never felt I could spend. If I had fooled myself about him when I was younger, well, I didn't anymore. He was out there, living not so far from Rochester. (I'd seen his return address.) But I never saw him and didn't think of him as family. With Mom gone, I was nobody's daughter.

When Aunt Brat and I had gone to the post office to arrange to have the mail forwarded, she'd put Mom's name on the form. Then she'd turned from the counter. "We better fill out a form for you too, Lydia." Immediately, I'd thought of those cards.

"I never get any any mail," I'd said. I'd felt a wash of relief. *No more cards. Done!*

But what about the bunch I'd already received? They'd been the last items in my "undecided" pile as I'd packed up.

Aunt Brat had popped her head into the room to say, "If you aren't sure about something, bring it anyway. You can always *divest* of it later."

Divest. Good word.

When we'd come down to the wire, I'd quickly double bagged the cards—with two thoughts in my head. First, keep the cards together. Second, keep them from touching my good stuff. Then I'd thought, *Don't contaminate the goddesses.*

The boxy car hummed down the highway. I'm not sure when or where I drifted off. Last thing I heard was Aunt Brat saying something about the Berkshire Mountains and losing the radio. I fell asleep leaning forward, with my right cheek and ear on the top of that box.

I woke up thoroughly confused, willing my eyes open and trying to bring my mother's face into focus while she gently touched my shoulder. . . .

Wait . . . you're not Mom. . . .

"Oh. Aunt Brat," I said.

"Sorry to wake you," she said. "I need some coffee. Anything for you? French fries? A bathroom break?"

"No. No thanks," I said. "I'll wait here." I used my sweater sleeve to wipe drool from the side of my face.

Lydia . . . you probably look like a glazed doughnut. . . .

I was awake for the rest of the trip, but I played possum for a while. When we crossed into Connecticut, Aunt Brat turned off the highway onto long roads that narrowed into hilly, country places.

"We're close," she said. "Close to Chelmsford now."

I watched the miles of woods and meadows. A warm snow began to fall—the kind that makes fat flakes that fall so slowly you can pick one out and follow it down.

Well, I thought, *at least it's pretty.*

3

Up Pinnacle Hill

The hill was a challenge for the boxy car. I heard and felt gravel slipping out from under Aunt Brat's tires. But when we got to the crest the land flattened out for what must have been many acres. A pasture met a meadow, and the meadow met the woods. Everything was dressed in a thin layer of the wet snow. Light glowed in the windows of the farmhouse. This was my first look at Pinnacle Hill Farm.

I had landed inside of a painting, I thought. Then I got such a pang. Mom would have loved this. She had been a country person who because of her health had to live close to the city.

Aunt Brat had told me how she and her wife, Eileen, had come to live on the farm, which belonged to an old,

old man with an unusual name. It was one of the things we'd covered during our five-and-a-half-hour car ride.

"It was serendipitous," she'd said. "A good arrangement with good timing. Elloroy needed someone to come in and cook dinner, and stay a little while each evening. We started off that way. Meanwhile, Eileen and I had been searching for a place where I could be close to the university. Eileen wanted barns and a good patch of land for . . ." Aunt Brat had paused there. She'd shaken her head. "Well, she had a project at the time but she's taken a job at the local feedstore now. Elloroy felt he had more house than he could fill up 'all by his skinny self.'" Aunt Brat had smiled warmly as she'd imitated the old man. "So we proposed that we move in with him. We offered to buy food for the three of us. We'd cook, keep house, and pay a little rent. He said yes to everything except the rent, the old sweetheart." She'd drummed her gloved fingers on the steering wheel, tilted her head back and forth a few times. "The place splits up nicely for the three of us."

Three about to be four. . . .

"We'd never leave Elloroy now," she'd added. "We love him. It's been a few years. I'd say it's working."

I'd nodded. How would I fit in? What was my role? Maybe the "young and strong" one? I was going to look for ways to be useful.

Now, as we pulled up in front of the farmhouse a woman

12

came tottering out of the door and down the porch steps to greet us. She ran her hands through her short brush of brown hair. I looked at Aunt Brat.

"Is that your Eileen?" I asked.

"Yes. My Eileen," she said. The softness of her eyes said *love*. I felt a little bud of warmth at my core.

Aunt Brat popped the locks on our doors. We unfolded our travel-weary selves from the car. I turned to set my box on the seat for the time being. (I'd kept it on my lap the whole way.)

Eileen was beaming. We'd heard about her—Mom and I—but we'd never met her. I knew Mom was sorry about that. Aunt Brat and Eileen shared a pair of glad-to-see-you grins as we stepped out of the car.

"We made it!" Aunt Brat called. She stretched her back. "Eileen, say hello to Lydia." She presented me with both her hands upturned. I pushed out a smile for Eileen and noticed the tall skinny dog whose pointed nose kept bumping into Eileen's butt. It was one of those racing dogs—a greyhound—and it pranced around the car with moves that made me think of a carousel pony gone free from its pole. I wasn't used to dogs. But this one seemed okay—maybe even sweet. It wiggled, shivered, and bowed its narrow head. Brat cupped the dog's chin fondly. "Hello, Soonie! Who's a good girl?"

It seemed safe to take my eyes off the dog, so I focused

on Eileen. She was looking at me too, eyebrows high and a smile that sliced up into her two round cheeks. "So, Lydia Bratches-Kemp, is it?" (She emphasized the Bratches part.) "I'm to be living with Big Brat and Little Brat now, am I? Huh-haw!" Then she moved in close to me, put her arms around me long enough to say, "I'm sorry about your momma. Truly." She gave me a squeeze before she let me go.

"Thank you," I said. "We're doing okay." That sounded weird. I knew it. I was so used to telling people about Mom and me—that *we* were fine or *we* were managing all right—while she was sick. Her death was still new. I didn't feel done being part of a team.

Aunt Brat nodded almost like she was acknowledging my thought. I wondered, *Is she going to be able to read my mind?*

"Well," said Eileen, "guess you know it, I'm Eileen! And I'm called Eileen, because *I lean*!" She tilted sideways a little and bounced up and down on one leg.

Aunt Brat covered her own mouth with one hand as if she felt both embarrassed and pleased. "Oh Eileen, don't do that. . . ."

I plastered on a smile. What I really was, was surprised. All I could do was stare at Eileen because the thing was, Eileen *did* lean.

"Had a motorcycle accident once," she explained. "Shattered femur. Left me with one leg shorter than the other. I'm incapable of standing straight." She tried it just to prove her point. "So, *I lean*! Huh-haw! Lost my spot with the New York City Rockettes over it." She hooked her thumbs into her olive-green overalls and did little kicks, side to side.

"The Rockette part is a joke, Lydia," said Aunt Brat.

"Oh," I said. "Okay."

"But I do love to dance," said Eileen. She twirled— pretty gracefully.

Before there could be any attempts at high kicking, someone else came out onto the dusting of snow. It might be simplest to say he was the oldest man I'd ever seen. Still, he moved easily down the steps, holding only lightly on to the rail. This had to be the guy who owned the place. What was his name? Aunt Brat had said it at least once. Something unusual . . .

Before Aunt Brat could introduce me, the man spoke. "Lydia Bratches-Kemp." His voice rolled out slowly and sounded like he had a few marbles tucked into one cheek. "Pleased to meet you, youth and beauty," he said. I stepped forward to shake his hand.

He was as tall as the doorway he'd come through, in spite of a forward bend around the middle of his chest, which surely cost him several inches of height. A pair of super-thick glasses balanced on the bridge of his nose and made his eyes look extraordinarily large. His skin was brown and freckled all over. His hair was white and looked like it'd landed on his head much the way the light snow had landed on the earth all around us. *He's got a dusting of hair*, I thought.

He extended his hand to me, long and flat as a canoe paddle. I closed my hand around his. His skin was soft, his bones and veins close underneath.

He looked at me through ice-cube-thick glasses. "Don't mind my bug eyes," he told me. (Another mind reader? I was in trouble.) "Glad they work at all, I'm so old. I'm ninety . . ." He stopped to think, jaw slack and bobbing slightly. "Ninety . . . *something*," he said. He waved one hand in the air. "Eh, sometimes I know it, sometimes I don't. But at least I'm *almost there*," he added.

"Almost where?" I asked. I'm pretty sure I heard Aunt Brat let out a groan, as if she dreaded what was coming next.

"Dead!" he said. "I'm *almost* dead. I can hardly wait."

"Elloroy!" Aunt Brat's face pinked up. She looked at me. "He says that all the time." She seemed to want me to know that.

"Well, huh-haw!" said Eileen. She fidgeted.

I blinked. I knew what they were doing. Mom had said

it more than once: "You're going to find that some peo-ple are uncomfortable with death, Lyddie. Especially with dead mothers."

Now that I had one I was beginning to understand. As for the ancient man standing in front of me, well, maybe they'd forgotten to tell him why I was here. Or maybe he was like Mom and just didn't think everyone should be so uncomfortable about something that was going to happen to us all. I really wanted to ask him more. I wanted to tell him that I'd just seen a death come. Or a life leave. Or a vessel fail. Whichever you wanted to say about it, and I could make cases for all three. But now seemed not the time. I winched up a smile for the old man.

"Well, it's very nice to meet you, El . . . umm . . ." I wasn't sure about his name. It was like Elroy . . . or Ellery, but not exactly. I had definitely heard *roy* at the end. Con-fused, I finished with, "Sir."

"It's *Ell-o-roy*." Brat helped me out. I think she was relieved to be moving past the death thing.

"Rhymes with 'Jell-O boy,'" Eileen chimed in, and she pinched the air with her fingers. What a gift. Now I would never forget.

"Ell-o-roy," I said clearly. "Well, dead or alive, it's nice to meet you." I gulped. I'd been there all of seven minutes and I'd blurted at least two very weird things. That had to be a record.

Eileen snorted, then let out a laugh.

I decided not to speak again—possibly ever. But then I noticed that Elloroy was wearing a big, open turtle-mouth smile. "Dead or alive. I like that," he said.

Aunt Brat cleared her throat. "So. I assume we are all set inside?" She dipped her chin at Eileen. "The room?"

"Ready to receive," said Eileen. She'd somehow gotten past me and was reaching into the car to get my box off the passenger's seat.

"Eileen, Lydia will get that one," Aunt Brat said. She circled her arm toward the rear of the car. She popped the hatch. "Come help me here."

Eileen went around and they grabbed my suitcases.

"I can come back for those," I offered.

"We've got them," Aunt Brat said.

"I always carry the purse," Elloroy mumbled. He fell into line ahead of me with Aunt Brat's handbag on one arm.

I have got to be more helpful, I thought.

I wrapped my arms around my box of goddesses and waited for my three new adults and one greyhound to go ahead of me into the house, my new home.

4

A Room of My Own

I stood wiping my feet on a rag rug just inside the door. I took in the simple open space: living room and entry at the front, kitchen at the back, a round dining table in between, and a set of stairs on the right that was set in front of a massive brick chimney that was sending warmth into the house. A closer look and I saw the woodstove tucked back under the open stairs and the neat pile of logs stacked nearby. *That*, I thought. *I'll be the one who keeps that pile high.*

"A small house that makes the most of itself," said Aunt Brat, and I nodded. It was clear that there was more of it too; a door at the bottom of the stairs wore a tilted sign that said Suite Elloroy on it. Sure enough, he hung Aunt Brat's purse on a hook at the entry. He pressed the latch and on his way through the door he said, "Welcome again, Lydia Bratches-Kemp. See you at supper." Then he muttered something about "youth and beauty" again, and the door whined shut behind him.

Aunt Brat and Eileen and I climbed straight up the narrow stairs together. They carried a suitcase apiece, and I carried my box. Soonie, it turned out, had a habit of shooting the gap on the stairs. Nobody warned me. I bumped into the wall as the dog cruised by.

"Greyhound. She *must* win," Eileen announced. The dog stood at the top of the stairs stepping in place, her long toenails clicking on the floorboards. She blinked her fawn eyes. I made a note: *Get used to that dog*.

Aunt Brat lengthened all her verbs as we made a sharp turn in the narrow upper hall alongside the warm chimney. "We don't want you to *feeeel* like we're *duumping* you in a laundry room . . ."

"But we are!" Eileen said. "Huh-haw!" She hoisted my suitcase way up to her chest. I couldn't help thinking: *Eileen leans backward*.

"This was our storage room and we did fold laundry in here . . . ," Aunt Brat said. She pressed the black iron latch and pushed the door open. She took a look inside. I saw her turn to smile at Eileen. "But it's a real room," Brat said, "and it has light from the big window."

Eileen let my suitcase down. "Yeah, and we climb in and out of that to use the 'clothes dryer.'" She drew quotes in the air with her fingers. Soonie tip-tapped her way over to the window as if she expected someone to go out there that very second.

"The dryer?" I stretched up to look out. I saw a folding wooden clothes rack collapsed flat right outside on the roof. "Oh. I see," I said.

"Oopsy. Meant to drag that in," Eileen said.

"So that's the flattish roof over the front porch, isn't it?" I tried to orient myself. All the while I took in the sweet scent of old wood and cleaning oil.

"Flattish! Good word," said Eileen. "I like that. It's a little spongy out there too." She flexed her knees. "But I haven't fallen off it yet. I sure have smacked my noggin on that window jamb a few times, though." She gave her head a brisk rub.

Aunt Brat said, "We'll find a new place for the drying rack. You'll have privacy here," she promised. "We do have a *real* dryer downstairs next to the *real* washing machine. We just like sun-dried clothes. And besides, that machine lacks energy efficiency."

I was learning that my aunt Brat could be very precise.

"You mean rumbles like thunder," Eileen said, precise in her own way. "When that thing is running, I can't hear myself think; can't smell myself stink." My aunt Brat smiled. Apparently she liked a little dose of nonsense mixed into her precision—particularly if it came from Eileen.

"So Lydia," Brat said, "about this space, your bed pretty much has to go on this long wall, and the dresser on the end here. But it leaves a nice space near the window, and that's just my old sleeping bag opened over the bed. You can pick out a comforter. We'll do anything to help you make it your own. We can paint . . . oh, except for the bricks," Aunt Brat warned. "You've got the short wall of a two-hundred-year-old chimney going right up through here." She patted the old bricks with the flat of her hand. "These babies are antiques. The room is yours, but the bricks belong to Elloroy."

"Got it," I said. I set my box on the bed and went to the front window. I could see across the flattish roof into the front yard. Aunt Brat's car was in view down to the right. My art trunk and boxes were still in the back of it. I stood there gazing just to gaze.

Behind me Aunt Brat and Eileen were talking about a rug for the room and hooks for the back of the old Z-frame door if I wanted. They meant to include me in their conversation. Yet it was going fine without me. Besides, I felt fixed in place the same way it is sometimes impossible to wake from sleep.

"So Lydia," Aunt Brat said, and that did get my attention, "long journey." She laid her hand on her heart, and somehow I knew she meant more than the miles we'd covered by car. "Do you want to unpack a few things on your own while we hustle up supper? Or, would you like one of us to stay and—"

"Enough, Bratches!" Eileen nudged her toward the door. "Let's give her some space in her new . . . *space*."

"Right," said Aunt Brat. But she lingered. I made sure she saw me smiling. I knew she wanted to figure out the right thing to do and do it. But how was anybody supposed to know what that was?

"I'll get the rest of your boxes from the car and bring them up," said Eileen.

"Oh, no. It's okay. I won't need them tonight," I said. "I mean, thank you, but you've done so much, and I can get them in the morning."

"Sure. Whatever!" Eileen steered Aunt Brat and Soonie into the hall. Then she poked her head back in the door to say, "Whatever you do, don't jump on the bed, kiddo. You'll crack your head open." She pointed up. I looked up. It was good advice: the ceiling slanted low over the bed.

They left and I listened to their shoes and Soonie's toenails on the stairs, that descending click-click-click-click. Quiet.

Oh, I felt weird in that room once they were all gone. But I'd felt weird while they were there too. I was tired despite having slept in the car. But it was more than that. Brat and Eileen made me tired too, each in her own way. Or maybe it was just that I was trying too hard to smile at everything. There was so much to get used to.

I looked around the room. "This is it, Lydia," I whispered to myself. "*Your* bed. *Your* windows. *Your* bricks. Correction. Elloroy's bricks." My shoulders slumped and my arms hung from the sockets. None of it felt like mine.

I settled on the bed next to my box. I pulled my mother's sweater close around me and lay back on Aunt Brat's slippery old sleeping bag. I stared up at the slatted ceiling. The knotholes and wood grain looked like yawning faces of old bearded people. And some bears. And foxes.

I thought about the places I had lived. Six years in the first house with both my parents, seven more in Grandma's little-box house in the city.

Then I thought about Mom. Seven years is a long time to be sick and waiting with your name on a list for a donor heart that never comes. It's a long time to bewilder doctors who have given up on you and to be tethered to an oxygen tank when you want to be free. But seven years is also *supposed* to be a short part of any person's whole life. My eyes filled.

Don't do this—not right now.

Too late. The tears ran hot down my temples and wormed through my hair and into my ears. The bears and foxes in the wood grain blurred.

There in the room, where I best not jump on the bed, I missed my mom good and hard. She had been right when she'd said there'd be a lot I wouldn't like. But I thought I would do better than to spill tears like this before I'd even crawled into a new bed for the night. I pulled the cuffs of Mom's sweater over the heels on my hands and rubbed my eyes. The wool I loved to wrap up in so much was rough on my face. I dried my ears. The wetness inside squeaked. I took a breath and let go. Then I heard something else—no? I waited. Yes.

A scratching sound. Fisk-fisk. Skitch-skitch. I scanned the walls of my new room. I listened. Skitch-skitch-skitch. Fisk-fisk-fisk. There. It was coming from right about where the wall met the chimney. I sat up to look. There was a poster—tacked up oddly low—a picture of three woolly sheep, clustered together in a big snow.

Scratch-skitch-skitch-skitch. Scratch.

I gaped at those sheep. They looked back at me, benevolently. "Do not get yourself spooked on the first night, Lydia. Be rational. We've got an old house here, funky roof, tilty floors, and who knows what else?"

I got up off the bed, dragging Aunt Brat's sleeping bag with me. I went to the window at the front of the house, flicked the latch, and pulled it open. I let myself out onto the flattish roof.

5

The Sun-Maid Raisin Lady

I squatted on the porch roof with my back against the house shingles and Aunt Brat's sleeping bag pulled around me. I had some pretty great wet-proof sneaker-boots—lime green with orange laces. Our helper, Angelica, had found them for me, brand-new, at a consignment shop back in Rochester. They came up high on my ankles and had good treads. Good for gripping a slight incline.

Oddly, the air felt warmer now than when we'd arrived. The thin snow was gone and the light was fading. The setting sun had laid a glowing stroke of rose-petal pink behind the bare tree branches where the woods met the meadow.

I whispered, "Mom? Are you seeing this? It's a pink New Year's Eve."

She'd always said one of January's gifts was short days, at least where we lived, and now here as well. Nature was the thing Mom believed in. That's where everyday moments of magic happened. She'd loved all seasons, all kinds of weather. She'd been likely to finish off a goddess collage with a border of vines and berries, a curtain of rainfall, a sun or moon hung overhead. She'd known all the different moons, the symbolic names—and that little bit of instruction that came with each one.

January . . . the Wolf Moon . . . offers protection for all homes and all loved ones . . . write down spring dreams. . . .

The first week in January was the week Mom had always told me, "Lydia, you should start a moon journal." She'd liked to nudge me, always with her wry smile that said, I know you're not going to do this—and you don't have to. Then just last week she'd switched it up. "You could write it in the way of memories." I didn't disagree. But talking about it gave me worry. Each mention of that word—memories—was like fast-forwarding to the day I wouldn't have her anymore.

This day.

Out on the roof my folded legs grew tingly and I wiggled my toes inside my boots. I knew I should get down to the kitchen and see if my new adults needed help with supper. But I stayed, staring out at the open space, imagining that the thin sticks poking up from the meadow with their clumpy heads bowed might be remnants of wildflowers. We'd had a flower garden back in the house from my first six years—the one where I lived with both my parents. We'd called it the House of the Sun-Maid Raisin Lady. That was because of me.

When I was little, I believed that my mother *was* the lady on the raisin box. She had the same chin and the long chestnut curls. Mom didn't have a bonnet, but she had a red canvas hat that she wore for both sun and rain. Mom was a knitter, and while Miss Sun-Maid had her basket full of bunches of green grapes, my mother had one for her yarn. She sat with it across her lap, sometimes in the garden, sometimes on the sofa in front of the window. I'm telling you, those two looked alike.

The first time I used a pair of kiddie scissors it was to cut the flaps off a raisin box. I carried that box around with me all day. I loved the picture of my mother, and I loved the way the box folded flat or stood square at my will. I propped it here and there on windowsills, or with our salt and pepper shakers at the table, and at the back of the sink while I brushed my teeth.

One night my dad came in to hug me good night and found me holding my raisin box and gazing at the picture.

"What do you have there?" he asked. He was a gentle person.

I said, "She's mine."

"But who is she?" I remember him pointing with his pinkie.

"Holly," I said.

"Who?" A smile pushed his beard out on both sides.

"It's Holly."

"You mean Mom?" He started to laugh. He picked me up, raisin box still in my hand, and trotted me to my mother. She was always exhausted by sunset, but even so, she worked at her knitting. She looked worried at first. Why was I out of bed? Was something wrong?

Dad asked me about Miss Sun-Maid again. Again, I said it was Holly. I felt shy. Was this funny? I pushed my face into my father's shirt and he hugged me tight. I felt him chuckling.

"Oh, Lyddie, that is lovely!" Mom said. She reached for the box and I let her take it. She cupped it in her hands. "Look at me," she said. "I'm forever young. I'm famous and delicious. Tah-dah!"

My collection of Sun-Maid boxes grew. I carried them around in a straw purse. I framed the maidens in flower stickers, drew borders on them with markers and crayons. At night I stood them up on my bedside table. Mom called them tiny works of art. The Sun-Maids stayed with us for a long time. They saw some good; they saw some bad. They saw my father leave us.

Now I heard voices below me. Aunt Brat and Eileen were down there beside the car. They must be getting my last two boxes. Oh. Why? I had said I'd get them in the morning. I was afraid they'd see me on the roof and be freaked out. I scrunched myself back against the house with the sleeping bag creeping up around my ears.

"You all right, Brat?" Eileen asked.

"Honestly, I'm exhausted," Brat answered. "But hey, we made quick work of the house. We had a good trip down. And Lydia's holding up like a champ."

Oh . . . yes . . . me . . . the champ. . . .

I wasn't sure about that.

6

Lacking Unpacking

I heard Aunt Brat and Eileen coming up the stairs—
greyhound first, by my guess. I hurried to straighten the
old sleeping bag back over the bed.

"Lydia? Everything okay?"

Flash of panic. I hadn't made a single move toward settling in, unless tucking my box of goddesses under the bed
counted. Did I have time to unzip a suitcase before they
came through that door? Pull the drawers open on the
dresser for the appearance of progress?

I felt a freakish burst of adrenaline. I hefted one suitcase
onto the bed—accidentally slammed the thing against
the wall just as my new adults and their long-legged dog
walked into the room.

There they stood with my boxes in their arms, eyes popping, an O forming on Aunt Brat's lips while Eileen's mouth turned up at one corner in a quizzical way.

"Oh. That was . . . uhh . . . not as heavy as I thought," I said.

"Huh-haw," said Eileen, though a little dully. I think she was eyeing the wall for damage.

I knotted my fingers together. "I—I haven't gotten very far." I shrugged. "I was kind of . . . daydreaming."

"Absolutely fine," said Aunt Brat. She bent her knees and set my art chest down.

"Okay to put this one here for now?" Eileen was chinning toward a spot on the floor near that noisy sheep poster.

"Sure," I chirped. "Thank you. Thank you so much." I spewed enough thank-yous to fill the narrow room from floor to ceiling. How wonderful to finally stop long enough to take a breath in through my nose. I smelled something so good—oniony, garlicky, and tomatoey. Something was baking too; something was getting a golden crust. This was going to save me. "Dinner smells great," I sighed.

"There's a corn bread in the oven," said Aunt Brat. "We're warming up a pot of chili."

"Always better on the second day," said Eileen.

"My mom says the same thing," I offered.

"Holly loved to cook," Aunt Brat said. "I remember coming home for spring break one year. I walked in the door, and something smelled so delicious. I thought I was in the wrong house." Eileen and I laughed. My aunt went on. "There was my little sister—twelve years old—standing at the stove wearing big pot holders on the ends of her skinny arms. Her face looked rosy and warm and her hair was up in a loose bun and she was glowing like . . . I don't know . . . like a little kitchen goddess."

Kitchen Goddess. My heart took a hop. It was like someone had opened a little door on my forehead and looked inside my brain. Or inside the box below my new bed.

"Holly had made a full dinner—appetizer, salad, entrée, dessert—in honor of my visit home. I couldn't believe it," said Brat.

I loved the story. I could *see* my mother, younger than I was now, with her funny pot-holder hands. I saw the chestnut curls and—who knows why—a patchwork of sunny colors all around her. Her cheeks were as pink as a sunset in winter in my picture. There was no oxygen tank. No hint that anything was wrong at all.

7

First Morning

My first morning in the farmhouse was disorienting. For one thing, I was under the covers. Completely. I'd put myself that way the night before, believing there'd be no sleep. Sometime in the night I must have opened up a little breathing hole. Morning was coming in now—the daylight and the smell of coffee. My nose felt cold. I burrowed back under, but I trained my ear on the rest of the house. Was anyone up? Must be . . . because . . . coffee.

I needed to get to the bathroom down the hall. But what if Aunt Brat or Eileen happened to be in there? Or just coming out of their room to go in? I tiptoed into the hallway. The smell of coffee hit me again—stronger this time. I could hear my three new adults down in the kitchen. I padded into the bathroom and closed the door as quietly as I could. I did my thing, then washed my face and brushed my teeth. I pulled back the curtain and peeked at the tub. I got myself all acquainted with the linen closet: plenty of towels, toilet paper, and a variety of feminine products. Good to know.

The house was chilly. I patted one hand along the warm brick chimney wall on my way back to my room. I purposely did not look down off that balcony, because what if they were all below watching for me? Waiting for the new, odd creature in their house—*me*—the stick-skinny girl with the nest of pale hair? I dressed quickly, double tights and double socks. I stopped to warm my back on the bricks. Then I wrapped Mom's sweater close, took a breath, and went on down the stairs.

I wanted to be invisible. But I knew there'd be three pairs of eyes on me the second I rounded the stairs.

There were.

Only, it seemed like just two pairs of eyes and then Elloroy's, which looked like a set of large, wonky insects roaming around inside a couple of ice cubes and possibly working independently. They were so amazing I had to force myself not to stare. All the lips were saying good morning and asking had I slept okay. Aunt Brat and Eileen looked ready to drop their reading materials and launch from their chairs to wait on me. But both held back, as if they had agreed not to overwhelm *the Lydia* with hospitality.

Instead, the skinny dog came tapping across the floor to check me. So, now a fourth set of eyes, cloudy with age. She poked me with her damp nose as if to say, Oh, you stayed the night? I patted her head with just the tips of my fingers—and not for very long. She nudged and nodded and I didn't know what that meant, or if it meant anything. We'd never had a dog. It'd never even come up. Grandma would not have been nice to one. Mom could not have cared for one. Pet ownership wasn't on my radar.

"Well," said Elloroy. (He still sounded like he had a marble in his mouth.) "New Year's Day. I can't believe it."

"Can't believe what?" I asked.

"Can't believe I'm not—"

"Dead," Aunt Brat and Eileen finished his sentence in unison.

"Told you. He says that all the time," Aunt Brat said.

"Wait until you're old, too," he told her.

Aunt Brat smiled and gave her head a shake. "What do you like to eat in the morning, Lydia?" She pushed back her chair, ready to rise. "Hot cereal, right?" (She had seen me make oatmeal in the little kitchen in Rochester.)

"Oh, I'm set!" I said. "I'll . . . um . . . I'll just get my coffee." I made myself sound capable. I was. I was used to making the coffee—and much more—every day. Aunt Brat settled back into her chair. But she looked funny, I thought. Like she was sitting on an egg and didn't want to break it.

"Coffee . . ." Two voices said it. One seemed to be telling; the other seemed to be asking. Both drifted away at the ends.

I scanned the kitchen and spotted the coffeepot (on the counter); found the mugs (on hooks below the cabinet); discovered the spoons (standing in a pottery jar right in front of me). I swung open the door to the fridge, pulled out the milk, and poured my mug half-full. Then I topped it with hot coffee. Right about then I realized that they were all watching me.

"Ah! Honey," I said. I reached for the jar and dipper, which sat in the center of the table right where all the watchers were. "I know," I said, "honey in coffee is weird, huh?" I let an amber dollop drop into my mug, then let the thread drizzle in too.

"Hmm . . . the honey . . . ," said Aunt Brat, nodding gently.

"Coffee . . . ," said Eileen. Her eyebrows arched.

"I'd love a warm-up," said Elloroy. I brought the pot.

The clear brown stream, the steam rising, and that smell all made me think of Mom. She wasn't supposed to have coffee, and for a long, long time she hadn't. But the sicker her heart had gotten, the sicker she'd become of "joy-zapping rules and regulations," as she'd called them. She'd gone back to drinking coffee and she'd loved that. And I had loved bringing it to her.

"That'll do it," said Elloroy. He raised his brown-spotted hand. I blinked and stopped pouring. I stood with the pot in my hand.

Is this how it's going to be? I wondered.

I was a novice at being at an orphan. This moment surprised me—this brief check-in with my mom. Five mornings had passed.

Five mornings since she turned blue. . . .

Signs were there. She'd been sleeping a lot. Her speech had gone thin.

"Soon now," she'd said, and then on the day, "Come. Hold me, Lyddie." And I had, until Mom and her over-large heart had gone completely still. I'd taken the oxygen tube away from her nose before I'd made the phone calls. Weeks earlier she'd said, "Don't let that be the last you or anyone sees of me—all croaked out with a plastic plug in my schnoz, will you, Lyddie?"

No. I would not.

"And then sit with me a while after. Wait until *you* feel ready."

I'd sat with her body, feeling astonished at how real the whole "turning blue" thing had been. I'd talked to her as she was leaving, and I had cried. It'd been hard. But I'd stayed calm because I'd known what to expect. Mom hadn't gone for hospice. But I had. I'd studied their pages online. The notes had reinforced what she'd been telling me. I'd wondered if we'd been reading the same things.

"When you see the mottling, the blue, just remember that's science. That's inevitable when circulation slows," Mom had said.

"I know, Mom. I'll take care of you," I had promised her again and again. And I had.

8

Yard Full of Dogs

For perhaps the sixth time since I'd arrived, Eileen stood at the fridge looking at the flyer. She gave it a tap with her index finger.

I'd looked that page over. It was an announcement about a dog adoption day at some fairgrounds. Aunt Brat and Eileen were planning to go.

Eileen twirled, clapped her hands, and sang, "Hey, hey, hey! This Sat-ur-day! New doggie-o! Coming to this house—yo!"

"I know." Aunt Brat smiled. "Coming right up."

"Can't wait. Ants in my pants." Eileen wiggled her butt.

"Well, that's nice," Elloroy said in his low, low voice. "The dog. Not the ants."

"Do you want to come with?" Eileen reached and clapped him on the shoulder.

He looked at me and mouthed the word "Owww." Then he grinned. "No, I'll stay here and see what you bring home."

"All right, then, you and Soonie," Aunt Brat told the old man. She turned to me. "Soonie can't go. She gets carsick," she explained.

"And it's gross," Eileen added.

"Well, I'll stay here too," I said.

"What? No way!" Eileen said. "You've got to help us choose, Lydia."

I glanced at Aunt Brat. She gave me a nod. "Oh. Okay then. Sure!" I chirped, because that's what I did in those first days: I chirped so they'd know I was doing fine.

Chirp. Smile. Chirp.

If I had been in my aunt Brat's position—and Eileen's too, of course—I would not have been looking to get a new dog. They had just gotten *me*—somewhat unexpectedly. Who could tell how that was going to go?

But they'd made this plan before they'd known I'd be with them. So, on my third morning in Chelmsford, a Saturday (one week to the day after Mom had died), I was along for the ride.

We hopped into Aunt Brat's boxy car and took the trip

42

to the fairgrounds a few towns away. The place looked abandoned for the winter, with its long white buildings boarded with dark green shutters. But the long gate stood open. We parked while more cars rolled in behind us. *Dog seekers,* I thought.

"Come on! Come on!" Eileen urged both Aunt Brat and me along. If she'd had a few ants in her pants before, they were now an army. We filed into a fenced lot with the other humans.

Soon we were watching a parade of adoptable dogs come off a trio of transport vans. I thought about that word, "adoptable." Didn't that rely on perspective?

Some dogs were lifted off in crates. Some were leashed and led by red-vested volunteers. Others ran freely around the enclosure. The dogs were small, medium, and large. They were standing, sitting, tugging, barking, sniffing, and peeing.

I stood flanked by Aunt Brat and Eileen, wishing I'd worn my hat. It wasn't very cold. In fact, forty degrees was mild for January. However, the wind was gusting in bursts that made my hair wrap across my face. I pushed the strands behind my ears, only to have them fly loose again and sting my cheeks. Yes. The hat would've been nice.

But most of my discomfort was because of all the dogs.

First problem: They were *dogs*. Three days on the farm with one greyhound—old, sweet thing that she was—had not turned me into a dog person. Second problem: This was a lot of homeless circled up in one place. I felt for these creatures. Their ears blew inside out and they closed their eyes in the wind. All of them needed a happy twist of fate this day. But considering where they'd come from—kill shelters and other bad circumstances, according to Eileen's flyer—maybe the wheel had already turned in their favor. It could be a good day for some for them. Some.

I heard the call. "That's everybody!" The vans were empty. All thirty-two dogs were on the ground. People started to stroll among them. I felt Aunt Brat and Eileen pushing me forward, though neither of them had so much as a finger on me.

"Can you stand it?" Eileen said. "Look at these beautiful creatures. Still trying to find the way home even after a big push to clear the shelters before the holidays."

Oh . . . these are the leftovers. . . .

Why hadn't they been chosen before? Did they lack dog handsomeness? Some were pretty plain, others oddly shaped. Big heads and squat bodies, for instance. Yet a woman in tall-heeled boots and a short jacket bolted right up to the smallest, most bug-eyed dog of all, afraid, it seemed, that someone else might try to get to him first.

A family with three little kids knelt noses to nose with a waggy black dog with flop-down ears. But for me the dogs were so . . . so . . . *everything*. They were eager and nervous, barking and not barking, wagging, whimpering, shuddering, and endlessly peeing—*or worse*.

For a few seconds, I had to close my eyes to all of it.

"Let's divide and conquer," Aunt Brat said in a revved-up sort of way. "We'll each take our own look around the lot."

Okay. . . . Can't do that with my eyes closed. . . .

"And just holler if you meet that special someone!" Eileen clapped her gloves together. The wind gusted. The two of them split away from me in different directions.

I wanted to stop them and ask, Are you sure? Sure you don't want to wait to see how one rescue goes before you get yourselves into another? Not to liken myself to a dog, exactly. But I had been *taken in*.

While I was at it, I might have pointed out that there already was a perfectly good dog at the farm. Soonie was pretty low maintenance from what I'd seen. She ran circles inside the fenced pasture—top speed—once a day. Then she spent the remaining twenty-three hours and fifty-eight and a half minutes a day sleeping someplace soft. Or standing right smack in the way. She was like fine furniture—a long-legged sofa table that kept suddenly turning up beside you. She liked to follow, and of course, she mostly followed

Aunt Brat or Eileen, and Elloroy if he was heading into his suite to nap. She ate two meals a day—dry kibble soaked in warm water. I had made a note. I'd even made the food one evening, jumping in to be my helpful self.

What about Elloroy? I wondered. He'd seemed on board as we'd headed out this morning. But it was his house. Did he secretly mind that a second dog was coming to live there? Had he minded that a girl had?

One thing was certain: Aunt Brat and Eileen had discussed this. They were *not* always together on everything, as I was learning, but they were definitely together about this. We were going home with one of these "four-leggers," as Eileen called them. A dog could cost me a pair of shoes. And socks, wasn't that right? Didn't they chew all the things that people wore on their feet? I had just one pair of boots and I was fond of them. I walked into the wind to find a dog that didn't look hungry for footwear.

I looked at a spotted dog with a very big head and a chocolate-brown mama dog with empty-bag nipples. Then a blur of dogs ran by me—playing chase. Then—ugh—a stocky white brick of a dog ran into my legs and nearly took me down. He stood wagging at me afterward, mouth open and tongue out. I had the feeling he'd jump on me if I stuck around. So I didn't.

But there were dogs everywhere I turned. A little

46

black-and-white whatever-he-was (very big ears, a hairy plume of a tail) caught my eye. He was inside a small play-pen, biting the stuffing out of a dog bed.

Who'd take him home when he does *that*? Poor left-over, passed-over guy. Maybe he'd quit it. But, I wondered, if you don't know dogs how do you take that leap of faith?

I looked up and saw a boy in a red volunteer's vest and a big hat with earflaps. He was probably my age, and he seemed to be looking right at me. He was also smiling. The wind took charge of my hair again. I ducked and tried to gather the wisps in my hands.

Eileen startled me from behind. "Well? Interested in the little black-'n'-whitey, are you?"

"Oh. No," I said. "Well, he's cute." (Or maybe not so much.) "I don't think I could ever pick." I held my hair back with one hand. The ends whipped across my lips.

"I know what you mean," Eileen said. "Did you see that blond hunky one over there with Brat?" Eileen poked her thumb over her shoulder. "He's a good-looker. I think Brat's smitten. He could be the one."

I looked across the lot to where Aunt Brat was standing. A large yellow dog sat beside her, upright and alert. The hairs on his thick coat lifted in the wind while he surveyed the yard in a nervous, not-sure-what-to-do sort of way. He pushed out a bark now and then. But he also looked up at

Aunt Brat every so often and dipped his pointy ears and licked his lips. That looked like a happy thing somehow. I wondered if he liked plain or suede shoe leather best. Would canvas be just as satisfying?

"What say we go check him out?" Eileen said. "Huh-haw!"

"Sure," I chirped. I glanced back at the volunteering boy in the red vest. He was busy now, helping to untangle two dogs who had crossed up their leashes. He was still smiling. I turned and followed Eileen through the sea of canines and people toward Aunt Brat and the leftover yellow dog by her side.

9

Say What You Mean

On the car ride home, my head warmed up and my hair lay still. The deciding was done and all that homelessness was out of my face. All the dogs—save one—were out of sight, if not completely out of mind.

Eileen piped up in the front passenger's seat, "Phew. I'm glad we're outta there. You know, I could easily become one of those tortured types who adopts too many dogs, goes broke, and has to move in with relatives."

Aunt Brat let one beat go by. "No, Eileen. No, you could not end up like that." She said it slowly and clearly.

"You don't know, Brat."

"Yes, I do. Because you have *us* and we'd never let you come to that." Her face softened.

"I'm just saying, it's awful hard to walk away from that dog lot and not keep thinking about the ones that you *didn't* bring home, is all."

From my spot in the back seat, I silently agreed. I hadn't wanted any dog. Yet I was still thinking about the chocolate mama dog, the spotty one with the big head, even the busy little black-and-white one.

"Well, if you put it that way, then yes, I understand," Aunt Brat said. "Say what you mean," she added.

Three days, and this wasn't the first time I'd heard Aunt Brat say that to Eileen.

"Of course that's what I mean," Eileen said.

"Well, if you say it then I know—"

"Oh, Bratches, you're too literal!" Eileen flapped a hand at her. "And you sound like a priss."

Half a laugh escaped through my lips—a sound like "pu-uh!" I made a few more noises to try to cover.

Eileen turned back to give me a sideways grin. "Huh-haw!" Up in the rearview mirror Aunt Brat was giving me a smile.

"Hey, Lydia, how's he doing back there?" Aunt Brat asked.

I looked into the back of the boxy car where the blond dog lay on his side, head down. His eyes were shut tight. "Sleeping," I said. Then I checked again, half expecting to find he'd been faking. Would a dog do that—fake a car nap just for peace and quiet?

I had. Just three days before, when Aunt Brat was driving us to Chelmsford. My way of taking in the changes slowly, I guess. Maybe that was true for the yellow dog too.

10

Not Bullet

The yellow dog came with a name: Bullet.

"We're changing *that* as soon as possible," Aunt Brat had said as the dog yanked her about the yard that first afternoon. She and Eileen had decided the dog should sniff around before they introduced him to Soonie—and *sniff* he did. Brat flew by us, then back again, with not-Bullet urgently pulling her toward all the unseen scents.

Elloroy had come out on the porch in his slippers to watch. I heard him mutter the words "Oh" and "My" and "Isn't he handsome?" Then he quietly asked a question into the air—a place from where he'd get no answer: "Is the new dog teaching Brat to heel?" I'm pretty sure I was the only one to hear him.

"C-c-can we agree . . . ," Aunt Brat called out on one of her bumpy flybys, "that *B-Bullet* sounds too much like a prophecy that he's going to fulf-i-l-l-l-l . . . ?"

"Agree!" Eileen called out.

"We'll have to work on a new name!" Aunt Brat said as she returned, huffing and puffing now. "Maybe he'll *tell* it to us!"

The dog tugged Brat again like he had a rag doll by the arm. I watched them bolt away. A few dog-name possibilities came to mind: Runaway. Renegade. Rocket. I can't explain why I was thinking in Rs or why all the names that came to me seemed like more of those prophecies you wouldn't want to see come true. Raceway. Roller Derby. I did not share my ideas.

"Should we bring Soonie out to meet him?" Brat planted her stance and struggled to make not-Bullet stand still. "Boy! I tell ya! This is a *lot* of dog! Maybe he'll be interested enough in Soonie to be a little more tranquil."

"Huh-haw!" Eileen threw her head back. "*Tranquil? Really, Bratches?* Are we a bit delusional today? Here, I'll take a turn." She took the leash from Aunt Brat and doubled it around her hand. "Hey, Elloroy! Let Soonie out!"

Not-Bullet did take to Soonie—with enthusiasm. He quit dragging the humans and sniffed every inch of the greyhound. He opened his jaws over her head. "He's not biting her, is he?" Aunt Brat asked.

"No, no. Just measuring her—for consumption," Eileen answered. She burst out laughing. The old dog took a few seconds' worth of shenanigans, then she snapped her jaws at not-Bullet. The yellow dog bowed away like a big furry chicken.

Elloroy muttered, "Atta girl, Soonie," from his place up on the porch.

Although the new dog could tug us around like laundry, the truth was that he hopped rather like a rabbit and walked low on bent legs. It had been noted on the papers that had come from the rescue group's vet: weak hinds/check hips.

"Could be dysplasia," Eileen said. She explained that was a congenital hip problem, not uncommon in certain breeds. "Congenital means—"

You are born with it. . . .

I finished her sentence inside my head. I'd been hearing that word for years. I'd seen a cardiologist every year for most of my life. She checked my heart because of Mom's heart. She was looking for that anomaly that might have been passed from my mother to me, which would also make it hereditary, just by the way. When I'd turned twelve that doctor finally decided I was in the clear. Mom had cried over that news. "What a relief!" she'd said. "I'm so glad I have kept my cruddy heart to myself."

Well, weak hinds be darned, the dog could still pull. I was afraid to be the human on the end of his leash. But I jumped in and helped, especially that evening. He was, it turned out, an unstoppable indoor puddle maker. Poop too. He kept hitting the rug. He ruined the dinner hour— and he absolutely squashed my appetite.

My adults chalked it up to new surroundings. Dog jitters. But as the newcomer hauled me round the dark yard, I had my own thought: We'd managed to bring home the most troublesome leftover dog of the lot.

Great job, us.

Night Whimperer

The *big yellow* dog had to be crated downstairs for the night. "At least for now," Eileen said. "There could be whining. Be prepared to stuff your fingers in your ears."

"Oh. I do feel sorry about leaving him down here alone," said Aunt Brat. She turned off the lights. "But there's no denying, he's not trustworthy. Not yet."

Before I was even in bed, I could hear the dog crying. When I shuffled along the hall to the bathroom to brush my teeth, I peeked over the balcony. I could see him down in the dim inside his crate. He was sitting, crouched and looking up through the wires—a blond prisoner. I was pretty sure his eyes were following me. When I came back by I purposely did not look at him. I closed the bedroom door and slid under my covers.

The dog's cries stretched into long, pitiful sounds that ended in sharp huffs, as if he were saying, Harsh—harsh! I imagined Aunt Brat and Eileen pulling their pillows tight around their ears. Elloroy was probably hard enough of hearing to be all right with the door to his suite closed. We were to ignore the dog. We must not let him think that whining would get him anywhere.

"Just know that he's okay," Aunt Brat had said. "He's been well fed and watered. There is absolutely no doubt that he's peed—"

"Everywhere," Eileen had interjected.

"And he has a nice soft bed in his crate so he's comfortable." Aunt Brat had finished on that high note.

Bed, I thought as I lay in mine. It still felt so new and not quite right. I pulled Aunt Brat's old sleeping bag up over my head. I tried not to hear the mournful song of that impossible dog. When you do that, you end up waiting for every next cry, and if you are me, and if it seems like too much has happened in the past three or four or eight days, you want to join in. The sad dog sounds rose into the rafter space on the other side of my thin door. Then they faded and rose again.

After a while, the metal crate rattled, then thrummed

like the dog might be swatting the door with his paw. Finally, the silences grew longer. He pushed out a few little yips. I heard him grunt. There was a defeated sort of clunk and a sigh.

There, you fuzzy yellow mess. . . . Give it up and go to sleep. . . .

That dog had made this day a long one. Now that he'd gone quiet, sleep was going to come easy and feel good. I sighed. I drifted.

Scritch-scritch. Scritch.

No way. . . .

But yes. There it was again—the noise behind that sheep poster. I reached for the flashlight that hung beside my bed and waited. I heard the scritchy-scratchy sound again. I bounced to my knees and blasted those paper sheep with light. I squinted. Right under the lip of the shortest sheep, a flap of torn paper moved like a creepy old tongue. I held the light steady. A tiny pointed head poked itself out from under the flap. Out dropped a mouse— as if the sheep had spat it. The mouse scurried along the floorboards. I lost sight of it when it reached the brick chimney.

Hmm. But where was it now?

I traced the edge of the room with the beam of light. I noted the slim gap between the bottom of my bedroom door and the threshold. I'd heard that mice could flatten themselves to fit through a vent slot. That mouse could be down the hall and into the bathroom or in Aunt Brat and Eileen's room already. Or . . .

I tipped myself upside down to look beneath my bed. I reached under and pushed on the box with the goddesses in it. No mouse. I checked along the windowed wall. Nothing. But what ancient secrets did this room have? How many mouse holes and escape hatches?

I got out of bed and crouched in front of the poster of the sheep trio. I picked open that paper flap—like I was looking under that sheep's lip. I tested the spot with my finger. Sure enough, I found a hole in the plaster. I pushed my finger in all the way up to my first knuckle. When I pulled it back out, plaster crumbs came with it, and so did a really big question: What was back there? How big a space?

I wanted to thump my knuckles on it, see if it sounded hollow or solid, but I resisted. Surely I'd wake up the dog—or humans—if I went knocking about. I tried using the flashlight to look into the hole, but it was impossible to see anything. I pinched the flashlight in my knees so I could use both hands to pick at the corners of the sheep poster. If I peeled it back, maybe I'd find another hole—a bigger one.

Well, my knees failed and the flashlight hit the floor with a terrible *thunk*. The yellow dog let out one sharp bark. Then three more. I scuttled back to bed as fast as I could. I pulled the covers back over my head. Heart pounding, I whispered, "Hey, mouse—and hey, dog—this isn't over."

12

A Dark Spot in the Morning

Aiming to be helpful, I was the first one downstairs on Sunday morning. I planned to start the coffee. But the yellow dog was already standing in his crate, murmuring at me while his huge puff of a tail intermittently banged on the wires.

"Okay, okay," I whispered. I rushed my feet into my sneaker-boots, threw on my jacket, and sprang the dog from the pen. It was all I could do to clip the leash on him before he dragged me out the front door and down the steps. Then it was pull-pull, struggle-struggle, sniff-sniff *everything*. I tried to accommodate his every sniff wish, in spite of the fact that I was spattering my own legs—and the sneakers I loved—with mud every step of the way.

I spoke nicely. "Okay, Not-Bullet, big fella, big pal. Take a pee, a good long pee!" But he left only little sprinkles here and there. *How does one make a dog go?* I wondered. *Go* outside, *that is.* I could almost hear my new adults saying it: Give him ample time. . . .

So I did. We must have stamped around in the mud for ten minutes. *Forever.* Both of us were panting. The dog's tongue hung out one side of his mouth. I noticed it was pink with a lot of dark, bluish spots on it. "Hey," I said as he powered forward, "did you eat a basket of blueberries?"

At least half a dozen times he squatted like he was about to *do* or *make* whatever. But then he'd abandon the mission. I was about dying for my cup of coffee by the time I pulled him back up the steps and inside. I smelled the brew. Someone else was up too. I held his collar, grabbed one of the old towels, and began to wipe his paws. He drew them away and jumped backward. Then he lunged forward and tried to yank the towel out of my hands. He shook his head and his tags jingled.

"And how are we this morning?" Aunt Brat stood smiling down at the dog and me. Soonie stood behind Aunt Brat's legs, blinking her fawn eyes.

"Oh, okay," I said. The yellow dog spotted Soonie. His toenails scraped the floor as he raced toward her. I held him back, but pretty soon all bets would be off. He was too much.

"He had a reasonably good night," she said cheerily. "A few bumps, bangs, and barks, I guess."

"Yes," I said, knowing that I'd caused some of that.

"And this morning?" she asked, giving me a big questioning side-eye. "Any luck out there?" I shook my head.

"No significant pees, no poo," I said. I gave his feet a final swipe. He mouthed my knuckles. I tried to ignore that. "I guess he's empty," I said.

"Hmm . . . I think it best we keep close watch on him if he hasn't performed."

"Right. Where do you want him?" I asked. I kept my aching fingers curled around his collar. "Back in the crate?"

"No," said Aunt Brat. "Let's allow him to be with us. The goal is to make him part of the family. . . ." Her voice trailed off as she headed back toward the kitchen, Soonie still at her skirt.

"All right," I said. I let Not-Bullet go and he sprang away from me. I thought he'd bolt toward the poor old greyhound, but instead he began to tour the living room. I watched him nose the rug exactly where he'd made his first puddle yesterday. I narrowed my eyes at him.

I took in a whiff of coffee air and thought, *I want, I want.*

Eileen came teetering down the stairs. "Good morning! Good morning, big boy!" The dog came to her! He even wagged his tail a tiny bit.

"We're letting him move about freely for a while," Aunt Brat said.

"Good, good." Eileen stretched her arms up over her head and yawned loudly. The dog stared at her, his ears up and his head on a tilt. Eileen saw that and finished the yawn in a big laugh. The dog turned weird. He crouched and barked at her. "Oh, shush! Come here, you lump. Come for a patting," she said. She leaned forward and gently clapped her hands. The dog rounded away. "Oh, no? Not feeling sociable this morning? Okay, okay. I'll get my sugar in my coffee, then."

In the time it took her to reach the coffeepot, the dog reached the living room. He walked a tight circle, then in a split-second move dropped his rear end low. "Uh-oh!" I rushed toward him. Too late. He skittered away to one side and there it was, a new dark spot on the braid rug.

"Oh, no!" Aunt Brat moaned. The dog tried to weave himself between and behind the furniture, all the while looking at us like we were about to do him wrong. I did not know a dog could look so mistrustful. Aunt Brat shook her head. "We're not reading his signals properly." (I didn't think there had been a signal.) "Oh well. It's all right." She spoke up louder, cheerier.

"I'll take him out," Eileen said. "You're a good boy. It's fine. It's fine."

Right, I thought. I slid a leaf of newspapers under the rug below the spot and another leaf on top. I marched my feet on it. *Everything is fine here. We have a suspicious-faced, indoor-peeing machine. Pee-ewe! But it's fine.*

"Ugh," said Aunt Brat. She came over and shook a mix of vinegar and water over the rug. "Here we go again. Blot, rinse, and repeat."

13

Picking the Hole

Eileen had to work at the feedstore from noon to four. "I'll take you," said Aunt Brat. "I'll go on from there to get groceries and gasoline. I'll pick you up later."

"I thank you, and so does my cranky truck," Eileen said.

"I'll dog sit," I said, because that was what I figured they needed from me. "And I'll check Elloroy for signs of death," I added. I gave his shoulder a pat.

Eileen stopped still to crow, "Huh-haw!"

When Elloroy and Soonie retreated into his suite for their afternoon nap, I took the dog who still didn't have a name outside on his leash. He pulled me along the front yard. I tugged him toward the pasture gate. Once inside,

I unclipped him. He bolted away—*while* looking over his shoulder at me!

"Go ahead and run," I told him. "I've got you fenced!"

I hung one arm over the rail and watched him nose his way along. He took leak after leak. Steam rising. Good. Less for the house. I noticed that he took squatty pees, rather than leg-lifting ones. He squirted his own front legs almost every time. His deep fur sucked it up like a sponge. I rolled my eyes.

"Yeah, it's dog towels and vinegar for you," I told him. He gave me a shifty look. His hind legs kicked backward. There wasn't much about this dog that was funny, but I laughed at that twitchy kick. He went off to sniff and sprinkle some more. I looked back toward the farmhouse. I thought about the mouse, the hole in the wall.

I looked up to my bedroom window, then to the place where the chimney rose through the roofing. There were two ridges, one high, one low. The high one was over the main part of the house, the low one over Elloroy's suite. He didn't have a second floor, which meant my room kind of butted up to his ceiling. On the inside of the house the broad brick chimney rose up between my room and the bathroom. But from inside, and now from the outside too, I could see that the chimney didn't go all the way to the end of the house. There was a space at least as wide as a person behind that wall—right where the mouse had crawled out. "Huh," I said.

"All right, dog-face!" I clapped my hands. "Time to go in. Come!" I called. He sat down and looked at me. If I were to name that pose, I'd call it "unimpressed and unlikely to obey." "Come!" I called again. I reached into my pocket for some broken bits of biscuit. Well, that dog galloped, if awkwardly. He plowed into me, chin high, licking his lips, and his eyes fixed on my hand. I gave him the treat—barely avoided getting my fingers snapped. I grabbed his collar and hitched him up again. Score one for me.

"Good boy!" That was a lie. Not-Bullet was not a good boy. But he had come when I'd called. Sort of.

I pulled him back to the house because that was the game: pull or be pulled. In the entry I dried his legs with a towel. I held him still while I sprayed him with vinegar and wiped him down again. He did *not* like that, and he tried to circle away. "Ow!" My fingers got twisted up in the collar. I coaxed him to his crate and threw a treat in ahead of him. I added a gentle shove. "Yep, yep. Tough beans," I said. I made the words sound sweeter than they were. I slid the latch. I felt pretty good. I was not a dog person, yet I'd managed Mr. Yellow this afternoon. I showed him my palms. (That's what Aunt Brat and Eileen had decided we should do.) "Stay," I said. He started to mewl. I didn't wait around feeling sorry for him. Aunt Brat and Eileen would return soon. I took the stairs two at a time, careful not to stomp. I wanted a look behind that sheep poster.

The putty was cold and hard. The poster came away from the wall easily. I tacked it up off to the side where I could grab it again quickly.

There was that hole—the one the mouse had come through. I stuck my index finger in it. I felt air—cooler than in my room, I thought. "Hmm. But how far back?" I whispered. I went into my art box and pulled out a ruler. It wouldn't fit in the hole—not at first. But I jammed and pried. The plasterboard crumbled, almost like it wanted to.

I am breaking Elloroy's house, I thought. An ache of guilt caught me in my jaw. But I wasn't wrecking the bricks. When the hole was big enough, I fed the ruler in—back, back as far as I could slide it until I was pinching just the very end of it in my fingers. *Well, it's at least twelve inches*, I thought. "But it *must* go all the way back to the bathroom, too," I said. "It *must*." I poked about with the ruler, learning nothing, to be honest. Then I lost my grip, and the ruler dropped into the dark unknown.

"No!" I sat back on my heels. "Smooth move, Lydia!"

Now I wanted two things: a look at that space *and* my

ruler back. The answer to both problems was a bigger hole. That's all it took for me to set to the dishonorable work of snapping off more pieces of old wallboard. Soon, I'd made a hole I could put my hand into. This was going to be a big surprise for the mouse.

I pressed one eye up to the hole. But there was only darkness. I grabbed the flashlight and directed the beam in. I fit my face beside it and shut one eye. It was very hard to see. But just like I'd guessed, there was the back wall of the chimney to my left and the framing of the end wall on my right. The space in between looked wide enough for someone my size to stand—possibly with both hands on her hips. So, a skinny hallway to nowhere. To my right, I could see a close little roof peak, no taller than one of those pup tents, where raw boards came together. That had to be the low roof ridge over Elloroy's suite. "Cool," I whispered. I backed away from the hole. I'd just seen house bones, or house ribs—a place no one ever went.

I wanted to make that hole wide enough to crawl through. I wanted to do it right that second! Trouble was, that was the same second I heard the yellow dog bark— and the same second Aunt Brat arrived home.

14

How to Stop a Bus

School was one of the things Aunt Brat had talked to me about on our trip from Rochester to Chelmsford. I'd be going. I had expected that. Big change; I'd been home-schooled for two years.

Mom had known we were not going to get as many years together as most moms and daughters. She'd made the choice not to be bitter about it. She'd focused on making sure we spent as much time as possible together. We'd always covered the lesson packets first. Then we'd spent hours at the computer "hopping topics." One day, we'd started with a search on how cadmium-red paint gets made. That'd led us to zinc ore and zinc smelting, mining, and then sinkholes. Another day, we'd hopped from yeast (we'd been baking a harvest bread) to fermentation, to effervescence, to Prohibition and the Great Depression. I had many odd pieces of information to go with my standardized achievement.

I'd done the work and I'd met state goals. But Chelmsford was not Rochester—not even the same state. What if some things had been taught in a different order? Or a different way? Would I be behind?

There in Aunt Brat's car, I'd suddenly felt adrift.

What if I had to do a bunch of catching up—by myself?

Oh . . . Mom. . . . This is not good. . . . Do-over!

She would've said what she'd always said in this kind of moment: "We're going to need a goddess for this!" Only there wasn't any *we* now. *I* needed the goddess. *Me. Alone.* Mom had been the one who could conjure them up. I'd tried to think like her. She'd always given the goddesses titles.

So . . . the Goddess of . . . what? A Messy Education? No, no. Be positive. *The Goddess of Learning?* No. That was boring, unpoetic. *The Goddess of . . . Gathering a Complete Education.* I'd liked that better. But how would I make her without Mom?

"I'm inclined," Aunt Brat had said, "to suggest they enroll you in the eighth grade. Chelmsford has its own K through eight school. Very small," she'd noted.

"I am thirteen," I'd said. "That is usually eighth."

"Yes, it is," Aunt Brat agreed. "And they'll assess you."

Great . . . I can't wait. . . .

"With a November birthday, you're close to the cutoff. You'll be one of the youngest members of your class. I'm not so worried about that. I think it's good that you'll have a semester to be with a small class of kids from town—a nice transition from your years at home before you start high school. By the way, that's a big change for all our students," she'd said. "Chelmsford doesn't have its own high school. We send most of our students out to a private academy come ninth grade. . . ."

An *academy?*

Aunt Brat had probably heard me swallow. *Academy* sounded strict, and formal, and hard. I was worried enough about being in a classroom again after two years.

"How do you feel about all of this?" Aunt Brat had asked.

"I'll be okay in the little eighth grade," I'd said.

Well, the Weather Goddess of Chelmsford finally figured out that it was January, at least for the time being. On a suddenly frozen Monday morning—just five days after I'd arrived and two days after the big yellow dog had moved in—Aunt Brat and Eileen put on their boots. They leashed both dogs so that all four of them could walk me down to the bus stop at the bottom of the long hill. They were going to see me off on my first day of school in Chelmsford—my first day at any school in over two years.

I took a long breath in and let it out. I tapped my foot on the mica-thin layer of ice that had formed over one of Chelmsford's many mud puddles and cracked it. Never mind the academics, what about the kids? Only twelve students in the eighth grade. At first, I'd been relieved. But now, I was having second thoughts. My old school had been huge, like an ocean of kids. Chelmsford was a pond, I thought. No, a puddle, like the one I was standing over, and a puddle suddenly seemed like a small thing to try to hide in.

The bus came into view in the distance. Orange as a Cheeto on that gray band of country road, it crept slowly toward us. My sweat turned cold in my armpits. I shivered.

"I see it!" Eileen said. "Here it comes! You sure they know, Brat? They know where to stop for her?"

"I gave clear instructions," Aunt Brat said.

I glanced at my adults, then at their two dogs, one of whom was misbehaving at the end of his leash.

Gee, this isn't embarrassing at all, I thought.

It was especially *not* embarrassing when both Aunt Brat and Eileen stretched their arms and themselves out into the road to flag the bus down.

"Here! Right here!" Aunt Brat called. The yellow dog jumped up and boxed her with his front feet. She stumbled.

"No, no! Down!" she told him. Eileen and I asked if she was all right.

As the big bad bus drew nearer, the dog got more skittish. He hopped sideways on the end of the leash, straining and barking. He circled around my aunt and wrapped her up in the leash but good.

Since Aunt Brat was stuck, Eileen stepped forward. "Halt!" she called. She *Ei-leened* herself into the road, swinging one arm over her head just in case there hadn't been enough flagging down of that bus.

"It's fine," I said as gently as I could. "The driver sees me." I could see her looking down out of the long front windshield as she steered slowly toward us. She was concentrating—probably on how to avoid plowing over that rabble of dogs and women at the side of the road. The bus hissed to a stop. The yellow dog barked back at it. The doors opened. I stepped up and inside.

One look down the aisle of the bus left me feeling outnumbered. Small school, sure. But stuffed bus. Maybe there was only one for the whole town. I took a tight turn to fold myself into the first open set of seats near the front. As I spun, I noted a pair of faces beaming from several seats behind me. It was just a flash. But both faces wore welcome-y looks—the kind that say, We know who you are; you're the new girl. One of them waved a fat white mitten at me just before I turned to sit. Meanwhile, Aunt Brat and Eileen could be heard cheering. "Have a great day! Buh-bye, Lydia! Bye!" The driver closed the doors. I closed my eyes.

I pictured that mitten. Hand knit, I thought, on circular needles, with roving woven through at the end. Mom used to make exactly that kind of mitten, years back. They were the best. The roving felted with wear, making the mittens thick and warm. I thought about the last two evenings when I'd taken the new dog outside. I'd somehow come to Chelmsford with nothing but a thin pair of stretchy gloves. Oh, I should *so* make myself a pair of those mittens. I had wool yarn in one of my boxes and maybe some roving too. I wasn't a bad knitter, and if I botched up, which was likely to happen at the thumbhole, Mom could always get me out of trouble. . . .

Oh.

I opened my eyes and stared out at all the unfamiliar places.

15

Significant Facts

I was nearly the first one off the bus. Chelmsford Public School stood before me, its entrance set off in crisp white paint centered on red bricks. There was a black clock face up above the door. Little kids zipped by me on the walkway. I might be the youngest in my class, but I was one of the oldest kids at this school. I hooked my hands into the straps of my backpack.

Okay, Lydia Bratches-Kemp. Step up and let's find out what you know.

I'd barely begun to march when the two girls with the welcome-y faces ran around me and planted themselves on the path, smack in front of me.

"Hi! We think you must be Lydia. Are we right?" The

mitten girl spoke first, and she spoke fast. I blinked. Fine line between being welcomed and being accosted.

"I am!" I forced the friendliest part of me to say it. I even put on eyes of wonder to make them think I was surprised that they knew about me.

"Well, hi! Oops. I already said that." The girl laughed. "I'm Sari Winkle." She smiled and softly clapped the white mittens together. Blue eyes danced. Shiny beaded earrings peeked out from behind her spilling brown curls.

"And I'm Raya," the second girl said. Her voice was low and husky. She threaded her bare fingers into dark, plum-streaked bangs and swept the strands away to one side. Then she pressed both her hands into her pockets. "Raya Delatorre," she added.

"Oh. Nice to met you."

"Same," said Raya. "So hey, we're here for you, you know?" She raised her shoulders and dropped them again. "I mean, like, we're designated. Appointed. Whatever you want to call it."

I knew it.

Sari Winkle bumped against Raya and giggled. "We volunteered! We're excited to get a new class member. Never happens!" Her eyebrows arched. "We'll introduce you to everyone and show you around the school. It's tiny. You'll be fine." She flapped a wool mitten.

"Thank you." That was all I seemed able to say.

Students were trickling past us on either side—and by that I mean they slowed down and turned back to look at me. New girl. I shivered, partly from the cold, partly from nerves.

"Come on, let's go inside," said Sari. "Office first. Then you can meet our whole class before first bell."

"Sure!" I chirped.

Inside, the air was warm. I noted that dust-on-the-radiator smell, and paste and salt, too, which took me zinging right back to my old school in Rochester. At the door to the school office I caught a new scent: cinnamon and cloves. Potpourri. I was greeted by a secretary, who alerted the principal, who said things like "Welcome!" and "We were so happy to hear that we were going to get a new student." I was given a card with my locker number and combination on it. I followed Raya Delatorre and Sari Winkle. Both of them turned back every few steps to make sure I was coming along. I was, but slowly.

There was artwork on these walls—some by students, some by the great art masters. I walked with my head tipped back, looking up at a set of banners that hung from the ceiling, Animals of the Rain Forest, in bright geometrics. Just down the hall was a wall mural of the town, all made up of dots, like a painting by Georges Pierre Seurat.

"Ser-rot dot." Mom had once said that to me with a wry grin. But then she'd corrected to proper French. "Say it 'Ser-raw,' Lydia. But remember 'ser-rot-dot' anyway, because . . . how do you make a dot? With the point of a paintbrush. Point for pointillism," she'd said. "That was Georges Pierre Seurat's genius—his contribution to neo-impressionism."

Neo meant new. Impressionism meant that the art captures the feeling of the moment, less than the actual look of it. I decided I was having a neo-impressionistic morning.

I followed my welcomers to the eighth-grade homeroom. Twelve kids, as promised. I envied them; they knew what they were doing. They knew where their coats went (in hallway lockers), where to sit (assigned seats), who was in charge (Mrs. Ossinger, who would also teach language arts). I have to say, I was grateful that Raya and Sari stuck by me while I fouled up the combination on my locker *three* times over.

"That's okay. Twist to the right to clear it. You'll get it this time," Sari said. Meanwhile, sweat broke across my brow. But then there it was: the crunchy sound of the metal latch lifting inside.

"Boo-yah!" said Raya. She pumped her fist.

In the eighth-grade homeroom, I sat with Raya to my left and Sari one desk in front of me. Attendance was taken.

Then a horrible thing happened: I was singled out for a big introduction. All eyes on Lydia Bratches-Kemp. How can one feel anything but freakish at a moment like that? Mrs. Ossinger asked all twelve eighth graders to introduce themselves one by one—*to me*—and to please share a significant, memorable fact or two about themselves.

There was a Charlotte. Her house was the one just after the broken barn on Cullen Road. (Wherever that was.) "That barn is condemned," she said, "but my family is petitioning the town to have it restored."

There was an Axel. He lived with his family and a set of cousins in a farmhouse that'd been in their family for over a hundred years. "We are pig farmers and we're proud," Axel said. He grinned and puffed his chest.

There was a girl named Gilly. She told me she was a competitive gymnast. "I can't wait to get to Clover Academy next year," she said. (The dreaded academy; the school Aunt Brat had mentioned.) "They have a really strong team."

Raya Delatorre's turn came. "Well, first, hi again." She gave me a little wave. I smiled back. "So, significant fact: I would pretty much always rather be outdoors than indoors. And if I can be beside a river, that's the best. I already know I want to study environmental science. I want to be a part of a clean river initiative—like for the state." A supportive sort of murmur rose in the room. Raya gave a nod in return. Then she turned her palms up and grinned. "Of course, a few things have to happen first. Like high school and college." She sighed and our classmates laughed. "Anyway, that's me. Okay, so the second thing—and it's related—is about our school. Totally cool. We got two hundred trout eggs back in November."

Several voices chimed in. "Oh. Yeah!" "So awesome . . ."

"They've hatched," Raya said. "Hopefully, it'll keep going great, and our class will release a school of fingerling trout into the Bigelow River come April. So far, so good," she added. She put both thumbs up.

Next was Sari Winkle. She tilted her head while a smile overtook her face. "I'm Sari. You know that." She fiddled with her earring. "I guess what I would want you to know about me is that I love to make things." She breathed a little laugh, and again there was a little hum in the room. I had the sense that any one of these kids could have introduced the others, including at least two significant facts. "I love arts and crafts. All kinds. That's me!" Sari giggled. "I guess it's inherited. My mom's a graphic artist. She and I live here full-time and my dad works in New York City all week and comes home on weekends. I guess that's all," she said. "For now, anyway."

On they went. I kept listening. Or, I tried.

Last, there was a smiling boy. He said, "Hi. I'm called Moss." Then he told me his family had been dairy farmers for six generations. One of their cows once gave four gallons at a milking. He had recorded the whole thing on video. "I'd like to be a scientist. But I'll probably end up on the farm." He shrugged. "That's all I can think of. I guess I'm not very significant."

"But you're funny," Raya said, and my new classmates laughed. Moss seemed fine with that.

I didn't laugh. There was something sort of sad about what he'd said. I gave him a slight nod. I was already forgetting names and facts and how they matched up. But I was going to remember the boy called Moss. He had an interesting name and a big handsome nose, and he was funny in my favorite sort of way. *And* he had one last, very weird thing to say: "Anyway, Lydia, it's nice to see you again."

See me again? What did he mean?

Then something dreadful happened. Mrs. Ossinger asked *me* to introduce myself, and I had to come up with a few significant facts of my own.

Oh. Which ones, which ones? My father ditched? My mother had a bad heart and I watched her turn blue and die nine days ago, and this is her sweater and I can't bear to take it off, and I have a box of paper goddesses under the bed I'm sleeping in that no one here would understand, and there is a mouse living in the wall of my room. . . .

My head felt like it was full of those finger fish that Raya had just mentioned. Swimming all around up there, bumping into my skull.

Say something, Lydia.

"Umm . . . well, I moved here from Rochester, New York. I live with my aunt. Bratches. That's her whole name. Just Bratches. And her wife, Eileen O'Donnell. Eileen works at the feedstore." (I realized that this was a good mention; a lot of these kids had animals.) "You might know her. And we all live at Elloroy Harper's place on Pinnacle Hill. It used to be a working farm"—they probably knew its history better than I did—"but, um . . . there aren't really any animals there now. I mean not the farm kind." I paused. I needed my lips to stop sticking. Some kids were nodding. Some were just looking at me. "Anyway I'm here to . . . help them. They need it. They just got a terrible dog." A few kids laughed. "He's so bad they haven't even come up with a name to give him." More laughing. "So I . . . try to help them with the dog. And. Just. Everything." I was never so happy to close my own mouth.

Mrs. Ossinger said, "Welcome, Lydia. We're glad to have you join us. We're sure you'll love our community."

Why did people say things like that? Who knew if I

would love it? What if I never did?

When Mrs. Ossinger went back behind her desk, Raya Delatorre stretched out of her chair to tag my shoulder. "Don't worry about remembering everything," she whispered. "Just ask who's who. I'll tell you."

Sari leaned back to agree. "Yeah, we all know each other really well."

Later, they walked me around so I could see the whole school. (That didn't take long.) We ended up down in the basement library. Ah, books! Maybe art books. Somewhere. I squinted at the signs that hung above the sections. Books seemed to be sorted by grade levels.

We stayed there talking for a few minutes, my welcomers and I. I told them I liked their significant facts. "I don't know anything about trout," I admitted.

"I am big into fish," said Raya. "We can go see the tanks later. Those are up in the science room. It's in the part of the hall with the rain forest banners. We would've shown you but it's also a homeroom, so it's busy in there in the mornings. But the trout are about so big right now." She showed me with her fingers. "Their yolk sacs are almost gone. It's been pretty cool."

"I'd like to see," I said.

"You will. We're all responsible for the tank."

Then I turned to Sari. "You said you make things. Do

you knit?" I asked. "I noticed your mittens—"

"Yes!" she squeaked. "Oh my gosh, I love to knit! Do you?"

"I do. And my . . . I do a little bit, actually. I've always needed help."

"I noticed your sweater," she said. She took a little bit of the ruffle in her fingers. "I thought to myself, *That's handmade! Someone's an expert.*"

I nodded. But I felt myself pulling back. It suddenly struck me that I had a day of testing ahead of me. "I guess I should ask you to show me to that room I'm supposed to go to. The resource room?"

"Okay, sure," Sari said. Then she paused and leaned in just a little. Her eyes were big and blue and serious looking. She tucked her curls behind her ear and I noticed the beaded earrings again. "And Lydia," she said softly, "we just wanted to say . . . we're sorry. We heard that you lost your mother recently—"

"Oh, no. I didn't *lose* her." I gave my head a quick shake. I felt heat in my cheeks.

"Oh," whispered Sari. She and Raya both looked stricken.

"She *died*," I said. "It's better to say she *died*." There. I'd said what Mom had told me to say, except not the sassy, sort of funny part about how I hadn't *lost* her like you'd lose a wallet or keys. I had not left her on the bus or down-town or at the flea market. I *knew* where she was. Sort of. So why did I feel so terrible now? So rude?

My welcomers blinked. They swallowed.

"So . . . the resource room is upstairs," Raya said, look-ing out from under her purple bangs.

"Yes. Right. Lead the way!" I said, turning myself back into grinning, peppy Lydia Bratches-Kemp, new girl. Off we went, a little more silently than before.

16

A Stop at the Feed

Week one is done.

Those words played a refrain in my head as Aunt Brat and I walked down the empty hallway of the school together on Friday afternoon.

I'd been assessed. (In and out of the resource room all week.) Now Aunt Brat and I were fresh from our meeting with Ms. Abraham. We'd learned a thing or two about me.

Though I, Lydia Bratches-Kemp, had been tracked a little differently from my new schoolmates, the differences were not concerning; knowing *how* to learn was more important than *what* one has learned, apparently. I could stay with my eighth-grade classmates for all subjects. The teachers at Chelmsford would "bring me along in regard to all topics specific to its curriculum." I'd have some reading to catch up on in these first weeks. (I was not thrilled.) But Ms. Abraham had said I'd do just fine. "We will be delighted, Lydia," she'd said, "when you begin to contribute to discussions from your own areas of proficiency, which are evident *and* considerable."

She'd really sung that last part out. Aunt Brat had sat by, beaming. I didn't completely buy that song, nor had I missed the message that they wanted me to participate in class. Still, the news had been good, and as we reached the wide doors I smiled to myself.

Did you hear, Mom? We did all right . . . I'm smarter than they thought.

That made me snort—loudly—which meant I had to share the thought with Aunt Brat rather than just be rude. So I did. She gave me the wry grin—the one that made her look like Mom. We pushed through the doors together and stepped into the sun.

The temperatures had come up again in Chelmsford. It'd been a rainy week. But now, so bright. Go figure.

"Let's drop in on Eileen at the feedstore before we go home," Aunt Brat said. Our shoulders bumped together as she spoke—accidentally, I think. "Would you mind?"

"Fine with me," I said.

I'd been to the Feed, where Eileen worked, just once before. I'd kind of liked the place, with its sacks of feed stacked high as my chin and the square wooden bins full of birdseed and dog biscuits. Now I was trying to remember which day in the recent blur of days that had been.

This was January ninth. *The ninth!* I couldn't think of any other New Year that'd brought such a pileup of changes with it.

On the ride over, I figured it out. I'd gone to the feedstore with Aunt Brat on the evening before they'd gotten the new dog. So that was last Friday. One week ago. I was pleased to have that straight in my little mental calendar. Tomorrow would be Saturday again. Two weeks since Mom died. There in the car I fought the now familiar wash of sorrow. The great gray threat, I called it, though only to myself. I was quite good at beating it—resisting a crumble-and-cry session. At some point, I'd stopped counting the days, I guessed. But right now, I needed to hold on to them.

The shop bell jangled as we let ourselves in the door at the Feed. I took in the smell—a weedy, woodsy, faintly sweet scent that I could remember from nowhere else and yet found comforting—if a little sneezy.

Eileen happened to be coming across the wide pine floor with two huge bags of chicken pellets stacked on one shoulder. (Eileen, leaning.) "Well, glory," she said. "What a surprise! My favorite women come to see me at my toil. Huh-haw! Gotta load this onto the Perkins' pickup." She gave a little grunt. "Be right back. Pick out some treats for the doggie-os." She gestured toward the biscuit bins with her free hand, then backed her way out the door.

"She's so strong." I said it out loud without thinking.

"Oh, I know she is," said Aunt Brat. She grabbed a paper sack and shook it open. She held it out to me. "Care to do the honors?" she asked.

"Sure."

The Feed was candy-shop wonderful, with its bins of biscuits in whimsical shapes and muted colors. I didn't have to like dogs to appreciate the treats. I pushed the scoop into a bin of pink-and-ocher-colored pinwheels. Then I moved along to the tiny brown bones.

"Delicacies for dogs, hmm?" Aunt Brat offered. "It's so satisfying to spoil them. Especially rescues, given whatever heck they might have been through. And of course we're going through a lot of training treats with the new fella. Oh, that reminds me, I want to pick out a collar for him too. His is so faded, so ratty."

"And he slips it," I added.

I need not have said so. She knew. The yellow dog was an escape artist. At least ten times in less than one week he'd pulled out of the collar and run off on us. Six times he'd done it to me. I was having trouble not taking it personally. He'd trot away just fast enough that I couldn't catch him, then go slinking along between the old barns. Then he'd look over his big blond shoulder at me. So much sass! The worst was when he'd hop off into the woods, disappear behind the layers of tree trunks, and be gone for twenty or thirty minutes. Aunt Brat and Eileen would get so worried for him, they'd take dinner off the stove, and we'd all get into our coats and boots and search. Then, like an apparition, he'd be on the front porch just staring forward, the stinker.

"He knows! He knows where home is," Eileen would say, so pleased.

"Oh, he's really a good boy, isn't he?" Aunt Brat would return.

No! He isn't! I always wanted to say it. Still, I'd felt a spark of gladness every time he had shown up again because my new adults had an unexplainable fondness for their new dog. I did not want them to lose him. Most of all, I didn't want to be the one to lose him for them, even though I was starting to think it'd be an act of mercy. He was putting them through so much worry. And so many towels.

Oops. I'd been unconsciously plunging the scoop in and out of a bin of fish-shaped biscuits—and leaving few survivors. I dropped the scoop and rolled down the top edge of the paper bag.

Eileen came breezing back inside. She joined Aunt Brat at the rack of dog collars. "He'd be handsome in green, don't you think?" Aunt Brat said.

"I do," said Eileen. "If he had a name, I could cut him a nice shiny tag on the new laser, too."

"The name is still in the works," Aunt Brat said.

"Yep," Eileen agreed.

It seemed unbelievable, and not a good sign, I thought, that they'd had the dog almost a week and still hadn't managed to come up with a name that'd stick to him.

17

Shiny Prize

It was my job to get the old collar off the dog while Eileen snapped the new one on. Not-Bullet struggled against us. Soonie stood in the way of the entire operation. I accidentally caught her under her chin with my elbow and made her cry. I started to sweat.

Doesn't anybody get it? . . . I am not a dog person. . . .

I pinched and pushed at the webbing of the old buckle-style collar, trying to unnotch it. Eileen held on to the dog. Not-Bullet kept twisting. Eileen's knuckles got in the way of my knuckles. How could it be so hard to get a collar off a dog when he'd managed to do it for himself so many times?

I was about to suggest we use the dog's trick and pull it over his head, when, success! The faded red collar dangled from my hand. The dog immediately closed his jaws on it and began to pull, tail wagging, butt in the air, slobber flying. Eileen still needed to clip his new collar on so I held firm, though now I had hold of nothing but the metal tags. (Not so comfortable, digging into the soft part of one's palm, let me tell you.) Eileen snapped the new collar on.

"Phew!" she said. She sat back hard on her butt.

Mr. Yellow and I continued our tug-of-war for the old collar. Aunt Brat chimed in from the kitchen, "Looks like he wants that back." She and Eileen laughed.

"And he may have it," said Eileen. "All we need is that shiny prize. The new rabies tag. Bling for the baby." She chuckled, then made a little gesture that somehow let me know that *I* was to get it. Great.

Actually, two tags hung from the collar on a metal S hook—one shiny, one not. I was loath to close my hand over them again, but I went for it. I leveraged a twist to spread open the hook. The tags bit into my hand! The dog shook his head. Ow-ow! I held on. Twist. Twist. I yanked upward—and I got those tags!

I let go. Not-Bullet slipped backward. He ran off, whipping the collar side to side as if *he'd* won. Huh!

"Did you get the tag?" Eileen asked.

I held up my fist. I forced a smile. "Yep!" I said.

"Amazing! Brava! Lydia victorious!" Aunt Brat crooned from the kitchen. She waved her cooking spoon in the air.

"Huh-haw!" said Eileen. She grunted and pushed herself up off the floor. The dog had taken his own prize to the living room rug. He held it between his paws while he gave it a good sideways chewing.

"Oh, look at him. So content," Aunt Brat said. Her voice oozed with affection.

"Sweet old lion," said Eileen.

Yeah . . . lion . . . after the kill. . . .

"Okay, let's just let him enjoy that for now," said Aunt Brat. "Our supper is ready. Don't lose that tag. We'll hitch it to him later. I imagine we'll need the pliers."

Pliers? We have pliers? I just ground the skin off my palm! I managed not to roll my eyes.

"We'll catch him when he's napping," Aunt Brat went on. "Wash hands, you two, and let's call Elloroy to supper."

In the bathroom, I soaped the tags and my hands together. I let the water rinse the suds away. The new rabies tag was all shiny copper paint and shaped like a shield. It was engraved: 0967 Blountville, TN.

The old tag was different—shaped like a dog bone. It was dull silver, dented up, with only traces of green paint left on it. It was exactly the sort of thing I scavenged for art projects.

Mom will love it, I thought. I *almost* kept myself from the realization that she'd never see it. *Almost*. This was

96

one of those moments when I felt like I was a visitor here. Soon I would go back home to Rochester and find Mom waiting for me in the little box house. I drew a big breath in through my nose. I dropped the old worn tag into the pocket of Mom's wool sweater.

"Done in here, dolly? My turn." Eileen wedged into the bathroom. She reached around me for the bar of soap.

"Done." I held up the shiny copper rabies tag between my finger and thumb for Eileen to see. "I gave it a bath," I said as I headed out the door.

"Our sweet lion will surely appreciate that," she called after me.

Can a dog do that? I wondered. *Appreciate?*

18

Facing South

The dog who was not to be called Bullet looked handsome wearing his new green collar when he squatted and peed in the living room during supper that night. It only ever took him a split second to get that done.

"Oh! Oh! No!" Aunt Brat cried.

"Dang it!" said Eileen. She threw her napkin on the table.

"Uh-oh," said Elloroy. But he sat right where he was and did not break the rhythm of his spoon dunking into his soup bowl.

My knees banged the underside of the table as I hopped up. We all knew *I* was the fastest way for *us* to get the dog outside. I grabbed the leash and pulled my jacket on in one

98

motion. "Here, here, here! Let's go! Outside! Outside!" I called, and clapped, and since he liked being outdoors so much, he came right to me.

The dog dragged me to the enclosure, where I let him go. He trot-hopped a few yards—escaping. "Because you always have to *escape*, now don't you?" I said. He ignored me, marked a tuft of winter grass. Then he sat down.

It'd dawned on me that these suppertime interruptions never turned out to be about the dog's urgent need to relieve himself; they weren't about needing exercise or running away either. (He saved that for dusk and daylight.) Once it was dark, he wanted to come outdoors and sit and stare.

I looked at the dog's long pale back. "You always face the same way," I said. "Why? What's out there?"

I oriented myself; I knew where the sun rose and set on this farm. "You face south," I spoke to his back. "And you came from Tennessee. Blountville, was it? Are you facing home?" Then I asked him, "Does it help?"

I turned my back on him and pointed my own toes north. Well, Rochester was actually to the northwest, so I shifted my heels a few degrees. I stood staring into the evening until two things happened. One, I started to shiver, and two, I decided that this was ridiculous.

Later, in front of a rewarmed bowl of minestrone soup, I asked my new adults, "Is there something—anything—you know about dogs that suggests that they prefer to face a certain direction?"

Well. That stopped all the soup eaters in midsip.

Eileen pulled her double chins in, turtle style. "Hmm . . . not sure what you mean."

"Does a dog know where it came from? Where its old home is?"

"Wow." Aunt Brat thought for second. "That's profound. An internal compass? That sort of thing?"

Elloroy stopped spooning his soup. "Why do you ask?" he said.

"Because I've seen the new dog facing south. A lot."

"Oh, I don't know, then," Elloroy said. "Because that's not my dog." Eileen snorted and gave the old man a tap with the back of her hand.

"Well," said Aunt Brat, "we know the earth has a magnetic axis, right? Although, it's not perfectly stable. Prone to disturbances. . . ."

"And so are we," said Eileen.

We're prone to disturbances because we have this dog. . . .

Meanwhile, Aunt Brat had gotten up and gone to the kitchen window for the best signal. She was doing a search on her phone. "Oh, interesting. So what I'm seeing here is, there have been studies. It says, there is some evidence that dogs choose to position themselves on a north-south axis when they pee or defecate." Aunt Brat laughed. "My apologies for being scatological during suppertime. But they did have to isolate the collection of data to times when the earth's magnetic field was most undisturbed." She put her finger in the air and looked at me with wide eyes. "And that would be at nighttime," she said. "There could be something to your theory, Lydia."

"You know, I think I've seen him facing south, too," said Eileen.

Then Elloroy said, "I've just seen him face his dinner bowl." They laughed, and I had to smile too. Elloroy reached over and tapped one finger on the table next to my bowl. He gave me a kind smile, big buggy eyes twinkling under his lenses and all his tiny brown moles magnified.

That night I went through the same little bedtime ritual I'd been doing since I'd come to the farm: I took off Mom's sweater, changed into my sleep shirt and pajama pants. Then I put the sweater back on and wrapped it close. Normally, I'd fold myself right into bed and start warming it. (My room got cold once the fire died.) But this night I set my hand into the pocket of the sweater and found that old dog tag. I rubbed my thumbs over it. I held the tag under the reading light beside my bed. I squinted. Wait. Was that somebody's name? And a phone number?

I read: "Ci . . . ci . . . Cici. Hoo . . . ver. Cici Hoover." I snapped my hand shut on the tag. "Whoa!" This was not a rabies tag. It was an ID. Were we supposed to have it? If someone surrendered a dog, shouldn't that be it? A done deal. No trail back.

We'd been trying so hard to decode not-Bullet. Now I wondered, did this Cici Hoover know all his secrets? Was she the thing he yearned for, the thing he wanted to go home to?

I held that tag between my hands. Maybe this person could help us. Maybe this was something I could do for Aunt Brat and Eileen—and Elloroy too, since it was his house—and his floors. I could make a call.

But what would I say to Cici Hoover? Hello. Have you ever owned a difficult yellow dog? Then I wondered this: What if Cici Hoover had never meant to give him up? What if the yellow dog was lost?

No, Lydia . . . unlikely. . . .

Someone would have called the number on the tag long before we'd gotten the dog. The rescue group would've checked. I was certain. I pulled my art box out from under my bed and opened the lid. The smell of wooden pencils, paint and wax, and glue came at me like a thousand memories. My heart thumped. A set of colored pencils lay in the open tray at the top. I rolled my palm over them.

When would I use these again? Would I still know how? I tucked the dog tag between crimson and pomegranate and put the lid back on the box.

I pulled Mom's sweater tight around me again and climbed into bed. I pulled Aunt Brat's old sleeping bag over me, leaving a tunnel for my face to look out. I fixed my gaze on the sheep poster across the room. I had not messed with the hole behind it all week. Opportunities were slim, what with Aunt Brat home most afternoons. In less than two weeks she'd go back to a new semester teaching at the university. But I wanted to pick more plaster before that. Maybe tomorrow. I sighed a big Friday-night sigh and watched for the mouse until I couldn't keep my eyes open anymore.

19

When Girls Come to Go Walking

I took in the quiet of Saturday morning. The weekend had arrived—a welcome break from a string of days of getting used to new people at that impossibly tiny school.

Aunt Brat and Eileen and Elloroy were all seated for breakfast with various reading materials in front of them. Soonie was asleep on her cushion at Aunt Brat's feet. The yellow dog had been outside for a haul around the yard with yours truly, and now he was settled, with his chin resting on one tucked paw. Aunt Brat and Eileen had managed to fasten his rabies tag to his new green collar. There was something dog-proper about the look of him. But I knew better than to be fooled.

Funny, this scene didn't feel so strange to me. I was still

hoping to spend most of the day alone in the narrow room upstairs. I wanted to open the box of goddesses. I also had a wall to pick open, and I'd been thinking about both all week.

I poured my milk and coffee, added my honey. I held the mug up to my nose just to breathe in the scented steam. My new adults didn't seem to notice my coffee drinking this morning. Hmm. Were we all getting used to one another?

I put my lips to the rim and took the first glorious sip—

Rap-rap-rap!

My coffee sloshed. Soonie leapt onto her spindly legs and let out a sharp bark. The yellow dog rose. He fired off a throaty alarm. Aunt Brat slapped her hand to her chest. "Whoa!" she said. Two barking dogs streaked toward the door.

"Umph!" Eileen stiffened in her chair. "Dogs! You disturbers of the peace!"

Elloroy, several beats behind, peered over his milky-blue glasses. "What was that?" He looked left and right.

"Door." Eileen angled toward Elloroy while she pointed to the front of the house. *"Somebody's knocking at the door."*

"Someone was barking," said Elloroy.

The yellow dog crowed again while all his back hairs stood on end.

Aunt Brat raised her voice. "Lydia, could you get it? Since you're up?"

I nodded in answer. Dog vocals would have drowned me out. I set down my mug and hurried over. The yellow dog was slinking back and forth, sniffing at the doorsill. I grabbed his leash, then had to step around Soonie to get to him.

"Encourage her out of the way!" Eileen flapped her hand helpfully from her spot at the table.

"Excuse me, Soonie." I sounded meek, even to myself.

I would *never* be used to dogs, even this sweet one. I leaned over her and hitched up the bad boy. Only then did I glance out the window to see who had knocked on the door. There stood tall Raya Delatorre right next to short Sari Winkle.

Oh . . . shoot. . . .

They had said they would come get me and take me walking—something about a tour of Chelmsford. Something about the farms. But nobody had said anything about *today*.

The dog was using all his different barks now. I called back toward the breakfast table, "I've got it!"

"Whomever it is, explain the invisible dog drill to them," Eileen called as she settled her eyes back on her newspaper. "Arms crossed over the chest, look up, and ignore. Shun that bad behavior."

"But don't shun the dog," Aunt Brat added.

"Well, you have to act like you don't see him," Eileen began to argue.

"Right, right," I said. All I could think about was how much I did *not* want to take a walk with the girls who were waiting just outside the door. Not even a little bit. It was going to mean more new people. And more strange places. Since we were talking about farms, some places were likely to smell bad. I had to come up with something—some way out of this.

I opened the door. Not-Bullet yanked me out onto the porch boards—in my socks. Raya and Sari stepped back to make room for us. The dog stopped and stared at them. He coughed out a few barks. His hairs still stood high on his spine. Soonie followed me, her nose right at my hip.

I caught sight of my three adults leaning from their chairs and peering at my situation. I reached back and pulled the door shut. I didn't want them to hear the lame, lying excuse I was about to make. And what would that excuse be, anyway? *Think, think, Lydia.* I looked up at my classmates.

"Hi!" I said, faking friendly.

"Hey-hey," said Raya.

"Hi, Lydia," said Sari.

"So . . . this is that bad dog I mentioned. Still no name.

He won't hurt you," I assured them. "He's sort of a scaredy-cat," I added, realizing only then that I was exactly right about that. How funny it was to hear myself talk about this dog—any dog—as if I knew what was up with it.

They stooped down and held out their hands to him. "Good boy, good dog." He sniffed their fingers, then jumped backward as if they'd stuck him with pins. More barking.

"So, what we do is, we ignore him," I said. "Like this." I modeled the shunning pose. They gave it a try. Trouble was, it was hard to visit with humans when you had your arms over your chest and your chin in the air.

And then there was sweet Soonie, who nosed forward, practically speaking the words "love me, love me." Before long, she was resting her chin in Sari Winkle's mitten-soft palm. Meanwhile, the yellow dog had quieted.

"So," I said. "Surprised to see you."

"The walk," said Raya. "We're going to show you around."

"Right," I said. Then I realized, maybe I didn't have to lie. The truth was, I didn't want to wreck my boots. I had just the one pair and I was kind of in love with them. I wanted to keep the lime green bright and the orange laces unmuddy. I'd seen enough of the farms of Chelmsford from Aunt Brat's car and from the school bus to know that they were fields of wet brown glop in this weird, warmish January. But as I took the breath to speak, Raya swung a pair of old brown hikers off her shoulder by the laces and dropped them at my sock-covered feet.

"You'll want these," she said. "Yours are too nice."

I caved like a sinkhole. I'd be taking that walk—through every cow pie and pee puddle in Chelmsford.

Darn it!

Aunt Brat was thrilled when I poked my head back inside to tell her the plan. She fetched my jacket and phone for me. She took the dog's leash so that I could step my feet into the old boots.

I remembered to introduce my welcomers to my new adults. Then they, along with Brat, counted the ways in which they already sort of knew one another. It was easy to make connections in Chelmsford, especially once Eileen arrived at the door to chime in. It became clear: the Feed was Chelmsford's hub of communications.

"Oh, it's so nice of you girls to come for Lydia," Brat said. "Thank you."

"Oh. Yes. Thanks," I echoed. I pulled the bootlaces tight. One end snapped off in my hand and I tried to hide it. I opened the boot up and did a hasty rethreading. That's when I noticed the initials lettered with a black marking pen inside the tongue of the boot: MCAP. What did those have to do with a girl named Raya Delatorre? I finished tying and stood up, ready as I'd ever be.

"Have fun," Aunt Brat said. "Touch base if you need to." She pantomimed a phone. I wondered if that meant, Call me if you can't stand it. Did she know how much I did not want to do this?

Elloroy had come to join Brat and Eileen. The three of them, and both dogs, stood in the door frame—with some pushing—as they watched me slog away.

"So long, youth and beauty," Elloroy said.

"What did he say?" Sari giggled and bumped up against me. I hummed a little nothing of an answer. For some reason that made Raya laugh out loud.

Well, the boots were at least a full size too big for me. That was obvious halfway down the hill from Pinnacle Hill Farm. Walking on the flat road was easier, though I scraped the pavement noisily. Both Raya and Sari looked at my feet as if to check on the oddball. I filled with dread as we turned down the driveway of the first farm.

I followed them, ducking under fence rails and navigating sloppy corrals. I had to crimp my toes to keep the mud from sucking the borrowed boots off my feet.

Those girls led me right up to animals. We walked between living, mooing cows, so close I could feel the heat from their huge bodies. A powerful stink rose up from the ground and into my nostrils. I held my breath. I got dizzy.

Mud and manure slipped away underfoot, like the earth was leaving me. Clumsily, I grabbed for tall Raya. Without a word she clapped her hand under my arm and helped me across the mud and up a high step onto the floor of the barn. Wood. Something solid. I stood with two hands holding the jamb and looked back across all the black-and-white cows' backs.

Raya and Sari were used to this. I was not. I didn't even want to be used to this. Why had I not come up with a reason to stay on Pinnacle Hill today? Suddenly, I was thinking of my mom again. She'd loved rain and mud, and now I wished I could ask her if she liked mud that had a lot of manure mixed into it. There was something I'd never know. Mom had had that way of marveling at small things. She hadn't loved the concrete all around Grandma's neighborhood; she'd missed her garden and the clover-filled lawn after we'd moved. But she'd always been the first to notice where a weedy little wildflower had pushed through in a crack in the concrete.

I walked up Raya's heels twice inside the barn, just trying to stay close. Problem: I was afraid to be behind cows or next to cows. I'd heard they could kick. I'd read about a boy being crushed between two of them. Once we were by all those enormous rumps and swatting tails, I could breathe again.

We walked out of the barn and into a long field. Partially

frozen pumpkins that had long ago split and leaked their seeds lay beside their dry stems. *Pumpkins not chosen*, I thought. *Like leftover dogs—except not.*

Even in winter there was work happening at every house, every farm. Some places we heard stories. Other places we got a friendly nod as we leaned on fence rails and stared out at resting winter rows. I didn't speak, except to say hello, but I paid attention. I learned that people either invited you in at the door or told you to go ahead in from the yards and barns and fields. There were cider dough-nuts on the tables, granola bars in the pantries. Might be some tea left in the pot but maybe not, but you could put the kettle on if you wanted to. This was normal for a Saturday, according to Raya and Sari. Welcome mats in Chelmsford meant what they said.

"Come on, I'll walk you all the way to the back of the property line." A Mr. Blasey made the offer proudly, and we went. There was nothing there except a pasture that ended at the base of a hill, much the way Elloroy's meadow met the woods. I caught on quickly: you walked out there for that look at nothing because you'd been invited. Never mind that mud creeping up to the laces of a pair of borrowed boots. Mr. Blasey's brother—also Mr. Blasey—rolled up on his noisy tractor with a flat wagon in tow. We were invited to have a lift back to the barn.

Yes! I boarded most ungracefully—jump, belly flop, legs kicking the air. Raya and Sari laughed as they dragged me onto the flatbed.

Mr. Blasey took us up to the road, where we jumped off. I could not have been happier to hear Raya announce, "Last stop before home."

20

The Onliest Few

I was pretty sure I had blisters on both my heels, and for sure, I had cramps in both my calves. Raya and Sari and I swished our boots through a clear puddle in the gravel of the last driveway. *Rinse cycle*, I thought.

We'd come down a long, long drive to reach this place. I expected to head to the front door with its plaque that said Gerber. My stomach would've been pleased with another snack. But Raya and Sari turned toward a small gray barn in the side yard instead. I shuffled after them.

"I hope Florry's here," Sari said, and she skipped ahead a step.

"Of course she'll be here," Raya scoffed. "She'll be with her bun-buns."

Bun-buns?

I followed close behind Raya. Instead of walking up her heels, I paused and let my eyes adjust to the low light.

"Florry? You here?" Raya did have the huskiest voice.

"Yee . . . ah, I am," came the answer. This voice was funny—like a very little child—and the reply sounded like a question because of a lilt at the end.

I could see the girl now—Florry—crouching in front of a row of wire cages. One door hung open. I saw a pair of little shining animal eyes in the dark corners. But mostly, I saw Florry. She was small and probably a few years younger than us, with nut-brown hair that hung forward in stringy pieces and brushed her jutting jaw. Her arms were wrapped close to her body as if she were holding her coat shut. She scrunched up her nose and snickered. She seemed distant and dreamy, and just as it hit me that she was special, Sari leaned close to me and whispered, "She has an intellectual disability. Should have told you. Her speech is unusual, but if you listen, everything makes sense. She loves animals."

"Hey, Florry," Raya said. "We brought a new friend. This is Lydia. Can we come in?"

"Yee-ah," said Florry. "But you be'er be quiet round here. Y'on't scare 'em." She gave us a bit of a big blue eyeballing.

"We'll be quiet," Sari said. She kept her voice warm and whispery. Florry stood up, still pulling her coat close. Was she cold? Poor kid. No. She was holding something in her arms—a bundle with some weight to it.

Then she turned and I could see the creature she held against her chest—a beautiful curl of rich reddish fur with long ears laid neatly back.

Oh, a rabbit. Bun-bun.

"Who do you have there?" Sari asked.

Florry formed the words slowly and deliberately. "Bellshin hey-yaw." She set her lips against the rabbit's head. She looked up and fixed large eyes on us. Then she nuzzled a smile into the rabbit's fur. She said, "We just got 'em. And we're the onliest few what raises 'em."

Raya leaned toward Florry. "Wait. You're what?"

Florry twisted gently side to side but did not repeat herself.

"Only a few?" Raya said. Then her eyebrows popped up. "Oh, you're telling us not very many other people raise this kind?" Florry didn't speak but her face changed. She brightened—ever so slightly. "And what're they called? What was that you said before?" Raya asked.

Again, Florry didn't answer. This was her way, I decided. She wasn't being sassy or rude. But if you didn't get it at first, she waited you out.

Sari said, "I heard bell and shin, and something like hey-yaw."

"Me too," I whispered. Raya and Sari both looked at me, probably surprised that I had spoken. "Bell shin," I whispered. I ran the sounds together. "Bellshin. So, wait. Is it *Belgian*? Belgian something?"

The pleased look filled Florry's face—like the first fraction of a second of what might become a smile but then it doesn't quite break open.

"You're right, Lydia." Sari gave me a gentle nudge. "Now what's hey-yaw?"

Raya shook her head. "I got nothin'."

"Well, it's something to do with rabbits, right?" I took a look into the wooden enclosure, where two more of the red rabbits hopped along on their fine-boned feet. They stood tall off the floor, ears high. Then one stretched upward with forefeet on the wooden wall. The poses reminded me of illustrations from an old book of fables Mom had. Fables, including the story of the tortoise and the hare—

"Hare?" I said. "Belgian Hare?" I wondered, *Was that a thing?*

Florry's face wakened again. She might have even nodded a little.

"There it is." Raya drew a check in the air. "You're good, Lydia."

117

"Thanks," I whispered. I crouched in the hay. A rabbit came near, then bumped its nose on my sleeve.

"They so soff," Florry said. She tilted her head until her ear touched her shoulder. I wanted to know more about Florry Gerber. And I wanted to draw the gorgeous Belgian Hares.

"Florry," I said. I slid my phone from my pocket and showed it to her. "Is it okay if I take some pictures?"

"I yon't cay-yaw."

I don't care.

My ear was adjusting.

She stooped and let the rabbit she was holding gently to the floor. The other two hopped right over to it. Touched base, nose to nose.

I did photograph those Belgian Hares—from overhead and down low in the hay, face on and tails turned.

By the time I finally stepped out of the stall, Raya and Sari were at the open door, out of earshot, I figured. I turned back to thank Florry Gerber. Then I whispered to her, "Hey. You're the Goddess of the Rabbits, aren't you?"

She wrinkled her nose at me and snickered. Then Florry Gerber said the strangest thing of all. She called right out loud, "I know your muh-tha!"

My mother?

21

Paper Friends

As we left the Gerber driveway, Raya and Sari were walking just ahead of me, our boots scraping, once again. My two welcomers were quiet. I knew why. Mom had been right: dead mothers make people uncomfortable. They'd heard Florry announce that she knew my mother. Raya and Sari had both blanched.

Now, on the road, Raya turned back toward me and spoke. "So. Man. Sorry about that."

"Florry must have gotten confused," Sari said. "It takes a little longer for her to understand some things." Suddenly I was walking between them. Sari patted my shoulder with her mitten-covered hand.

"It's fine," I said. Maybe I should have helped by saying

what we all knew: Florry Gerber couldn't possibly know my mother. But it was so much more interesting to me that she *believed* she did.

"That was sweet what you said to her," Sari said. "The Goddess of the Rabbits. . . ." My blood rushed. I hadn't meant for Sari or Raya to hear that.

"Florry liked it," Sari went on. "She knew you were saying something special about her. What made you think of that? Goddess?"

"It just popped into my head." I shrugged.

"That's so cool," said Sari. "I like thinking of Florry as a goddess."

"Yeah," said Raya. Her eggplant-colored head bobbed and her eyebrows arched. "And ya know, it's accurate."

Accurate but *strange*. That's what she really meant.

I probably seemed so weird to these girls. Whatever. They'd been nice to bring me out. Soon they'd drop me home. I'd see them at school and we'd say hello because our class was tiny, and we really couldn't get away with not greeting one another. We knew significant facts. We were raising tiny trout.

I pulled my jacket closer. Checked the sky. Something was changing here in the middle of the day. The wind was slicing through the sun's warmth. *Hello, Weather Goddess.* I drew my hands up inside the sleeves of my jacket, into the cuffs of Mom's sweater. I gathered her knitting around my fingers. We walked on. Raya and Sari began to chat again. I dropped several steps back, where my mind could wander.

I thought about the last year that I'd gone to school. Fifth grade. Just another Monday . . . until I'd walked up on something in the lunchroom—something I wasn't meant to hear.

Beth-Anne Carlo had been to my house the Saturday before. We'd planned on a trip to the city flea market, but we'd had to scratch that because Mom's energy had tanked early that day. (It happened a lot. We couldn't predict.) So we'd spent the day baking cookies instead and making collages. We'd gone through old magazines and had cut out colors and patterns. We'd found the best faces, best noses, eyes, and mouths. We'd cut them at funny angles, mixed and matched them. "Cubists for the day," Mom had said.

The new faces were weird, fascinating, and plain hilarious. We kept playing, dropping a large eye on the same face with a small one. That sort of thing. Beth-Anne and I had both fallen on the floor laughing.

"Look! We *Frankensteined* them!" she'd said.

Then Mom had had an idea: we should create Great Goddesses of the Flea Market. For the first time, I'd thought about that—how the goddesses had so often replaced, or stood in for, the things we'd had to miss. Mom let us pick photos from the Wasserman Studios folio. Beth-Anne and I "dressed" our goddesses in bright, paper-scrap colors. We surrounded them with trinkets and baskets full of ridiculous things for sale, like pink fish heads, spotted apples, and even spare hands, just to be bizarre. We cut and tore, pasted, and painted for hours. We'd had a great day. Or so I'd thought.

On that following Monday I'd come up behind Beth-Anne, who'd appeared to be holding a lunch-table audience captive. Slowly, I'd tuned in. "So there I was," she'd complained, "stuck for my *entire* Saturday with Lydia, her mother, and all their *paper friends*. . . ." She'd waggled her fingers beside her ears.

There'd been a lot of snickers at the table. Sympathetic groans. Then Amelia Sykes had spotted me standing there and she'd cleared her throat. The girls had ducked their faces. Lunches had been left and Beth-Anne had looked truly horrified.

I'd gone home that day and I'd sifted through the papers on our table. I'd unearthed a few fairly recent goddesses. I looked at the faces, some serene and some intense, some a little angry, I suppose. It was funny, I couldn't always remember which ones were more Mom's handiwork and which were more mine because we'd passed them back and forth. But Mom hand lettered all the titles—like "The Goddess of an Early Spring," "The Goddess of Perfect Sleep," "The Goddess of Home Repairs."

Anyway, I'd told Mom what had happened at school. Then I'd said, "I'm not really upset. I'm surprised. It seemed like Beth-Anne had a pretty good time here."

"Hmm. I thought so too," Mom had agreed.

"She made a goddess. A great one," I'd said.

"But you know what, Lyddie, probably both things are true. Beth-Anne had a fine time. We saw that. But she also expected something different on the day, and so she felt stuck here too. From there it's a matter of attitude and how she chooses to tell the story. You know, what will get the biggest rise out of the friends at the lunch table." She'd waited, then asked me, "So, what did you do?"

"Well, Beth-Anne was embarrassed. I felt bad for her. So I just said, 'Yeah, we had to totally change our plans.' Then I ate my lunch. Some of it."

"Yeah." Mom had nodded, her usual sweet smile on her lips. "Well done, Lyddie."

I'd never said anything more about goddesses—not to friends. I'd never invited Beth-Anne or anyone else over again. Turning point. My friends could not understand—not really—what it was like to have a mom who was so sick. (And no dad.) My life was too different from theirs.

At the end of fifth grade Mom had decided to take me out of public school, and I hadn't fought her on it.

"Man! Do you guys feel that?" Raya said. She stopped still. I was jolted out of the memory. She stood on the road, turned her face up to the sky just briefly. "It's turning out here. Brrr . . . ," she said. She made a funny shivering noise with her lips.

"I know," Sari said. She made mitten fists. Her teeth chattered. But her jacket was flapping wide open.

"Zip this!" Raya scolded. She grabbed the two halves of Sari's jacket and pulled them together.

"I c-c-can't!" Sari squeaked. "I'm too c-c-cold to take my hands out of my mittens!" Raya sighed, hitched the zipper, and brought it up under Sari's chin. "Th-th-thank you!" Sari chattered.

"What are friends for?" said Raya. "By the way, you're a dork."

"Y-y-yeah," said Sari. Then they laughed as they walked, stamping their feet to make themselves warmer.

I couldn't help it, I smiled too. But inside I felt a weird split; I was half-happy and half-sad.

22

Ornery

My old fifth-grade feelings stuck to me as I climbed the driveway to Pinnacle Hill Farm by myself. There was nothing wrong with Raya and Sari. They'd been all kinds of nice. But all morning, I'd felt like a log in tow. My life had a lot of unshareable parts—not things I was ashamed of, but things that seemed so exhausting to explain that I didn't even want to try.

When we'd parted at the bottom of the hill, Raya had checked with me. "You know where you are, right? This is your hill." She'd pointed it out. I did know, but she was right to ask. As small as Chelmsford was, I felt spun around. We'd traveled off-road, and in fact we'd cut across a hilly field and a good patch of woods after that last stop at the Gerber farm.

"We'll come get you again, so keep the boots," Raya had said.

I'd looked at my feet. I'd never seen them in anything uglier than those brown boots.

"There are more places to see," Sari had told me as she'd waved her mitten.

No, no . . . we are done. . . . Please don't come back. . . .

I'd felt bad for feeling that way, and that's why I was crabby as I climbed the drive. I scuffed my foot hard on the gravel, watched a grassy wafer of damp manure fly off my boot. "Oh! Pee-ewe!"

Aunt Brat's boxy car was not in its spot outside the house when I crested the hill. Eileen's junky truck was there, but with any luck, she'd gone with Aunt Brat, and maybe Elloroy had too. Then there'd be *no* people home. The nameless yellow dog would be in his crate, the old greyhound would be sleeping, and I could do what I wanted, which might be go upstairs and cry awhile. Or maybe even pull the lid off the goddess box for the first time since I'd arrived. I was dying to do it as much as I could not seem to make myself do it.

You are a mess, Lydia Bratches-Kemp.

I stepped onto the porch and the yellow dog crowed an alarm. Great. Now he was jumping up to the glass part of the door. Someone was home—or he'd escaped

126

the crate. "Shut up," I muttered. I cracked the door open. "Get down! Back! Back!" I called. He barked his head off. I stuck one arm and one knee inside and forced my way in through the smallest opening possible. I used my body to shove the dog back. If he got near the open door, he'd try to bolt. I had fresh blisters on both feet; I was in no mood to have to go tromping after him.

I closed the door behind me, and the dog slinked away. He threaded himself in behind the furniture and gave me his suspicious look and a few deep woofs.

"Lydia, you're back!" Eileen came to greet me.

"Yep." Now Soonie came clicking across the floor as well. I gave her head an obligatory pat. "Okay, okay," I said. I hoped she'd get it; I was done.

"Good walk, was it?"

"Oh, Yeah. Interesting. Farms," I said. I let out a sigh.

"Wonderful," Eileen said. "Well, Brat's at the grocery, but big news here. We've done it!" She wiggled a little cha-cha.

"Done what?" I asked. (Had they won a lottery?) My blisters burned. I began the tender operation of stepping out of the borrowed boots.

"We named the dog!"

"Oh?" I said. I stood on one leg with one boot in my hand.

"He's *Guffer*!" she cheered. "But only if you agree. Like it?"

"Guffer? Sounds fine," I said. The newly named dog galloped forth. He snatched the boot right out of my fingers. "Hey!" I spoke sharply. "Give that back!" I lunged toward him. Wrong move. To the dog, that meant the chase was on. He leapt. He shook the boot for the kill.

"Try the 'Leave it!' command," Eileen suggested. "He's catching on to that one. Sort of."

I was fuming. Maybe it was the blisters. Or maybe it was feeling that this Saturday morning, which I'd wanted to myself, was now gone. Or maybe it was hearing Eileen suggest that this dog—this Gumper, or Gruffer, or whatever—had caught on to even a single command. He had not! He was plain bad, and now he had a dirty, borrowed boot in his mouth and he was knocking mud and manure off it all through the house.

"Leave it!" I snarled at him. "I said, leave it!" He dropped the boot, tucked tail, and ran, sideway-ish, behind the couch. Then he peeked around and stared at me while I swiped the boot off the floor. "Yeah . . . you sneaky piece of . . . ," I spoke under my breath. But I knew Eileen could hear me.

"Well. There, then," she said, obviously a bit surprised.

I could feel her looking at me as I set both boots into the tray by the door. I excused myself up the stairs. I kept my mad-hot face turned away from Eileen.

Not much later I heard Aunt Brat arrive home. She and Eileen spoke in mumbly voices down in the kitchen. I guessed that they were putting groceries away. I guessed Eileen was telling on me—recounting my tantrum for Aunt Brat. I should go downstairs. Be helpful. But I didn't. I sat on the bed popping the liquid out of my foot blisters and making decisions about whether to peel the skin off or flatten it back down to cover the raw spots.

I heard Aunt Brat call up to me, "Lydia? We're going to take the dogs around the perimeter." They had a theory: this was how the new dog would learn where home was. Well, the edges of home, perhaps.

"Okay by you?"

"Sure is! See you soon!" I tried to find that chirp in my voice, but I don't think it quite came up. I waited until I heard them go out. From my window over the flattish roof I watched them cross the yard. It was all of them: two dogs, two women, and Elloroy. Aunt Brat took long strides, Eileen lurched on her shorter leg, and Elloroy plodded, laying his long flat feet down in front of his body with care. The newly named—what was it? Goffer? Goofer?—led, of course, on the leash, turning back to lightly gnaw on

129

Soonie if she trotted alongside him or passed him, which she did. The greyhound must win.

They would not be out for long, I thought. I was alone and just a little cranky. Seemed like the perfect time to bust a bigger hole in that wall behind the sheep poster.

And I did.

23

The Other Side of the Bricks

The hole I made was roughly rectangular—and quick work. I set the flashlight inside and crouched down. I'd fit myself into small spaces before. I was long, but I was thin and foldable.

I led with one arm and one shoulder, tucked my head, and pulled my body in sideways. I crouched in the chilly space, then stood up slowly, unsure how far above me the roof rafters would be. I stretched to my full height and shone the flashlight upward. I had at least a foot and a half to spare. I stood there grinning. How cool to be standing on this side of this ancient chimney—the side that no one ever saw!

I laid one hand on the bricks. I felt just a little warmth . . . and cobwebs. Wow. Everywhere! They stuck to my bare hands. They stretched themselves into strings that wrapped between my fingers. "Ew! Ew!" I tried to shake them away, but they clung and made me feel freaky. I wiped them onto the hip of Mom's sweater with rough swipes.

"Ew!" I said again. "Okay, okay." I calmed myself down. The bricks stretched six feet or so, the same as on the other side in the upstairs hallway. That made sense. But how surprising that there was a passageway behind the chimney. At the far end, I could see the plumbing pipes that fed the bathtub.

I started forward but quickly saw that there was more framing than flooring underfoot. I made a point of stepping on the joists. Between them lay tattered rows of insulation, the old kind made of pink fuzz and brown paper. I'd heard that you weren't supposed to touch that stuff. It'd make you itchy. I did wonder what was under the rows. One thing I was sure of: mice.

I spotted little chewed-up nest bundles everywhere, and some nutshells, and turds. "Come out, come out, wherever you are. . . ." Generations' worth of whiskery ones must have crawled through here.

Oh . . . a crawl space? . . . Is that what this is?

I ducked under another swag of webs and reached into the peak with my open hand. It was nearly as cold as the outdoors up there. My adults would not be pleased that they were losing heat through this hatch.

That reminded me, they and their dogs would be back from that walk soon. I stooped down to exit and something caught my eye—my ruler! I'd forgotten about it. I grabbed it and squeezed back through the hole.

Well, the crawl space wasn't the cleanest, warmest spot on earth. Far from it. But when I turned back just to poke the flashlight in and have one more look up and down, I knew I had found something that I'd been wanting: this was a home for the goddesses.

24

A Name to Stick To

In the evening I stood at the kitchen counter topping the two bowls of dry dog food with a dollop of the stinky wet stuff. Eileen brushed by me, mumbling something about croutons for our salad. That was disconcerting for one who was looking into a pan full of kibble. But then she stopped abruptly right beside me. "Goodness, Lydia. You've got a webby thing here," she said. She raised an eyebrow as she pinched the sticky strand off my hip. She walked partway around me, still pulling. "Extraordinary," she mumbled.

Eileen unraveling me.

"That's a nice decoration," said Elloroy.

"Oh, and looks like another on her sleeve." Aunt Brat pointed at me with a cooking spoon. Great. I had everyone's attention. With any luck, they wouldn't ask—

"What did you get into?"

"Oh . . . who knows?" I said. "I did do some dusting earlier." (Not a complete lie.) "Oh, hey, the dog! You've named him!" I said. "Guffer, right? So how'd you come up with that?"

"Well," said Aunt Brat with a coy grin, "he said it to me. In fact, he says it all the time. This morning after you left I was giving his coat a brushing. He was mouthing my hands—you know the way he does?" (I did.) "There's a little sound he makes. He says, 'Guff-guff.' So I said it back. I said, 'You're an old *guffer*, aren't you?'"

"That's right. And he said yes!" Eileen piped up.

"He what?"

"He said yes."

"Ludicrous," said Elloroy.

"Oh, tuning in, are we?" Eileen teased him. "And here I thought you were a little bit dead or something." Then she argued, "It's *not* ludicrous. As soon as Brat said it, the dog turned belly-up, tail wagging. That's a sign of extreme well-being. He was saying he likes the name."

"Says you," said Elloroy. He offered Eileen his pinkie and she hooked hers into it.

Aunt Brat laughed at them. Then she said, "I hope you like it, Lydia."

How funny. Why would I have a say? "Sure!" I gave a shrug. "I just hope it sticks."

135

"Well, we spent all morning saying it out loud and giving him treats if he looked our way," Aunt Brat said.

Elloroy leaned toward me. "And you want to know what happened right after that?" I narrowed my eyes at the old man. "He *pooped*!"

I snorted. I snotted a little, too. Couldn't help it. I grabbed a napkin and buried my face in it.

That set Elloroy off. He laughed so hard his eyes closed up tight. Great, magnified tears wet his magnified lashes. He had to mop them on his sleeve. Elloroy laughing made Eileen laugh and that made Aunt Brat laugh. Then the yellow dog—*Guffer*—came over, head on a tilt, ears askew, to check on all of us. He rumbled, then barked the sharp bark at us. That startled Aunt Brat. She made a big O with her mouth. We all burst into a new round of laughter.

All the next week they worked on teaching the dog his name. We had to be consistent, my aunt and Eileen kept reminding me and each other. "At least we, the humans, are remembering this name, after all our failures," Aunt Brat pointed out. "We probably had him thoroughly confused, poor thing."

Maybe she was right. Sometimes I thought the dog was getting it, and I don't mean just his new name. There were times he actually cooperated, and I'd wonder if it was true compliance or just that in certain moments he wanted to do the thing we all wanted him to do.

Regardless, at least once a day, he still botched it all up by peeing or pooping indoors or giving us the slip and running off. Aunt Brat's shoulders would drop every time he messed up. One day I overheard her talking to Eileen. "We know the adage: It's training the owner as much as it is training the dog. I'm perplexed. Soonie arrived with plenty of baggage from her days at the track but we worked through that. Was it this hard? Have I forgotten?"

Eileen just sighed and said, "We'll get there. We knew where Soonie came from. We had a little greyhound hand-book. This dog didn't come with operating instructions."

I'd hear those conversations and think about the old dog tag up in my art box and that name, Cici Hoover. I had her phone number. What if I could learn something that would make life with the yellow dog go smoothly?

For my part, well, I used his name when I walked him to the enclosure at night, where he sat looking south and I stood looking northwest. I spoke to him; I even confessed. (Our back-to-back poses seemed good for that.) "I've put a serious hole in the wall up there, Guffer. Yep. Inside the house where these good people have taken me in. Taken both of us in," I clarified. "But you know, Guffer, at least *I* didn't use it for a toilet."

In fact, I'd been cleaning the crawl space whenever I'd

had the house to myself—or almost to myself. I'd taken bags of felted cobwebs, mouse nests, and plaster pieces out to the trash in secret.

"Guffer, I'm going to move the goddesses in," I told him. "Ya hear what I'm saying?" I faced his back, then said his name sharply. "Guffer!" He turned suddenly to look at me. He let out a pitiful little yip like something had stung him. "Oh, what?" I said. Not for the first time, I had the thought that he might be a bit of a crybaby. But then he came over on his hoppy legs and waited in front of me to get his treat.

"Good boy," I told him, being consistent. Then I gushed at him so I'd sound even more like Aunt Brat and Eileen.

"Gooood boy!"

25

Looking Forward and Back

Looking through the glass wall of the fish tank, I saw a bloated version of Moss Capperow looking back from the other side. I had not come here to see him; I wanted only to see the baby trout. Still, Moss looked pretty funny. I might have been smiling about that—right up until I realized that I must be looking bloated too. I stepped back from the tank.

"Hi, Lydia."

"Hi, Moss."

"How's it going with your dog?" he asked. Funniest thing, I wanted to answer the way Elloroy would: That's not my dog. Moss had probably watched our troubles from the windows of the morning bus.

"Hmm. Not so bad, I guess. They finally gave him a name. It's Guffer."

Moss gave a nod. "That's a cool name."

"Well, seems to fit him," I said. "But so would a lot of other names."

"Oh really? What other names?"

I shrugged. "Like, Run-away. And Rug Wrecker."

Moss laughed again—not the kind of laugh that makes a lot of sound, but a wriggle that started in his shoulders and ended in his hands. Goofy. And a little bit sweet.

"I just saw one of the other dogs from that day," Moss told me. He seemed to think I'd be very interested, but I was confused.

"From what day?"

"Oh. Sorry. The adoption day. Maybe you didn't notice me. I volunteered that day. I saw you. It was really windy," he said as if that would jog my memory.

So that's why he'd said it was nice to see me again back on my first day of school here—the "significant fact" day. "I—I noticed you," I said. "But then I forgot. I mean, I got to school and had it in my head that I'd never seen anyone before, so . . . You know. Besides, you had a hat on."

He smiled. But then again, he never really stopped smiling. I thought to ask, Hasn't anyone ever told you, if you keep that up your face will get stuck like that? You'll be terminally cheerful. . . .

No, no. Don't say that. . . .

Instead I asked him a question. "So, where does Moss come from?"

"Spores, I think."

I sputtered a laugh—clapped my hand over my mouth so I wouldn't spray Moss Capperow. He wriggled again.

"Mossimo," he said. "My mother's maiden name."

I recovered and managed to say, "Oh . . . interesting."

"What about Bratches-Kemp?" he asked, and for once he looked like he was thinking instead of just smiling.

I wished I'd had something clever to say, like that Bratches-Kemp was a species of salamander, or a team of brilliant physicists, or the cross streets near my birth home, or, better yet, something to do with a renowned artist.

"Mother. Father," I told him. I flipped my thumb from one side to the other.

"I figured," said Moss.

I thought about how much I didn't like wearing "Kemp" on the end of my name. All my life, I'd heard and liked the story of how my aunt, who'd been named Anna Lois Bratches, had decided to legally shed two-thirds of her name and just be "Bratches." Mom had once said Aunt Brat was trying to free herself of anything that my grandma, her mother, had given her because they'd had a terrible relationship. Why did I have to keep Kemp when the real Kemp had chosen to up and leave me?

"No dead ones," Moss said.

"What?" Then I realized he was looking into the fish tank again.

"We lost a few in the beginning. Did anyone tell you?"

I shook my head no. I looked at the fish hovering close to one another in the tank. "What did that . . . look like?" I asked.

Surely a fish does not turn blue . . . does not tell the others how much she loves them. . . .

"Floating," said Moss. For the moment, his smile was gone. "We felt bad about it," he said. "But when it happens we take the dead out and look them over with a magnifier." He shrugged. "A dead fish is sad. But it's interesting."

Moss had to go. I was surprised when I didn't want him to. It was my turn to record the water temperature. I added it to the trout log. I pulled a chair beside the tank, sat down, and watched the trout wiggle their tails.

Moss Capperow had me thinking about floating fish and things that happen *last*.

Mom and I had made a last goddess—of course. We called her the Goddess of Looking Forward and Backward. Mom had started her in early December when she was thinking about the coming of the New Year. This goddess was unusual for us. She'd gotten her start as a female version of a male god from Roman mythology—Janus.

He was the guardian of doorways, the protector at the gate. He gave his name to January. Mom had seen a sculpture in her favorite art magazine—a rendering of the god Janus—but as a female. We'd always invented our own goddesses, but Mom had felt inspired, and she'd set right to altering one of the Wasserman gallery portraits. She'd given the woman two profiles that faced opposite directions. Looking forward and looking back. We nicknamed her She-Janus.

Our She-Janus sat around unfinished longer than any other goddess we ever had. Mom had less energy. I'd known it and she'd known it. She'd say, "Put a little paint or something on our She-Janus, will you, Lyddie?" I'd stood over that goddess and had tried to think what she needed besides two faces.

One afternoon I'd mixed white paint with clear gel medium and I'd painted over her entirely. It looked like I had drowned her in milk; she was nearly gone. I dabbed some paint off to reveal her again. "Nice," Mom had said. "Conceal and reveal! Now lay down some lace for pattern. Lift more white off." So I had, and that left a wintry frost on She-Janus. I'd held her up for Mom to see. Mom had relaxed back into her pillow, wearing a smile of pure approval. But I'd had the thought that Mom, too, was paling into her own background.

In the days after, I wondered at the coincidence of Mom dying so close to the New Year—leaving at that traditional time of looking forward and backward.

Mom . . . it's all I do now . . . I try to see forward . . . but I keep looking back. . . .

26

Two Little Goats

The third week of January brought changes. Aunt Brat went back to her position at the university. That meant that on Tuesday, Wednesday, and Thursday mornings, after doing the bus stop thing with Eileen and the dogs (I hadn't the heart to tell them that they were cramping my style), she took her long walk, then was gone until early evening.

She was worried about not being home for me after school. I reassured her I was fine without saying I was actually kind of pleased. I'd hop off the bus and check in with Elloroy and Soonie to see if they needed anything before their nap. I'd take Guffer outside, get him to do his business, then I'd do my homework. "I'll start dinner if you need me to," I offered. "I know how to cook."

"I know. But you need to be a kid too."

It was just a few words, but I felt them in my chest. Our helper, Angelica, used to say that to me too.

"Oh, if only I didn't have afternoon classes," Aunt Brat muttered.

"But if you had to be in for early classes, you'd miss your morning walk here," I said.

"You're right," she said.

We decided she'd pick me up on Fridays. (I think she liked the idea of us checking in with each other at the end of each week.) As planned, she was waiting for me in the circle inside the boxy car on Friday afternoon. Her head was bent. She was studying her phone. I opened the door and she jumped. "Hi, Aunt Brat. Sorry I startled you."

"It's okay. I have a message from Eileen," she said. "She wants to be picked up."

"Did the truck die again?" I asked. (I swear that truck was held together by rusted safety pins.)

"Hmm . . . she doesn't say, but I don't think so. I'm not sure what this is about. But I think we best hop on over there."

"Right now?" I was surprised. The Feed didn't close until six p.m.

"Yes," said Aunt Brat. "Seat belt." She pointed at my lap. She dropped her phone into her purse and off we went.

We found Eileen in tears. She'd had an awful day. I heard her say so as she buried her swollen face on Aunt Brat's shoulder. There, she chugged out sob after sob. I stood near. I alternately stared down at the pine floorboards and watched my two adults working their way through some unknown awfulness. I listened for clues.

"They dumped them," Eileen said. "Right out on the front porch here at the Feed. I didn't even know what I was looking at, not at first—" Eileen lost it in another flood of tears. "It's two. Little pygmy goats. Alive. But bloody as . . ."

Bloody?

"They've got no hind hooves, and three out of four ears were taken."

Taken? Off goats? For what? My guts lurched.

"Oh, dear God!" Aunt Brat cried. "Oh, no, no! How awful. Oh, Eileen . . ." She tightened their hug. "I'm sorry. So sorry. Oh, who could do such a thing?"

"No idea. It's a crime, is what it is," Eileen said.

"Yes. It's inhuman."

Aunt Brat held Eileen while Eileen cried and swore. I tried to figure out if I'd heard right. Eileen looked at me over Aunt Brat's shoulder. "S-sorry, Lydia. Sorry."

I shook my head. I was aching and bewildered. "I—I'm sorry for you, Eileen." I truly was.

147

Barley, the owner of the Feed, came up the ladder at the loading dock. "She told you, huh?" He came around to the checkout counter, eyes on Aunt Brat. "Been a rough day," he told her. "Brutal."

"Do you have any idea who, or how?" Aunt Brat asked.

"Nothing yet. I hope we can get an investigation. Cruelty case, if I ever saw one." He shook his head. "The vet will come as soon as she can."

"Oh, she'll have to put them down, don't you think?" Aunt Brat asked.

"It's her call," Barley said. "She can't get here until closing. I laid down straw and penned them in the corner so they won't try to move around on those injuries. They each took a little feed and water," he said. "But they're listless. Look for yourself, if you think you can take it." He jabbed a thumb over his shoulder.

It was hard *not* to look where that thumb was pointing. I wanted to see them. Was that awful?

"No, no. Don't look at them, Brat," said Eileen. "And Lydia, not you! Don't do it." Eileen shook her head. She blew her nose on a wad of tissues.

But Aunt Brat did cross the room to the corner and I walked with her. Eileen covered her face while we looked inside the makeshift enclosure.

It was bad. Very bad. Aunt Brat touched my shoulder and whispered, "Are you all right, here?"

I think I nodded. I might have said yes. But mostly, I stared.

The two small goats lay close together, their chins on the floor. They were mostly white with spots of brown. At first I couldn't see what was wrong, but then, I couldn't *not* see it. Their legs were tucked partway underneath them as if they were trying to hide what had been taken—or protect what had been left behind. Curls of bloodstained bandages lay on the straw, having unraveled from at least one hind foot. The ears were just as Eileen had said, three of four gone—sliced away, leaving a raw red circle of folds. I could see partway into the tunnel of an ear—a place I was not meant to see.

The pale curly coats of both goats looked clean. Had someone tended the wounds? Maybe Barley?

The little goats looked back at me through their weird, sage-yellow eyes with the pupils like thick hyphen dashes. Their gazes seemed to reveal no shock—unless that was exactly what they were revealing. What did I know of goats? I only knew that I felt sick, and embarrassed to be a human—the same species that had done to them what had been done.

I lifted my trembling chin. I swallowed. I nearly stumbled stepping backward away from the makeshift pen. "Th-they look like babies," I said.

"They do," said Eileen. "I haven't looked at the teeth—I just can't—but I'm guessing just weeks old."

That seemed like an interesting thing for Eileen to know. When I turned she closed her eyes and tears streamed over her round cheeks.

"Dear God," Aunt Brat muttered again as she, too, came away from the goats. Her tone thickened with outrage. "What possible reason could there be for such a vicious act? What is wrong with people? And I suppose someone dropped them here at the Feed so someone would find them."

"Animals have been left before," Barley said. "But not like this."

Eileen caught her breath. "But Brat, if the vet can fix them up enough . . . somehow . . . if she says she can treat them then we should take—"

"No. No." Aunt Brat shook her head—adamant little shakes. "I sincerely hope she can help them, Eileen. But *you* can't." She leaned toward her and whispered, "This is not for you. You'll suffer *again*. You can't. And I can't." Aunt Brat held her and whispered, "You know I'm right."

I stood alone. My cold fingers held my other cold fingers.

What did *suffer again* mean? There was much more to know about this—about goats and about Eileen, I thought. I looked down, I toed the floor.

"I should go home," Eileen said. "I barely made it this

150

long." She choked back another sob. "Sorry for dragging you here. And Lydia too. I needed you, Brat," she said, though barely above a whisper.

"Of course you did. I'm glad you called." Aunt Brat turned to Barley.

"Yeah, yeah. Go," he said. "Eileen, take the rest of today and wait for me to call you back in. Let me get the vet here, and get this figured out."

Outside, I opened the car door for Eileen. "Thank you so much, Lydia," Aunt Brat said. We stood together watching Eileen settle onto the front seat. When we shut the door, she let her head drop against the window. It was a strange sight. Ever since I'd arrived to Chelmsford, Eileen had been jovial—Pinnacle Hill's own comedian.

Through the evening, Eileen sat wrapped in a blanket on the couch. She sipped the tea Aunt Brat brought to her. Elloroy had been told, and he sat with one arm around Eileen's shoulder. Soonie nestled on her other side and put her head in Eileen's lap. Eileen stroked her over and over again. Even wild Guffer seemed to pick up on the mood. He settled on the rug with a humph of a sigh and laid his chin on one paw. None of us humans wanted much supper. Aunt Brat and I made up little plates of leftovers and brought them into the living room.

I needed to be out of the way. There was a *thing* in the

room, and if they weren't going to talk to me about it, I might as well help us all and get out. It seemed almost right when Guffer rose, circled, and took his evening squat over the rug. I jumped to my feet. I took the dogs to the fenced pasture and wandered along the rail while they did their thing: Guffer pursuing Soonie, Soonie avoiding Guffer, night falling. I looked back at the house, windows glowing pumpkin gold. I thought about the little goats— the damage—and then tried not to.

I took my pose facing northwest, and sweet old Soonie came alongside of me. She was funny that way, such a stand-beside-you dog. I offered her my gloved hand to rest her chin in. She took me up on that. Guffer stood, or rather sat, his ground, being his serious, south-facing self.

27

Another Hard Story

I know that Aunt Brat would have knocked on my door if it had been closed. She was good about that. But the door was open so she brushed her knuckles on it, then entered. Only a minute before, I'd secured the sheep poster back on the wall over the hole. Two minutes before that, I'd had my head in there.

How lucky that she hadn't caught me. However, she did see that I had the box out, the one I kept the goddesses in. The dreadful afternoon had brought me to them. Objects could be places of comfort—especially these objects. There needed to be a Goddess of the Goats. But they probably weren't going to get one from me. I hadn't made anything since the She-Janus. Nothing since coming here. But I had braided some yarn and I'd started tying it to the goddesses—something to hang them up by.

Now, I tried to be nonchalant about sliding the box back under the bed. Aunt Brat's eyes darted from me to the spot where it'd disappeared and back to me again.

"Sorry," she said.

"How's Eileen?" I asked.

"A little better. She'll be okay. I want to talk to you about that." Aunt Brat parked herself on the bed and I joined her. "She knows I'm up here. We agreed that we need to share some history with you. But it's too hard for Eileen to talk about, so you have me." She pressed her hands on her knees and spoke slowly. "I think it doesn't feel right to keep secrets from people you live with, Lydia—"

Whoa. Uh-oh.

I felt my heart bang against my ribs. What secrets did she mean?

"—and I didn't mean to do that." She went on. "*We* didn't mean to."

"Is this about the goats?"

"Yes. I'm sure you could tell that something was wrong—I mean something besides the obvious. And I am so sorry you saw that. I should have protected you. Just because I needed to see, doesn't mean you needed to. You've been through so much. I know that you're grieving,

154

and you haven't said a lot, and that's okay. I respect that. Silence is one way to feel strong, especially when something is so new." She pressed her knuckles up under her nose. "I hate to burden you with another hard story." She paused and gazed at me until I had to look away.

"Aunt Brat, I'm all right. You can tell me," I said.

She nodded. "So . . . one of the reasons Eileen and I came here to Elloroy's place is that she wanted to start a business. She wanted to manage a small herd of goats."

"Of goats? Ohh . . ."

"Everything she needed was here: pasture and barns. We were both excited—and Elloroy was too. Eileen had visited other goat farms. She'd done all her research, had a meticulous plan for building a small herd. She took out a loan for repairs and new fencing. Along the way we learned about leasing as a side business," she explained. "People will actually rent goats to control vegetation—they're like a team of environmentally friendly lawn mowers. The state was interested."

"The state government?"

"Yes. For tending public lands. Eileen won a nice contract. She worked to the point of exhaustion, but she loved it. She did everything right. She got rolls of special fencing. She took the very best care of the animals, but it did mean installing them at various sites for days at a time. And Eileen always went with them. Believe it or not she pulled a tiny camper behind that old truck of hers." Aunt Brat laughed a tiny laugh. "But then one evening, she was on a site not too far from home and she started to feel sick—so sick. She drove herself home—barely—and we took her to the hospital, they rushed her into surgery and removed her appendix."

"Oh my gosh, Aunt Brat."

"Yes. So scary. And poor Eileen, she'd barely been awake when we got the most horrific news. Vandals had trashed the trailer and cut down the fences—"

I gasped. I clapped my hand over my mouth.

Aunt Brat shook her head. "The herd got loose—or was chased—onto a highway. Every animal was lost."

"Lost?"

"Either struck and killed, or just never recovered from injuries. Four were brought here, and we tried to nurse them back to health." Aunt Brat shook her head. "They didn't survive."

"Oh, poor Eileen," I whispered. "And the animals . . ." I balled my hands into a knot.

"She was devastated. And full of guilt. They were like pets to her. It turns out goats can be very affectionate." Aunt Brat gave a little sigh. "Eileen felt conflicted about making money off them. It's one of the toughest things about animal husbandry, at least from what I have observed," she said. "I think of the farms around here . . ." She shook her head. "Anyway, all those feelings compounded the loss and—"

"And then today happened," I said. "Oh, Aunt Brat, it's terrible."

"Exactly—and goats, of all things!" Aunt Brat looked at me intently. "So you can see, it's salt in the wound. Eileen and I didn't mean to leave you in the dark. This story just hadn't come up yet here at home, but honestly, I would've hesitated to tell you if it had, Lyddie."

Lyddie. That was Mom's name for me.

"But after today, how could I *not* tell you?" she said.

"I'm glad you did," I said. "Are you sure that Eileen can't have the goats from today? Shouldn't have them?" *If they're still alive*, I thought.

"Oh, Lydia. I am *so* sure," Aunt Brat said. "The damage looks serious—and that's just what we can see. There could be infection. That lethargy worries me. Their heads should be up. Then there's the question of how they get along from here, the treatment. If we brought them home Eileen would become invested. And then, if they didn't make it, well, I love Eileen too much to watch her lose like that again." Aunt Brat's voice cracked as she finished.

We sat in the quiet. I was trying to accept what my aunt said. But I wondered if it wouldn't somehow help Eileen to be a part of giving the goats a chance. But maybe that was just it: it was goats. Again.

"Aunt Brat, you should go back down and be with her," I said.

"Are you all right? Want to come?"

"Well, I'm sure it's you she really wants."

Aunt Brat reached forward and covered my hands with both of hers. Then, in a warm sort of whisper, she said, "In this house, we all need each other."

28

The Word at School

On Sunday afternoon Aunt Brat took a phone call from Barley. She went outside for a better signal. (So it was up on Pinnacle Hill; cell phones worked in my room, at the kitchen window, or outdoors.) She paced back and forth for what seemed like forever. Finally, she came in to say, "The goats have been placed, and the vet said there was hope." It was vague news, but good news.

"Sheesh! Took Barley long enough to spit that out," Eileen said. "You looked like you were doing a five-miler out there, Brat." (I was glad to hear her make a joke.) She followed with a big sigh of relief, which I know was for those little goats.

Eileen went back to work on Monday. But there remained a sort of gentleness at home—and zero talk of the incident. It wasn't until late that week that I heard Eileen sounding like her jovial self again.

Meanwhile, the kids at school had heard the story: two maimed goats left at the Feed, and since not much happens in Chelmsford (their words, not mine) it was the topic of the morning. Everyone was indignant—so much so, I felt a sense of kinship. But accounts of the incident were different from what I knew to be true.

Someone had heard all four ears were gone; someone else thought all eight hooves had been cut. I listened. I remembered the bandages, the raw circle around the three ears. I pictured the goats with the hyphen pupils in their eyes, the way they'd looked back at me and how unreadable I thought they were. But I was sure that no one at school had actually seen the animals. Nobody except me.

"Hey, Lydia," Raya said, "your aunt's wife works at the Feed, right? What did she say?" Then rather grimly she added, "Did she see them?"

"She was super sad," I said, and that was all I said. I was feeling protective of Eileen.

Everyone believed that the goats had been brought from outside of town. "Yeah, because who has pygmies right now?" Someone asked the question, and I could see everyone mentally counting up their neighbors' livestock. "Nobody, right?"

They speculated as to what had happened: It was a tractor accident. A cult thing. Wild dogs.

I heard two true things: the vet had seen them, and a farm had agreed to take them in.

"Sorry to say it, but it's not practical," Axel said. "If they heal, they're going to need fake footsies—"

"Prostheses." Charlotte supplied the word.

"Right. And you can't just walk into a farm store and buy that like you'd buy a bottle of caprine vitamins. That has to be custom. Probably need a 3-D printer."

He couldn't possibly know it, but that actually gave me hope.

"Who has that kind of cash? And who'd spend it on that if they did?"

"That would be expensive?" I asked. Every head turned. *Quiet girl talking.*

"So expensive!" Axel said. "You could get a new goat for a lot less."

"Not the point," Raya spoke up.

"Exactly," Charlotte added. "The idea is to heal them." This was the girl who wanted to restore a barn, I reminded myself. I rather admired her.

"I'm just saying, it gets expensive," Axel pressed. "Whoever took them in, they probably can't afford to keep them—not indefinitely."

At home, I waited to be alone with Aunt Brat. I told her what I had heard. "Do you think the kids are right? It will cost a lot?"

"I imagine," she said. "There might be an animal rights group that could help, and I gave Barley something for the vet's bill."

"Oh, Aunt Brat, that's so good of you."

"I had to," she said. She gave me a thoughtful look. "Did the kids say anything about who took the goats in?" she asked.

"I don't think anyone knows. In fact, now that you ask, there seems to be a little mystery about that. The kids would have said if they'd known. They don't have any secrets."

"You seem to know your classmates well," she said, and she smiled. "Do you feel like you are finding friends at the school?"

Segue! The friend thing. . . . Oh, darn. . . .

"Sure. I mean, this town—the kids are all nice. Nobody gets left out because it's so small. They've even said it. They *have* to get along." We laughed about that. The trouble with Aunt Brat's question was that she was asking it of *me*. How could I tell her? If I didn't have friends, it was because I didn't feel like I could let my insides out here. I was catching up on schoolwork, being in a new home,

162

managing the unruly Guffer, getting used to Aunt Brat and her people.

Trying to hang on to my mother. . . .

"Raya and Sari sure seem like sweet girls."

"The sweetest," I said.

It was true. They'd been tireless, at school, and on another weekend hike. (I'd discovered that doubling my socks inside the ugly brown boots solved the fit.) Raya and Sari had been my escorts all across Chelmsford's acres. I'd been to their houses. I knew the place where the six roads came together. I'd sat on the cold hearth of the first chimney in town. It was all that was left of the very first house in Chelmsford, and it jutted up out of the ground like a freestanding monument. They called it the Soldier's Chimney because the place had belonged to a Union soldier who never made it home from war.

Raya and Sari talked and talked and always tried to include me. I knew, and I felt bad, that I didn't offer much back.

Funny thing: when I did talk, it was mostly about Guffer. "The troublesome yellow dog," I called him, as if that were his title, which made Raya and Sari laugh. "Three weeks and he's still not house-trained," I'd say.

They knew he was quirky. He still greeted them rudely, racing up and then drawing back, barking.

One day, Raya (who tended to touch things, I had noticed) picked up the handles of a wheelbarrow that'd been sitting in the yard for at least as long as I'd been in Chelmsford. She pushed it forward all of five feet and Guffer went batty, leaping away and circling back. He barked wildly, and all the while he kept his eyes trained on that small black wheel. "Wow," Raya said. She let the wheelbarrow down. "He doesn't like that."

"He barks at wheels," said Sari, which sounded funny.

"Yeah, he's kind of slinky all around, huh?" said Raya. We watched Guffer as he skimmed his body along the fence. Every so often he'd look over and stare at us as if we were a trio of goblins about to do him harm.

All I could do was shrug and say, "Yeah, he's weird."

He's a dog with an unknown past.

29

A Gallery

Lydia Bratches-Kemp, you are dirt.

That's the thought I had as I pulled myself, and my armload of goddesses, into the space behind the chimney. I was going to turn the crawl into a gallery of goddesses.

What about your new adults? The kind, kind people. . . .

"There won't be any damage," I whispered. Well, no further damage. All my cleaning must count for something, *and* I was making sure that no harm would be done to Elloroy's ancient brick chimney.

I was going to need something to stand on in order to reach the rafters. My art trunk was good and sturdy, and narrow enough to make it through the hole, and long enough to span the joists. But it was also heavy. Easy fix: I lifted all the trays out of it. I dropped the lid back on and hauled it into the crawl. It raised me up about a foot, which was enough.

I set to work putting up the goddesses, one by one, on their yarn hangers. By the time I was done, I had raw fingers and aching thumbs from pressing pushpins into the wood—and I was about frozen. But there they were. I'd staggered the heights like the rain forest banners at the school. I had a gallery of goddesses. "Yes!" I whispered.

Check it out, Mom!

I could step along the joists and be among the goddesses; I could brush my fingers against them and set them gently swinging. I breathed in the smell of paint, paper, and paste—three of my favorite scents in this world; three scents that made me feel like I could turn and find my mother right beside me.

I was shivering when I finally stepped back through the hole and into my room, which felt warm and was bright. I turned and shone the light into the hole. Our She-Janus was closest to the entrance—looking forward and back. It seemed just right.

Later, when I tacked the sheep poster back over the opening, I had the thought that I was a little sorry to *entomb* the goddesses like this. But it was better than keeping them boxed. I could drop in and see them and not have to explain them.

I smoothed my hand over the sheep poster. "Take care of the goddesses, you sheep," I said. "Those who are usually guarded must now guard."

Twice in the night I got up and peeled the poster and shone light on the goddesses. I wrapped up in Aunt Brat's sleeping bag and sat outside the hole looking in.

Skitch-skitch. Skitch.

Oh! Where?

I rolled the light through the crawl until I spotted the mouse scurrying across one of the joists, nimble and quick. The creature didn't seem to mind my light. It stopped on its haunches—looking adorable—and worked a little tuft of stolen yarn in its wee muzzle.

At home with the goddesses. . . .

30

A Bad Green Machine

There had been a couple of inches of snow, which made things prettier and more interesting as I walked Guffer out around the yard early one Saturday morning. Of course, he made dozens of stops and a lot of yellow snow.

"You're ruining it," I told him. "You think you are artistic? Trust me, that's not beautiful." I pointed at the pee-spotted snow. He followed my finger with his nose, hoping for a treat, I am sure. "Snow should be white, not citron," I said, drawing my hand back. I yawned. I needed coffee. I gave him a gentle tug and coaxed him around the corner of the barn. The house was in sight but still a long way across the yard. "Come on, Guffer. Come— Whoa!"

I squinted, eyes on the porch. Raya Delatorre and Sari Winkle were sitting on the snowy steps, facing each other. I turned Guffer as quickly as I could and pulled him back behind the barn.

I thought most teenagers—the ones who were not me—slept in late on winter Saturdays. Not the case with those two. I didn't have my phone with me, and I would not have taken the time to look anyway, but I was pretty sure it wasn't even nine a.m. yet. I was short on sleep—my own fault for goddess gazing in the middle of the night. I did not feel like walking with Raya and Sari, not today.

I marched beside the barn right at the tree line, thinking I'd wait them out. Trouble was, if Guffer spotted them he'd start his big chicken-dog barking and give us away. "Come on," I whispered to him. "Come!" I rattled his leash, and he came bouncing at me—then past me. My arm jerked at the socket. Guffer headed into the woods. I let him lead. Within seconds he found what seemed to be a path.

Guff's nose was to the ground, his legs going at a hop. I hustled behind him. I kept one arm up to knock back the branches. I figured we'd go ten minutes out, then I'd turn him back. Raya and Sari wouldn't wait twenty minutes. I followed Guffer, and before long he got me into a run under some low-hanging limbs. I ducked, but tree-branch fingers picked my hat right off my head. "No!" I cried.

My mom made that hat!

I tried to set my brakes. Guffer, the engine, hauled forward. "Stop!" I demanded. I dug my heels in, slipped on the snow, then stumbled forward a few steps. I looked back at my bright blue hat bobbing over the trail.

"Guffer! Stop!" I said firmly. We were going back for the hat. I tightened my grip on the loop of the leash. I pulled. "Come! Come!" He resisted. I was so *sick* of battling him.

The leash grew tense as a tightrope between us. His big blond ruff gathered into a circle around his face like a furry hood. He struggled, twisting his head left and right, backing himself away from me until—pop! He was out of the collar. I fell on my butt. I sat in the slush, leash in my hand. I cursed. How many times had I seen him pull that trick?

Well up the trail, I saw the flash of his pale tail sailing away from me. "Well, I guess that's what it means to high-tail it out of somewhere," I mumbled.

I stood up and started after him, aware that it rarely helped to chase. I called his name. Darned if he didn't stop and look back at me. He even cocked his head. "Come!" I said. He looked like he might be thinking it over. "Yeah! Come on, boy." I put my hand in my pocket, a sign that I had a treat for him. He threw his head up, jaw open like he was letting out a big dog laugh. He dove away at a gallop.

"No!" I hurried after him. Here I was with a dog who supposedly had weak hinds and yet he could out-dodge and outrun me. Why was he like this? Why did it scare me so much? That was the worst part. I was afraid *for* him. All the time! I worried he'd run into the road when we were at the bus stop or getting the mail at the bottom of the hill; I worried he'd get lost in these woods where the trees all looked the same for as far as my eye could see.

I caught a few glimpses of his blondness through the tree trunks. But then I lost him again. I followed his broad paw prints in the soft, shallow snow. Finally, I saw a clearing up ahead. Well, more like the end of the woods. *Where am I?* I wondered. "Perhaps I'm not in Chelmsford anymore. . . ."

I heard a buzzing sound—a machine—not too far off. Then barking. Definitely Guffer. Definitely his scared bark. I saw a flash of bright green. Then the buzzing stopped.

"Guff? . . . Guffer?"

I picked up my pace. I stepped over a crumbly rock wall and into a field. I saw a bright green four-wheeler—just sitting—and several long white barns off in the distance.

"Hey!" An angry voice cut the air. I turned and froze. About twenty feet from me stood a man in a grubby brown jacket. His face hung in a mean frown. His mud-brown hair was perfectly straight and looked like it'd been buttered flat to his head. "Is that your dog?" he asked.

Guffer bounded forth from the edge of the clearing where we stood. He barked and slinked, first at the four-wheeler, then at the guy. His fur stood up along the ridge of his back—scared hairs like I'd never seen on him.

"Guffer, come!" I tried. "Come!" He came toward me but stayed just out of reach. I had no choice: I lunged and grabbed his ruff. He yipped out loud. I pulled him toward me and wrapped my arms around his chest.

The man stepped closer and raised a weathered finger. His knuckle looked like a crust of dried cement. Slowly, he dropped his fingertip so that it pointed right at me. "I said, is that your dog?"

"Y-yes," I said. Guffer rumbled long and low. I straddled him and pinched him between my knees. I thought about explaining that he was more my aunt's dog, and I'd never wanted him, and that I certainly didn't want him right this minute. Yet I clung to the dog like both our lives depended on it.

Behave, behave, behave.

"He's been coming around here," the man said. "Troublemaker. And I'm telling you, I won't hesitate to defend my livestock."

"Defend?"

172

"Happy to pump him full of lead."

I gulped. What was he saying? He'd *shoot* Guffer? Poor mixed-up, crazy, scared Guffer? I began to shake—a lot. I willed my knees to be strong and steady. I kept hold of the dog.

"S-sorry," I said. "H-he doesn't really run. I mean we don't p-purposely let him go—"

I stopped talking when I saw a boy coming across the field—a smiling boy. I squinted. Moss Capperow. He came jogging up behind the man in the brown coat. Guffer twisted excitedly. His front feet came off the ground. His paws cycled in the air.

Moss called out, "Unc! Hey, Uncle Mick!" He slowed to a walk. "The dog's okay. I don't think he'd hurt a flea. Well, maybe a flea since he is a dog."

The uncle wheeled on Moss. "You think this is funny?" Moss's smile dropped away. "Think you know better than I know? Tell me yes, and I'll kick your ass from here to home."

My breath stopped. I stared at the angry uncle.

"No, Uncle Mick. I don't think that."

Moss found a little bit of his ever-smiling boy self. He nodded at me. "Hi, Lydia."

"Hi," I said back. I barely heard my own voice. I had all I could do to hang on to Guffer. He was so nervous, rumbling and twisting. He got loose from my knee vise. "Guff, no!" I said as sternly as I could. He bounced forward, then slipped back behind my legs. I snagged him. Held him. Moss's uncle watched, stone-faced. "I'm sorry, he's a pretty b-bad dog," I explained. I trapped Guffer in my knees again. I pressed his hinds down. "Sit!" I hissed.

"I'm going to be frank," the uncle said. "A bad dog is a *dead* dog as far as I'm concerned."

"Aw, Uncle Mick, this guy is a rescue. He's still in training." Moss looked at me. "Right?"

"Y-yes," I said. "He's just—a dog with an unknown past and we, well, we are trying to train him. It's just taking a while." My jaw shivered uncontrollably.

The Capperow uncle lifted his chin at me and said, "I strongly recommend you keep him tied. *Tied*," he repeated. He poked his callused finger at me again. "Keep him away from this farm and *all* the farms around here." The Uncle Mick person said, "If you don't, you will have trouble. You'll be paying for dead livestock."

"Dead livestock . . . oh—" I flashed on the pygmy goats. My heart pounded. "This dog—I don't think he'd ever k-kill—"

"Then you don't know dogs," the uncle snapped. "Don't let me catch him around here again, or you'll find yourself digging a hole just his size. You understand?"

I was speechless. Shaking inside and out. Knees collapsing.

"Uncle Mick, really, the dog's only been here for—"

"Moss!" the uncle cut him off. "Get the girl and her dog on a path out of here. Then get to your chores in the barn." He turned and strode to his four-wheeler. From the back, Moss's uncle wasn't anything but a loose pair of pants and a jacket that looked uncomfortably short. But I was not going to underestimate him. I held tight to the dog while the uncle threw his leg over the seat of the four-wheeler. Guffer wriggled and whined. He twisted harder in my arms when Moss's uncle started up the engine. "It's okay," I whispered. It seemed like he wanted to look at me but couldn't risk taking his eyes off that machine.

The wheels . . .

Neither the dog nor Moss nor I moved until his uncle was well across the pasture. Moss sighed. Guffer settled, somewhat, against my legs. I stopped shaking. (Mostly.) I opened up Guffer's collar.

"Can I help?" Moss asked.

"No. Thank you. I got it. And I don't need to be put back on the path," I added. I circled Guffer's neck with the collar and snapped it shut. He jumped up and down at the end of the leash. Moss Capperow laughed. He held a hand out to the dog, and he tried to pat him. Guff wagged his tail slightly, then leapt away.

"What's the matter, big guy?" Moss offered his hand again. But Guffer looked back at Moss like the boy had fireworks for fingertips. "He's a really great dog," said Moss.

"Yeah, well, I don't think your uncle would say so," I said.

"Well, I don't usually agree with my uncle." He shrugged in an embarrassed sort of way. "Sorry. He thinks he's fighting for the good of the farm. But really, he's just plain fighting. I'll talk to my dad about it because, honestly, that's not how we treat our neighbors," Moss said.

I knew it wasn't Moss's fault. I tried to meet his eyes, but he was looking at the ground near my feet, and smiling, of course. I shifted to one side, fearing I was standing in a dog poop or something. That would be fitting. "Y-you should let me walk you back to the path," Moss said, and then I saw him glance down *again*. Then up at me. Then down. His smile recharged twice over. Why was Moss Capperow so fixed on *my* feet! Finally, I looked down at them myself.

Oh. Is this about the ugly boots . . . really?

I stabbed the toe of one boot into the ground. "These are my dog chasers," I explained. Then I wondered why I had bothered to say it.

"Oh, yeah. That's good," he said. "Hey, as long as they work, right?"

"This is what I figure," I said.

"And who cares where they came from," he said, and right then I felt like I'd missed something. "Well," he said, "are you sure I can't help you get back on the path? You're still new around here."

"I'm fine," I said. "Sorry for the bad behavior. And the barking."

Moss Capperow laughed out loud. "Did *you* bark, Lydia? So sorry I missed that."

I turned my face away from him before he could see me crack a huge smile. I shortened up on Guffer's leash and followed my own soggy footprints toward home—and oh yeah, my blue hat.

31

Calling Tennessee

It didn't matter that the very last thing Moss Capperow said to me was pretty funny. The morning had left a rotten hollow in my chest. I could still feel it as I brought Guffer through the door.

"Lydia! There you are!" Aunt Brat was moving toward me from the kitchen, pressing her hand into her breastbone.

"Oh, phew!" said Eileen. "We sure did wonder."

"We wondered? No, we were *worried*," Aunt Brat said. "Please take your phone with you next time." She swept her arms toward the front porch. "The girls were here for you—"

Oh yeah . . . Raya and Sari. . . .

I had forgotten.

"Sorry," I said, though I'd already decided that I was not going to take a lot of blame for this. The dog had run off; that'd happened to all of us. "I didn't mean to be out there so long." I pushed my hat off and unclipped Guffer. He hustled to the water bowl, took a long drink, then went over to dribble on Soonie's head. I pried off my boots and found myself staring down at the peeled-back tongue and those initials in black ink: MCAP.

Moss Capperow . . . of course. . . .

I sank back against the wall and puffed out a long breath. That's why he'd been staring at my feet. These boots had been his boots. "Whatever," I muttered. I had much more serious business. I straightened up—full height—and looked at my adults. "I have to tell you something," I said. "It's about the dog."

I recounted my encounter with the Capperows. Aunt Brat and Eileen were not pleased about the way the Uncle Mick person had spoken to me and threatened the dog. Like me, they simply didn't believe Guffer was a killer.

"But best we acknowledge that our Guff has probably prowled around the Capperow farm," Aunt Brat conceded.

"Never guessed he'd gone that far. We've got to put a stop to that," Eileen said. She gave her head a scratch and a shake.

"Fine," said Aunt Brat, "but I am furious that Capperow treated Lydia that way. That's intimidation."

"Capperow is not a warm guy," Eileen said in a thoughtful sort of way. "He comes into the Feed, and when he's not unpleasant, he's silent."

"Nobody needs to berate a child who is merely trying to collect her dog."

Not my dog. . . .

"Agreed. But you're forgetting one thing, Brat," said Eileen.

"What? What am I forgetting?"

"He's a farmer. Hard enough living without someone's naughty doggie coming around to nip the hocks of his herd."

Aunt Brat let out a huff. "Do we know that's what happened? Did *this* dog do that? For that matter, were Mr. Capperow's cows even injured?"

As soon as she said it, the image of the two maimed goats flashed. My classmates had suggested it was a dog attack. I didn't have to be a dog person or a farmer to disagree. Nothing about their injuries had looked like a dog attack to me. A dog's teeth would puncture. Tear. The goats had been *cut*. Ugh.

Eileen put one hand up. "Point of view, Brat. To a farmer, the Guffster looks guilty just for having four paws and a mouth that says woof."

I sighed. They could talk all they wanted. "We have to keep Guffer from roaming," I said. "We have to do better at—" I stopped and shook my head. "I wish we knew his past. That man Capperow, he was riding on one of those four-wheelers and Guff was out of his mind over it," I said. "Why? And why does he act mistrustful? Why does he poop and pee inside the house? Still! Why doesn't he like us?" I said.

Aunt Brat and Eileen looked surprised.

"Like us?" Aunt Brat said. She looked at the dog.

"He—he likes us." Eileen said this slowly. "He's just independent. Not as affectionate as Soonie girl. As for his past, we can only guess at that and it probably won't do a lot of good. We have to go forward."

"We'll redouble our efforts to keep him close," Aunt Brat said. "Lydia is right to feel worried, especially after such a hellacious encounter. Vicious accusations. Nightmarish threats—that's what you're saying, right? You're worried about him?"

I nodded yes.

"Me too. We'll tighten his collar so he can't pull out of it—and we'll keep trying to make him feel secure here at home. I'm committed," she said.

"Of course," said Eileen. "He's our dog."

I looked at Guffer, who was settling his huge yellowness

beside the couch. He laid his head down on the floor and let out a sigh that fluttered his black, rubbery lips in a noisy way.

Aunt Brat and Eileen laughed right out loud.

"There's our pretty boy," said Eileen. "He's tired." She cooed, "Our *Guffster*, our buddy, our pal."

They love that dog. . . .

Alone in my room, I opened the old art box, lifted out the first tray, and picked the old dog tag out from between the two colored pencils. I turned it over in my fingers. I squinted at the phone number. I took out my phone. Slowly, I tapped Cici Hoover's number in. I looked at it a good while before I hit the green button.

The ringer purred in my ear, must have been at least six times. With each ring, I came closer to chickening out. Then it seemed like Cici Hoover was not going to pick up. I should hang up. Then there it was, a little set of clicks. A woman with a gravelly voice said: "This must be the place since you called it."

"R-right. Hello," I said. "My name is—"

"Leave me a message," said the voice.

Oh. Answering machine . . . landline. . . .

"I *might* call ya back!" The woman cackled. Then of all the crazy things, I heard dogs barking in the background of the recording. A lot of dogs.

In the next couple of seconds, thoughts flew at me: *Do I leave a message? Try again later? Hang up? Have I even reached Cici Hoover?* She hadn't said.

Meep! The answering machine was ready for me.

"Ummm . . . yes, hello. My name is Lydia Bratch—"

No, don't give your full name!

"Uh . . . I'm just wondering if maybe you are Cici Hoover? Because, well, I live in New York—I mean Connecticut, and . . ."

Don't say where you are!

"W-we adopted a dog a while ago and, um . . . I found your number on his tag. He's pretty big and blond like a shepherd, they said, with spots on his tongue, and, well, we're having, um . . . trouble and I wondered if you know him and if maybe you could tell us anything that might help us. So, I'm just here. At this number. Okay and so thanksss you—I mean, thank you. Okay. Bye."

I hung up and clapped my phone to my chest. I looked at the ceiling. Oh man! What was *that* going to sound like coming out of her answering machine? Whoa, what a mess! Maybe Cici Hoover would think she'd been pranked on and ignore the whole thing.

Still, for the next several hours I kept my phone close. What if she did call back—but during dinner or some other moment when I was sitting right beside Aunt Brat and Eileen and Elloroy? How was I going to take that call?

I started willing Cici *not* to call me back. I guess it worked. Sunday evening came and I hadn't heard a word.

32

The End of a Ragged Day

I slid the art trunk out, thinking I'd put away the dog tag with Cici Hoover's name and number on it. I pulled out all the trays full of postage stamps and paper scraps. The one on the bottom had little square compartments where I kept odd charms and tokens, coins and keys—all from flea market days with Mom. "Artifacts of everyday life." That's what she used to say. I dropped the dog tag in and stirred everything with one finger.

My door latch clicked. Guffer burst in—big, panting Guffer, who'd never come up the stairs as far as I could recall. He saw me and stopped panting. His tail wagged. His ears dropped down in the sweet-dog way. His nose stretched forward and twitched.

"Oh no . . ."

Please don't pee. . . .

He strode straight at me and right over my wooden trays—big paws landing in them. Pencils shot out and rolled across pine floorboards. Tubes of paint crumpled out of shape—but didn't puncture. Phew! Guffer hopped up and hind kicked as if something had insulted his delicate fat feet. He skittered away. I spread my arms over the trays to protect them. But back he came, stepping over my arms and onto my treasures again.

"Guffer—pffff . . ." He brushed the long, long side of his body right across my face. "Oh! Pitoo-pitoo!" I spat dog hairs off my lips. He lay down, half-off and half-on my trays. He settled in with a big sigh. How was this comfortable? He tipped to one side, then turned himself upside down, belly-up, chest high, and throat exposed.

The extreme well-being pose. . . .

His full tail swept side to side. Paper bits went flying.

"What the heck?" I said.

I don't pat you much. . . .

I realized this as the dog stretched before me with his buttercream belly all laid out and a tiny triangle of blue origami paper stuck in the pink pit of his leg. I sighed.

You are magnificent . . . you stinking runaway. . . .

I reached and scratched his chest. One hind leg came

186

up and kicked a few times. I scratched faster. The leg whisked the air. When I stopped, the leg stopped and Guffer waited, still upside down.

He drew breath. I thought he might sneeze. Instead he said, "Guh-guh-guff . . ." He made the same sound again in a higher pitch. He held a whiny little note on the end—one I thought might go on endlessly.

"Guff." I started to laugh. "You big baby." His tail twitched and swept. "Guffer, get off my stuff. Come on, buddy." He stretched a leg toward me and pressed his huge paw and big black toes against my shin. "Guff! Ow!" He pushed harder. I started to laugh in spite of the sizable toenails that were pressing dents in me.

Aunt Brat came to the doorway and saw me laughing. "Oh my goodness! Guffer? What's he's doing up here?"

"Don't ask me," I said, still giggling.

"He's pushing on you, isn't he?" She laughed lightly. "Guffer! Don't hurt Lydia. Oh, you funny, funny dog!"

With that, he gave me a final shove. I was laughing so hard now, I tipped over onto my side. "Umph!"

"Oh, Lyddie! Wha-ha!" Aunt Brat burst out laughing. She bent forward and hugged herself at the waist. "Are you all right?" she could barely ask. I could barely answer.

He stayed in my room all evening, even when Aunt Brat went back downstairs. I tugged my art trays out from under him. He picked up his head and looked at me but then set it down again. He dozed, with his lionlike eyes tightly closed. He began to dream and I watched the black dots on that twitching muzzle—the places where his pale whiskers grew from. I almost reached out to stroke that butterscotch fur. But I stopped to think, What did the dog really want?

To sleep . . . to dream. . . .

To have peace from what this ragged day had shown him—a cold-souled man shouting threats and a noisy machine on four fearsome wheels. I remembered the feeling I'd had while holding the dog to my chest at the edge of the Capperows' field. We'd been two shuddering creatures in that moment. Hugging him had comforted me.

I let the dog sleep.

I made perfect order of everything in my art trays—I handled every piece of thread, paper, yarn, every old button, each secondhand ribbon.

Make something, Lydia. . . . Make something. . . .

33

The Perimeter

Guffer had seemed so afraid of Moss Capperow's uncle and his four-wheeler that I didn't believe he'd been to that farm multiple times. I wondered what Moss would say about that. But I didn't want to ask him.

Aunt Brat and Eileen and I buckled down on the dog with what they dubbed "perimeter training." (They made that up.) Eileen brought a long leash home from the Feed and we took turns walking Guffer around the inside edge of the woods. We reeled him in if he went beyond the clearing. We were careful not to let him get into the dreaded backward position where he could pull out of his collar. We gave him treats for staying inside the perimeter. We told him he was a good dog.

When Eileen went out with him, she tottered because of her short leg. (*I-lean.*) She kept the yellow dog fairly close to her side. Aunt Brat went striding with him, possibly rushing to finish so that she could get on with her own constitutional out to who knew where.

Aunt Brat's walks were sacred. I'd watched her disappear into the trees at the far corner of the pasture plenty of times. Eileen had said it more than once: "Rain or shine, or ice on the vine, she goes. She'll switch to her skis once the snow comes."

For Guffer, the week was a bit like boot camp and it seemed like "perimeter training" was beginning to stick. We tested him, letting him out on his own for a few minutes at a time. He'd settle on the porch, almost like the good guard dog he might have been if he weren't such a chicken. We were certain that he had not been back to the Capperow farm.

But often, around suppertime, Guffer would hear something from inside the house—something the rest of us couldn't hear. He'd rush to the back window, slipping on his toenails, back hairs high. He'd stare at the window and rumble. Then he'd bark so hard, his feet came off the ground.

"What, what?" Aunt Brat said. "Why so nervous, boy?"

"He knows there's something out there," I said.

"Like what? Raccoon? Fox? Bear?"

"Hmm . . . nasty farmer? On a four-wheeler?" I suggested.

"Oh. Do you think?"

I did.

I think all of us were holding out hope that "perimeter training" would somehow help with housetraining, too. He was still making mistakes. We needed a magic trick.

One evening, exactly as four bowls of butternut squash soup and four plates of green salad with apples and ginger and feta cheese had been set on our table, Guffer circled into the living room and squatted.

"Ack! No!" I unceremoniously dropped the breadbasket on the table. I let go a heavy sigh. "I just walked him around the perimeter. He had opportunity. Ugh! Cover my bowl," I said, feeling defeated. "I'll take him out again."

But there came Eileen saying, "Nope! Nope! He's not going outside." She took the dog's collar and ushered him straight into the crate.

"Uh-oh," said Elloroy. He was already sitting down.

"But he hates that. He has to pee," I said. I looked at Aunt Brat. She was as surprised as I was. Eileen closed the door to the crate and latched it. I have to say, Guffer looked puzzled too.

"He doesn't really have to pee," she said. "And yes. He

hates the crate. And we hate it when he does that." She pointed her finger at the dark circle on the rug and stared at the spot.

"But the crate is supposed to signal bedtime, and when we are going to be away, isn't that right?" Aunt Brat asked. "Are we going to eat our dinner while he watches us?"

"I am," said Elloroy. He scraped a curl of butter onto his knife.

Eileen snatched the throw blanket from the couch and threw it over the crate. "There!"

"Oh, Eileen!" Aunt Brat protested. "That seems worse! Poor dog! Now he can't even see—"

"Nope. Nope. No feeling sorry. We are going to try this, Bratches. Let's say the crate is for when we are *unavailable*."

"Well, I'm just wondering about consistency," Aunt Brat huffed.

We had a rather quiet, tense supper. Eileen kept reminding Aunt Brat and me, "Don't look. Don't look." In truth there wasn't much to see. Guffer was covered. And he was quiet.

After supper, I fixed eyes on Eileen and she finally gave me a nod. "Okay, go spring him and take him outside. No fanfare," she insisted.

Well, we didn't enjoy it, but we used the new strategy the following night too. We gave him the chance to "*not* violate the rug," as Eileen put it, but when he did, we crated him again. "It's the same as the shunning thing," Eileen reasoned. "When we don't like what he does, we ignore him. It works like a charm. With this dog, we just need more charms."

"I can't argue," said Aunt Brat. "Where did this latest tip come from?"

"I made it up," Eileen admitted. "But I got the idea from Lydia."

"From me?"

I'm not the dog person. . . .

"Yep. A few nights back the Guffster peed the rug, as the Guffster so does—or so used to do," Eileen said with optimism. "You went to take him outside and you told him, 'I'll take you out. Your favorite thing.' You mumbled it. Sarcastic-like. And you were right. Going outside is his favorite thing, next to treats. So I got to thinking about that—"

"So, you're saying, every time he ruins the rug we . . . *reward* him with one of his favorite things to do?"

"Huh-haw! You speak dog now. How does it feel?" Eileen beamed, and I couldn't help grinning.

On the third night Guffer circled into the living room and, surprisingly, he lay down. He rested his chin on his curled paw and moved nothing but his eyeballs as he watched us put our dinner on the table. While we ate, he closed his lids. Even Elloroy glanced into the living room and gave a nod.

Guffer's rug-wrecking days were done.

34

Being She-Janus

February . . . the time of the Storm Moon.

My mother was not there to say the words to me. I never guessed I'd miss hearing them. (To be honest, I used to roll my eyes.)

Mom . . . I was actually paying attention. . . . Storm Moon . . . time for planning your future. . . .

Mine seemed hard to see.

Begin spring cleaning . . . sweep out cobwebs . . .

Well, I'd been doing that.

Burn purifying incense and white candles . . .

Mom had loved candles, but they were too dangerous in a house with an oxygen tank.

Prepare for new growth . . .

Well, maybe somewhere.

The Storm Moon did bring storms—the first heavy snows I'd seen in Chelmsford.

There were school closings, and I was alone at the house with Elloroy and the dogs more than before. A plow came to clear the drive on Pinnacle Hill. But the porch steps and paths all had to be shoveled, snow had to be swept off the woodpile. I stayed busy, and most of the time Guffer was not far from my side—even at night. Ever since he'd quit soiling the rug, he could be out of the crate at night and free to choose where he wanted to sleep. Most nights, he chose me. He'd land beside my bed—a heap and sigh—and he'd still be there in the morning.

On the snowy evenings, while Aunt Brat was still making her way back from the university, I'd leash Guffer and go down the hill to pick up the mail so she wouldn't have to stop. (The boxy car did better on the snowy hill when it could have a running start.)

Here in Chelmsford we had a mail carrier named Jaycinda. I'd seen her often, wearing bright athletic leggings, tall boots, and an anorak. She'd hop out of the truck and sink her whole leg into the snowbank if that's what it took to get the mail into the box.

After a daylong storm with snow still falling, I doubted her. But when I popped the door to the mailbox, a neat stack of envelopes had been delivered.

"That's because Jaycinda is a goddess," I told Guffer.

Apparently, Jaycinda also delivered our firewood. I hadn't seen that firsthand—not yet. But it was a house-hold topic. There was a precise time to call to get on the delivery list. It gave me a little frosting of guilt to think how much heat was being lost through the crawl space—my goddess gallery.

Guffer's collar jingled as he shook the falling snow off his coat. I tucked our mail inside my jacket—well, not *our* mail; it was theirs: Aunt Brat's, Eileen's, and Elloroy's. Nothing ever came for me. I chirped to the dog, "Ready? Let's go home!" ("Home" was a word we were trying to teach him.) He bounced along beside me. This dog loved snow.

For fun, I crossed into the yard where the snow was over my boots. Guffer tucked his nose deep down. He came up, shook, and dove down again.

I bent low to scoop him a snowball. The handle of the leash slipped right over my hand. "Oops-oops!" I reached for the leash and missed. Guffer flashed me one of his dog grins and hopped away, the leash making a whip in the air.

"Come!" I tried. He didn't. But he didn't bolt either. He continued up the hill, staying just out of my reach.

I yipped into the air. Guff stopped still. He looked at me, head cocked. I let myself fall backward into the snow, arms flung. He was probably going to ditch me, but I doubted he'd go far—not so close to his own suppertime. I raised my head and saw him pushing a trail through the snow, going home.

I lay back in the silent hollow of snow. I watched flakes falling toward me. I felt them touch down on my cheeks and nose. Mom and I had made the She-Janus—how many weeks ago?

It was February now . . . counting back to early December . . . so maybe ten weeks? . . .

Cold white snow was falling on me. Layers of white, just like She-Janus. But I felt warm at my middle—like I could melt my way deeper into the bed of snow. Could the falling snow cover me? Take my oxygen? Would I turn blue? The thought filled me with an odd peace.

Mom . . . did it feel like this? . . . The quiet . . . it really is all right. . . .

"Lydia! . . . Lydia!" I opened my eyes wide. I pushed up to sitting. I blinked snow off my lashes.

Aunt Brat was charging toward me, plunging leg after leg into the snow. Behind her I could see the boxy car stopped in the middle of the hill. "Good God! Are you all right?" She halted in front of me, taking hard breaths, her long gray coat covered in snow.

"I'm fine!" I said. "Fine! I was just—"

198

"Lying in the snow!" Aunt Brat finished for me. "Didn't you hear me hollering? I thought you were—"

"Dead?" I said, and then I almost burst out laughing, because that was Elloroy's line.

"No, not dead," she said. "Just . . . I don't know. Oh, Lyddie." She let go a huge sigh. Actually, it might have been a huff—*at* me. I couldn't blame her. I realized what she'd seen: Girl in the snow. Not moving. Make that fairly recently orphaned, coffee-drinking, semisecretive girl with boxes under her bed, lying in the snow. Not moving. Oh. My poor aunt.

She reached both arms toward me. She opened and closed her hands as if to say to, Grab on. I felt so much like my six-year-old self that I was surprised to be tall when we finally got me to my feet. I paused, taking in the scent of snow and something else—like sweet hay, like the barns of Chelmsford.

"Wait, wait," I said, looking all around me. "Aunt Brat, did you see Guffer? We were playing. . . ."

"Yes. However, I became otherwise distracted," she said. (Little eye roll, but she was sounding precise again. A good sign.) "He was on an approximate course for home. Come on. We'll watch for him on our way."

"Sorry," I said as we got into the car.

"All is well," she said. She sounded tired.

199

"I got the mail," I offered. I reached into my jacket to tug it out.

"Glory be," said Aunt Brat. She pressed the boxy car up the hill for home. We found our big yellow dog. He'd curled himself into a nest atop the snow pile beside the steps. A thin blanket of flakes had already accumulated on his back.

"Well, there is a portrait of contentment," Aunt Brat said. She sighed.

"He's so beautiful," I said.

I could feel my aunt watching me while I watched the dog.

35

A Secret to Keep

Movement was keeping me warm, so when Raya Dela-torre halted us in the road, I continued to march, in place. "Who's up for a hike to the Gerbers?" she asked in her raspy voice.

This was the long, long driveway, I remembered, and it was the home of Florry Gerber and her Belgian Hares. I waited for Sari to reply. We'd been out for over an hour observing Chelmsford in the aftermath of a big snow. If she'd had enough, I'd go along with that.

"Oh, let's!" Sari said. "There could be babies! And Florry would be so proud to show us. Lydia? What do you say?"

"Footslogging we shall go," I said, and I swept my arm forward. (I owed these girls some enthusiasm.)

"Footslogging," said Sari. "I like that."

"How about floots-logging," said Raya.

"Or loots-fogging," said Sari.

We ruined that one word at least a dozen ways—some hilarious, some unsavory. When we laughed, we spread out so that we took up most of the snowy road. Then we regrouped into our usual triangle: them in front, me bringing up the rear and always looking off to the sides of me at the cloak of snow on the fields.

If Pinnacle Hill felt isolated because it was so high, the Gerber farm felt that way because it was low and down the long driveway. By road, the two were a pretty good trudge apart. But my geographic sense told me they were closer as the crow flies.

"Hi, Gwen!" Suddenly Raya and Sari were waving, arms stretched high. I leaned around them and saw the woman, elbow propped on the handle of her shovel, taking a break from snow clearing. She shaded her eyes with her other hand. I had not met Gwen.

"Raya? Is that you? And Sari?"

"Yes!" Sari called. We trotted the rest of the way in. "We've brought Lydia Bratches-Kemp as well!" Sari presented me with a sweep of her white mitten.

She's the new girl with the dead mother.

"Lydia." The woman smiled. "I know your aunt

Bratches, and Eileen, too. I heard we had a new resident here in little Chelmsford. Welcome!" Gwen Gerber was a young woman, younger than my mother had been. "Sorry we haven't met before this. I'm basically married to my place. Tell her I'm right," she said to Raya and Sari. "I don't get off the property a lot." She laughed.

"Especially in snow!" Sari added.

"True. It can take me days to plow out. But, as they say, snow is the poor woman's fertilizer. Good for the fields."

"Here, here. Let me," said Raya, taking the shovel from Gwen. She began scooping huge shovel loads onto a pile.

"Wow. Thanks. You're better at that than I am," Gwen said, "and I am not just pulling a Tom Sawyer on you. Really! I'm not!" We laughed. Raya went on clearing snow.

"Where's Florry?" Sari asked. She explained that we'd seen the beautiful Belgian Hares some weeks ago.

"She's in the barn," Gwen said with a sweet smile. "That's where she loves to be. She's got a gruesome little cold, though, poor kid."

"But can we go visit?"

Gwen seemed to hesitate but finally nodded yes. "Just don't let Florry sneeze on you. I sent her in there with a box of tissues. I hope she's not glazed in boogs," she said with a laugh. "It's one thing I can't make her understand.

Working on it. Maybe someday!" Her good humor made me think of Mom. I liked Gwen Gerber.

She reached to take the shovel back from Raya, who threw a few more scoops of snow onto the pile. "You're a good egg, Raya," Gwen told her. She offered her a knuckle bump and Raya took it.

Inside the barn we met Florry almost exactly as we'd met her before. But this time she was holding an armload of hay instead of a rabbit. I could hear her steadily mouth breathing. Her nose was red—and glazed. She seemed not at all surprised to see us. She spoke first.

"You wan' know what? I got a cold," she said. She dropped the hay and pointed to her nose. The Belgian Hares gathered at her feet, nosing the hay as if looking for the good parts.

"We heard. How do you feel?" Sari asked.

"I'm okay." She pulled a new leaf of hay from the bale beside her and shook it into the raised hutch.

"Want some help?"

"You 'on't have to. I could do it." She picked up a small hoe and dragged damp hay and droppings out from under the hutches. "This for compost," she said, more to herself than to us.

The Belgian Hares took elegant slow hops around us. They reached toward us with their noses. I wished I had come with pockets full of carrots. Instead we knelt and offered clean hay. I loved the feel—that bossy tug—as they took it from my hands. I was mesmerized watching long pieces of hay disappear into lips that looked like pairs of velvety brown pussy willows. Then the soft, comforting grinding sound as they chewed.

"Meh-eh-eh-eh-eh!!! Meh-meh-eh-eh!!"

Raya stood straight up. The rabbits scattered. Sari and I stayed low, waiting and listening.

"Meh! Meh-eh-eh-eh!"

"Was that bleating?" Raya said.

All of us looked at Florry. "Shhh," she said, and she ducked her chin in her bashful, almost flirty way.

"Did you get a . . . goat?" Sari asked.

"No." Florry shook her head. "Two! Bwoken ones," she said, eyes wide.

"Broken?" Raya asked.

"Yee-ah. Two of the feet. And the ee-yors. That's the onliest bad parts. You wan' see?"

My brain bell rang. My stomach rose. Florry Gerber led us out of the rabbit enclosure and down the middle of the barn. She stopped in front of a solid stall door. What was it with all these barns? Every one had stalls with walls just high enough that we couldn't quite see over them, and the boards were spaced so you couldn't quite see in.

Florry set a foot into the lowest board and climbed up. She put her hands and chin on the top rail. We followed, me squeezing up between Raya and Sari.

By then, I knew what I would see. I peered into the stall.

"Oh my God, it *is* them," I said.

"Them? Who?"

"The goats from the Feed," I said. But as I stared down, I could see the changes. The goats seemed calm—maybe drowsy, but their heads were up. What a difference. The bloody bandages were gone. The feet were covered in clean sturdy casts, wound in bright pink tape. The edges of those ears looked healed under a slick of ointment.

Raya and Sari were silent at first. This was a lot to take in, I knew that.

"Oh, wow," Raya breathed. "So these are the ones?"

"Look how awful." Sari's lip quivered. "Those pink clubs instead of hooves? It's just wrong," she whispered. "And the ears. That edge . . ." She pressed her forehead on her mittens, unable to look.

I ached to tell them that this was better. But that would mean admitting to Raya and Sari that I'd seen them before. I'd held that back when our classmates first learned about the goats; I hadn't wanted to be asked to describe what I'd seen. I remembered how stricken Eileen had been—how Aunt Brat had been so protective.

206

"They goin' get new feet," Florry said. "Those has to get made furst."

"They're going to get prostheses. . . ." I realized this out loud.

"Holy . . . ," Raya said. "So . . . it was Gwen who took them in." She turned to Florry. All of us were hanging on to the top of the stall practically by our chins now.

"Florry, when? When did you get them?"

"We 'idn't get um," Florry said with a tiny shake of her head. She was so earnest, I thought. But she was also wrong. Of course they'd gotten them. We were looking right at them.

"But Florry, they're here," said Sari. She spoke gently.

"Yee-ah. But they idn't ours." Florry stretched her chin toward us.

"Oh. Are you taking care of them?" Sari asked.

Florry broke into a wide grin. She nodded. She wiped her nose on her coat sleeve, leaving a shiny trail. I slipped down from the wall. I had to; my fingers were cramping. I sank down against the outside of the stall. A few seconds later, the others joined me, including Florry, who crouched on the barn floor in front of us.

Though it'd made me woozy to see them again, I thought that it was good that the goats had landed at the Gerber farm. It was quiet here and out of the way. They had this gentle girl to care for them, and they had Gwen, who already seemed super capable to me.

"You wan' know whose?" Florry said. "They hurs." She was looking directly at me. "Those goats are from your mutha."

"My mother?" I touched my fingers to my collarbone.

Raya shifted beside me. Sari let out a little breath.

Dead mothers make people uncomfortable.

I squinted at the Rabbit Goddess girl, who was nodding now with confidence.

"Hmm, Florry, I think . . . well . . . I'm not sure that's right," Raya said.

"But that's okay," said Sari.

"Oh yeah. Way okay," Raya said. She gave Florry's shoulder a loving stroke. Florry scuttled forward. She leaned into Raya the way a cat might.

"Not wrong," said Florry, another new grin breaking across her face. "Hur mutha got 'em brung here."

What?

She raised a finger between us. "We're the onliest few what knows. So 'on't you tell." She shook her head quickly. She wiped her nose again and gave us a shiny grin.

I was not going to try to explain to Florry Gerber why my mother could *not* have had anything to do with the goats. What if I upset this tender girl? But, oh, what a story she'd built!

"Uhh . . . Florry, my sweet." Gwen came striding down the center of the barn. "Did you forget?"

"We're the onliest few what knows," Florry said. She sounded defensive. I was surprised.

"If you mean the goats, it's not her fault," Raya told Gwen. "We heard them bleating."

"I see," said Gwen. "The better they feel, the louder they get." She looked at us, her eyes imploring us to cooperate. "Well, girls. You've just been made a part of a special contingent. My fault. I could have kept you out of the barn. . . ." She let that trail off. "You've probably heard about these poor little ones."

"Oh yeah, we did," Raya said. "But hey, Gwen, we won't tell anyone they're here if that's what you need."

"That's what I need," Gwen confirmed with a nod. "They've been entrusted to me—I'm a helper—until an owner is found, or it's otherwise sorted out."

"Oh. Gwen. You are so good," said Sari. "It can't have been easy."

I remembered now how Axel had said that taking in badly injured animals was costly. By all appearances Gwen was on her own, with a special daughter to take care of.

"Well, I'm providing shelter and some of the care," said Gwen. "But I couldn't do it if the goats didn't have a benefactor. We have a long way to go. They're still mildly sedated, and on antibiotics—"

"The mennissin," Florry said.

"The medicine. That's right," said Gwen. "If we can get them healed rehab will be next. They have to learn to walk again." She tilted her head and let out a worried sigh.

Florry slid herself along the side of her mother and into the space under her arm. Gwen kissed her daughter's hat-covered head.

On our way out, Raya took charge. "So, you guys, seriously, we don't tell. Okay? Not one person."

"What about my mom and dad?" Sari asked.

"Well, I'm not going to tell you what to do about parent stuff," Raya said. "But for me, unless mine actually say, 'Hey, Raya, do you know where those abused goats are living?' I'm not mentioning this. Because you know what happens?"

"A person tells one person who tells just one more . . . ," Sari said.

"Exactly. And the thing is, whoever did that to those goats is a total criminal. And there's no way to know what's up with them." She pointed to her head. "And I don't know if it's even a worry, but I sure wouldn't want them to find a path to Gwen because of something I let slip."

"I won't say anything," I said.

210

My aunt doesn't like secrets . . . but I keep some any-way. . . .

"Wow. Is Gwen Gerber a good person, or what?" Raya said.

"One of the best," Sari added.

A goddess.

36

Sick in Bed

By Tuesday it was clear that I had caught Florry Gerber's cold. Only it seemed like more than that. I had a fever and aches, with a sore throat radiating out to my ears. My nose needed blowing, constantly. I finally crept downstairs in search of hot tea—no coffee.

In the kitchen I announced that I was sick. Aunt Brat immediately put the kettle on, then insisted that I come over to the window for her to have a look "down my hatch," and, of course, Eileen came too.

"Ahhhhhhh . . ." They said it with me. They took turns peering into my throat.

"Oh, yes," said Brat. "Looks angry in there."

"Red rager, red rager, get the doc on the pager!" said Eileen.

I shut my mouth so my breath wouldn't poison them.

"I wonder where you picked it up," Aunt Brat mused. "Well, I guess any school is basically an oversized petri dish."

"No, I think I got this from Florry Gerber," I said, and instantly wished I had not. "We hiked over there this weekend."

Okay, Lydia . . . stop talking now. . . .

There beside the light of the window I thought I caught an uneasy look on Aunt Brat's face. Before I could slide away, she grabbed my head, pressing one hand firmly across my forehead, the other at my crown. "You're definitely warm." She no sooner let me go than Eileen, too, palmed my head.

Aunt Brat poured my tea. I sat at the table, listlessly dunking the teabag.

"Sorry for you, youth and beauty," Elloroy said. "Have an extra hit of honey." He pushed the jar toward me with the back of his hand. Eileen intercepted it and drizzled a big dose into my cup.

"I'll call you in absent," said Aunt Brat.

"Already on it," Eileen said. She produced her phone. "Got the number programmed in. Huh-haw. This is a first. Call the girlie in. . . ." She wedged up to the kitchen window and poked at her phone.

"Let's try to get that fever down." Aunt Brat reached into the narrow cupboard where they kept medications and pulled down a white bottle. Every motion—the twisting of the cap, her splayed fingers, and the way she held out the pair of pills to me—bore sister-likeness to Mom. I double-checked that, yes, I was looking into my aunt's face. I gingerly picked the pills out of her hand. This was the first time I'd been sick since Mom had died. You want your mom. You just do.

I thought about how she'd always managed to rally to take care of me when I needed her. Those were the times she fretted most about her lousy heart. I longed to hear her say it: We're going to need a goddess for this.

Sick days, I realized, had always smelled like paste and paint. Then again, maybe most days had. Could I do it? Could I use this sick day to make art? Did I have a goddess in me? Maybe once my chills were gone. But, right now, I didn't have enough strength to work a pair of scissors.

"All set," Eileen said, triumphantly coming away from the window and pocketing her phone. "They know."

"Perfect," said Brat. "Now then . . . I'm going to message my students and cancel my classes. Eileen, do you have time to take the dogs out for a little exercise before you leave for work? They're going to miss their trip to the bus stop today."

"On it," said Eileen. She headed to the front door, dogs at her heels.

"Elloroy, are you all set for the rest of the morning?"

"If the rest of the morning comes," he answered. I smiled, even as the hot tea rode down my aching throat.

"This will work," Aunt Brat said. "I'm going to grade papers for a couple of hours. I'll check with Lydia afterward. If she feels okay, I'll go out for my ski. Now Lydia . . ." She put her hands on her hips and her head on a sympathetic sort of tilt. "What else can we do to make you comfortable?"

I pointed up the stairs. With teeth chattering, I said, "I'm going back to bed. With this." I raised my mug.

As I climbed the stairs the mug felt heavy. So did my feet. But I made it to my bed. It wasn't long before I heard the dogs come back in. Eileen's truck cranked up a minute later. I floated in and out of sleep.

Goddesses circled. I was amazed. I was dreaming them. "This is a first," I was saying. I saw faces—all shades of flesh—with cheeks painted in "the colors of fevers"— that's what the dream told me. There were rose-petal lips and shiny noses. Rings and wreaths floated around my field of vision: leaves and berries and sticks of hay. Everything changed in pops of color. I saw goat faces, then dog faces—laughing ones—with spotted tongues lolling between the canine teeth. I stood in a field of white flowers and insisted to some unseen person that they were snow. The flowers changed to red bee balm. I asked my mother, "Can you see the goddesses and dogs? I'm keeping them . . . for you." My eyes flew open. All of it was gone.

Mom! . . . You didn't answer.

My head throbbed. The skin under my eyes felt hot and tender. I reached over the side of the bed for my tea—now cold. I sipped. I shivered. I tucked my arms back under the covers. I think it was only minutes later that I woke to a lapping sound: Guffer, with his nose in my mug, was finishing the last of my tea.

"No, no. Not for you," I said, and I took the mug. He sat staring at me. I put my fingers into his fur. He sighed and lay down beside my bed.

I was awake when Aunt Brat came to check on me. "Did you sleep?" she asked.

"Yes."

So weirdly.

"Feeling any better?"

"Somewhat." I yawned. My throat ached.

"Hmm . . . well, I think I'll stay home with you—"

"Aunt Brat, you can go for your ski. All I'm going to do is lie around."

"Are you sure? What about Guff? Want me to encourage him back downstairs? I can crate him."

"No, he can stay." The truth was, I wanted him.

The other truth was, I might not have wanted Aunt Brat to leave me. When I heard her go out the front door I got out of bed. I took her sleeping bag to the window with me, then nearly burst into tears as she went planting her poles and gliding on her skis. I watched her knees alternately popping angles into her long skirt as she slid along the outside of the enclosure to the corner of the clearing. She disappeared into the woods.

Aunt Brat skis through trees.

I heard that almost like a whistled tune. I loved that. I loved it enough to buck up and not get weepy.

I dragged my art stuff out but ended up just sitting on the floor with the sleeping bag around my shoulders while I sifted threads and paper scraps through my fingers.

Mom. I hate this! . . . Art doesn't happen anymore. . . .

A hot tear rolled down my cheek. I pushed the box back under the bed. I scuttled over to the sheep poster, peeled it from the wall, and sat next to the opening. I needed to look at these goddesses—mine and Mom's—and not the ones from my dream, which seemed upsetting to me now.

A certain big yellow dog came over, shoved me aside, and stuck his nose into the hole. He picked up a scent— mouse, no doubt.

"No, no, Guffer." I gently elbowed him away. He turned and followed his nose to the poster, which he stood on and creased. Great. Then he sniffed along the edge of the floor all the way to the crack under my door.

I wondered, *Does the dog know where the mouse goes?*

Later, I met Elloroy in the kitchen. He turned from the stove. "Up and around," he said brightly. I nodded.

"No sign of Aunt Brat?" I asked. "Hasn't she been gone over an hour?"

"Stays out quite a while on the non-university days," he said thoughtfully. "Today turned into one of those. I'm warming up soup for lunch. Got some here for you, too."

"Really?" I smiled. I hadn't even known I wanted soup, but now I felt both parched and hungry.

"This will fortify." He gave the pot a stir. "Did you get some sleep?"

"Yeah. Sort of crazy sleep," I answered.

"Oh yes?"

"Dreams." I shook my head. "I was seeing dogs and . . . more dogs. Their tongues," I said. He tipped his head back and let out a silent laugh.

We ate our soup together. Elloroy noticed that we were both slurping.

"Yeah, sorry," I said. "It's because I can't breathe through my nose."

"And I'm old," he said. Then a long noisy sigh filled the air. "Was that you, Lydia?" Elloroy glanced about.

"No, that was Guffer," I told him. "He's under the table. He just lay back on my foot."

"Oh! He's being good. You women have brought that dog along by a good measure recently."

"He is much better," I said. "Maybe goodness is always possible." I slurped another spoonful of soup. "Elloroy," I said, "were you always good or did you have to work at it?"

Elloroy set down his spoon. "I don't know," he said, his eyes wandering around behind his glasses. "It seems like you'd have to ask the people who knew me a long time ago. Trouble is," he said, "they're all . . ."

"Dead?" I said.

We were laughing when the dogs rushed the door to greet Aunt Brat. Both dogs sniffed her up and down as she stepped out of her short ski boots. She stopped to pull dry grasses from the ankles of her woolen snowflake socks. She tilted her rosy face up and raised her arms to sweep her hair back and retie her ponytail. Circles of sweat dampened the armpits of her shirt.

She has such good health.

"Hello, Guffer! Hello, Soonie!" She crouched to pat them. "And hello, humans," she said, laughing. "I see you two found the soup. Lydia, how are you feeling? Maybe time for another dose of meds? More tea and honey?"

She came across the floor. She reached up into the high

cabinet, one sock-covered foot coming up behind her. I had to smile; there was more of that grassy stuff caught on the hem of her skirt. But I quit looking at that because I wanted to watch her open the bottle of pills again—just like Mom had.

37

Orange Envelope

The last of the worst of my cold coincided with the start of yet another big storm. I'd missed three days of school, and honestly, I wanted to make it back on Friday. But snow fell from Thursday night right up to suppertime on Friday. Pinnacle Hill had been plowed once midstorm but was ready for another pass anytime. None of us were sure there'd be mail. But Aunt Brat thought she'd heard rumbles down on the road, including, she said, the putter of Jaycinda's mail truck. Guffer had sounded a few alarms in possible agreement—maybe the uncle Capperow was riding the scary four-wheeler nearby, or maybe, like me, the dog was feeling pent up.

I'd already set the table and fed the dogs. Anytime was a good time to get Guffer outside, "to do his biz," as Eileen would say. So the dog and I started off down the long hill to the road.

The fresh snowfall lay like an endless deep felt on the meadow. It weighed down the pine boughs so the trees looked like closed umbrellas. Even the narrow fence rails held tall slices of snow.

Guffer bounced just far enough ahead of me that I felt a tug every tenth step or so. He was reveling—being adorable. He tucked his nose into the powder, came up as a white-faced dog, then shook off the frost. Energized, he galloped forward. I tried to trot along and leave slack in the line. A dog should have his joys. If only we could trust him completely.

When I saw the height of the snowbanks where the plow had come through, I double doubted there'd be mail in spite of the indomitable Jaycinda.

Our box looked like it was sitting atop the snow with no pole. But the bank had been disturbed enough that I could tell our faithful mailwoman had done it again.

The snows had made the roads narrow, and drivers weren't likely to be watching out for a girl and her naughty dog. I shortened Guffer's leash to keep him close. Then I plunged into the snowbank.

"Be good. Be good," I told the dog, and he seemed to take a patient stance, looking majestic, with a scarf of little snowballs all stuck to his ruff.

A fat roll of mail had been wedged into our box. I drew it out and tucked it under my arm. "Done! Good boy!" I said. Well. You would have thought I'd told him ready-set-go!

He started jumping away from me. "Guffer, no! Heel!" I wasn't sure it was a fair command in this ocean of snow. I was in thigh-deep and Guffer well up to his chest. He scrambled now to get unstuck. He let out a little whine. He made his way forward a few yards.

I heard something drop behind me—just a whisper of a thing. I glanced back and saw a bright orange envelope sliding away on the snow. "Shoot!" Legs pinned in the bank, I reached back with one arm. I lost hold of everything at once. The bundle of mail slipped from under my elbow. I let go of the leash. Guffer hopped back to the trail we'd made and started away.

"Come!" I called. But he was done with the business of collecting mail. "Oh! And you were being so good!" He stopped for a split second and looked right at me. Then he was off again, pushing his way through the snow without me. "Okay, okay. But stay out of the road. Head for home." Under my breath, I added, "Please!"

I gathered up the mail and rolled it tighter this time. I checked on Guffer. He was heading in the right direction: up the hill toward home.

I had only that stray orange envelope left to grab. Even facedown it looked like something important, with its triangular back flap all sealed shut—a personal letter, perhaps, for Aunt Brat or Eileen or Elloroy. I took my glove off with my teeth. I twisted back and laid myself across the snowbank and got my fingertips on the envelope. I flicked it toward me and tucked it into the roll of mail.

"Got it, Guff! If you care. . . ."

Where was he? I squinted into the dusk. I found our path of broken snow and started back up the hill.

Soon I saw the dog's handsome form—the up ears, long back, and low tail. A sense of calm and gladness wicked through me. He was moving easily through the snow, like any creature going home for the night, though this one was dragging his leash beside him.

"You are missing your person," I whispered. "But I'm right here."

I followed as he pushed ahead, opening up the path. We were going home together, the yellow dog and I. My next thought was so unexpected, my eyes filled with water.

I love him . . . so much.

He went up the front steps and sat. The blond bowl of the back of his head waited in front of me, ears in the happy, sweet-dog position.

When I reached to let Guffer in, I heard that same papery swish-whisper I'd heard down at the mailbox. That orange envelope—again. This time it stabbed itself into a crack in the snow-dusted deck boards. Guffer cocked his head at it. "No," I said. I stooped to pick it up. He didn't challenge. "Good boy."

I held the envelope under the porch light just to see which one of my adults it was for. My breath caught.

Lydia Bratches-Kemp

It was addressed to *me*. I knew the handwriting, and in the upper-left-hand corner was the same address sticker I'd seen off and on for the last seven years. "Kemp," I said.

He found me. That means he looked.

I unzipped my jacket and stretched open the neck of my shirt. I tucked the letter against my chest.

I did not tell Aunt Brat about the orange envelope from Kemp.

A thought kept striking me—one that I knew was sort of twisted. It had to do with Mom being gone now.

So stop . . . stop hurting us.

Every card that Kemp had ever sent had pierced both Mom and me.

Aunt Brat and I had not talked about Kemp, but I was sure she'd be as surprised as I was that he'd reached me this way.

My aunt didn't like secrets—and I was keeping a few: the hole in the wall, the goats at the Gerber farm, and now this letter from my walk-away father.

This one was hitting my bones. I felt like I couldn't afford it. I'd felt settled in the last few weeks—if not quite nestled. My new adults and I were moving pretty easily around one another. If nothing else, I wanted time to think before I told Aunt Brat.

I ate supper with that envelope in my shirt. I helped with the dishes, then climbed the stairs to my room, and by then, any importance that orange envelope had come with had faded. I stuck it into the bag with all the others and shut them all back inside the box that I'd brought with me from Rochester.

My father sent cards. That's what he did. This was just another one.

38

Snowshoes

Chelmsford had just gotten itself dug out, it seemed, when Sunday night brought another storm. School was closed again on Monday. I was no stranger to heavy snow-falls. Rochester averaged eighty-four inches of snowfall annually—a fun fact from my early elementary years. People had their snow day rituals. I'd known kids whose families had headed straight for the best sledding hills or ski slopes. Others popped corn and watched old movies. Mom and I had baking days, and that usually meant oat-meal-raisin cookies.

This was Chelmsford, and Raya Delatorre and Sari Winkle arrived wearing snowshoes on their feet. A third pair—well-worn and dented—waited with a set of poles stabbed into the snow beside them.

"Oh . . . I've been sick," I said, eyeing that third pair.

"We missed you," said Raya. She pointed at the gear in the snow.

"But I've never even tried—"

"Neither had I until this morning," Sari said. "But it's easy! You just walk. Well, you march. Or stomp."

"Come on. Get your hoofing boots on," Raya said.

So I doubled my socks and put on the brown boots. "Oh, hey, Raya," I said. "Did you give me Moss Capperow's old boots?"

Raya shrugged. "I don't know. Probably."

"Probably?" I turned the tongue of the boot out so she could see the letters: MCAP.

"Yeah, that's Moss," she said.

"Yeah, it is," Sari echoed.

"Well, how did you get them?" I asked.

"Hmm . . . my mom must have picked them up at the town clothing exchange. Had to be a few years ago, by the look of them. No way those would fit Moss now." She laughed. "Come on," she said impatiently. "Snowshoes!"

As we strapped me into the foot traps, Guffer cavorted. He lunged and barked at the strange metal monsters, which now had me firmly by my feet. "It's okay," I told him. He licked his lips and wagged his tail. Then he tried to lead me out for a walk. "No, no. You have to stay." I hated to leave him behind, but there was no telling how this would go. I'd have poles in both hands. If I tried to hold a leash, I'd be pulled down for sure.

Aunt Brat came out to corral the dog. She held up her fist, a treat buried inside. "Guffer! Come!" He did and she set the treat into his open mouth. (He was getting very good at taking them gently.) She stroked his golden coat while the dog leaned on her.

"Looks like fun, girls. Where are you headed?" she asked, one eye squinting closed against the low winter sun.

"Bushwhacking," said Raya with a shrug. "Kind of wherever the walking looks decent. But we'll be careful. I thought it'd be cool to head out that way." She waved toward the trees.

"Yeah? How far do you think you'll go?" Aunt Brat asked.

"Halfway to exhaustion and not a step closer," Sari quipped.

"Practical," said Aunt Brat with a nod and a smile. "Lyddie? Do you have your phone?" I assured her that I did. "Okay, then. Do be careful. This is a lot of snow."

She should know, I thought. She'd skied off into the woods every chance she'd gotten in recent days. It was her tracks that Raya and Sari and I followed while I was getting a feel for the contraptions on my feet. We went out along the enclosure and into the woods.

"These tracks are great training ground. Easy going," said Raya as we tromped along the parallel lines of packed snow.

"How does it feel, Lydia?" Sari called back to me. "Are you stable?"

"Yeah," I said. I was surprised. "The poles help a lot. The balance, I mean." I planted one of mine so that the basket fit into the circle of one that had gone before. *Aunt Brat's*, I thought, and I smiled.

"If you're good, let's head up," Raya suggested, and she punched a foot into the fresh snow on the uphill side of Aunt Brat's tracks.

I hated to leave that trail, but I followed my friends, sidestepping up the hill, then traversing behind them as we marched below the pines. The snow carried us so high off the ground we had to duck under branches in some places. I worked and breathed, step after satisfying step.

I grew warm at my skin, and my nose ran so much—no holds barred—I had to pull a Florry Gerber and use my sleeve more than once. But there was something about this trek in the snow that had me all pumped up. I liked this. A lot.

Raya stopped where a downed tree crossed our path. She leaned on her poles, turned around, and asked, "Everyone okay?" I knew she meant me.

"Woo-hoo!" I said. I stuck my poles, opened my arms wide, and faced into the treetops. "I am ready for the Winter Olympics!" I laughed out loud.

"Yes!" Sari cried. "We are the women's snowshoeing team from tiny Chelmsford, Connecticut! We will put this place on the map! Gold medal!"

I stomped in place, looking down at the snowshoes. "It's just so funny," I said. "Like going out with a pair of cookie sheets strapped to your feet, though not as slippery!" All three of us laughed.

"Hey, Lydia, you're not mad that I put you into Moss's boots, are you?" Ray asked.

"Not mad," I said. "Just surprised."

And I think Moss was too. . . .

"Everyone around here shows up in everybody else's old stuff. Recycling, you know? It just makes sense."

"Perfect sense," I said. I'd decided that I liked wearing the boots that had once belonged to Moss.

I looked down from where we'd come—our tracks the only human-made disturbance in the snow. The slope was not treacherous, but steeper than I'd realized. Almost dizzy making. I firmed my poles into the snow.

Stay on your feet, Lydia. . . .

We began descending. I tried to orient. I was sure we'd moved mostly eastward. What did that mean in regard to the places I'd come to know? Home was behind us, and the Capperow farm was even farther to the northwest. Soldier's Chimney in the village center was to the south.

We hop-stepped down toward a level trail in the side of the slope, a place where the trees began to thin. Down and away, a creek had managed to melt a thin, shining black ribbon through the snow.

"Look! You can see down to the Gerber farm," said Raya. She raised a pole and pointed to our right.

Ah-ha! I'd had a sense that the Gerber farm was over this hill. I squinted into the distance. The house and barn looked like toys from a train set. That watery crack I'd been tracing was the creek that ran behind Gwen and Florry's place. Raya began to move us forward again. It wasn't long before I saw that we were about to merge with a set of parallel tracks in the snow—the kind made by a pair of fat skis, just like Aunt Brat's.

We were rejoining her trail. I glanced down at the Gerber farm again. I flashed on Aunt Brat's woolen snowflake socks. I remembered the dry weeds—no. Hay! That was hay! That's what she'd brought home—stuck to her socks and her skirt hem. It hit me:

Aunt Brat skis to the Gerber farm. . . .

I took an inward breath.

She knows the goats are there . . . she must . . .

I could practically hear my brain locking pieces into place. At the same time I felt the kind of weight that comes from realizing that you've made a discovery that somebody didn't want you to make—even if you still aren't sure what it is.

"Hey, you guys? You guys!" I blurted. Raya and Sari stopped. Both turned to look at me. I huffed and puffed a bit. "This has been so great. But I'm thinking I should head back." I jabbed my thumb over my shoulder. "I'm tired." I grinned apologetically. "Would you mind?"

"Oh, sure!" came the answer. My two friends planted their poles and turned themselves around.

"You've been sick," Sari said. "You shouldn't overdo it. Besides, I'm getting tired too," she admitted.

"Glad you spoke up before we got any farther out," Raya said. "Much as I like you both, I don't want to carry you piggyback."

That made Sari snort. "Oh my gosh," she said. "Could you imagine us kicking you in the sides with our snowshoes? Giddy-up, Raya!" They laughed as I let them go by me.

I looked over my shoulder at those ski tracks. They sketched a perfect path to the Gerber place.

There was no doubt in my mind: my Aunt Brat, who didn't like secrets, was keeping one of her own.

39

Oatmeal Cookies with Raisins

Sometimes stepping along will click your thoughts right into place. I puzzled over my hunch that Aunt Brat was spending time at the Gerber farm.

Gwen had said the injured goats had been entrusted to her; she was providing shelter and some of the care. Someone else was bearing the expense. Could Aunt Brat be that someone? And what about the way Florry Gerber had so earnestly insisted that she knew my "mutha"? Did she think my aunt was my mother? There were times my aunt looked like my mother, and people had said that I looked like Mom. So was that what Florry saw? A family resemblance?

Meanwhile, I wondered if Raya and Sari were putting together the things that I was putting together. Maybe not. They were busy talking about school and our upcoming test on the major battles of the Civil War.

"Ugh," I called up to them, "I missed all the review days last week."

"The main part will be an essay—open book and open notes," Sari said. That was good news for me.

Neither of them said anything when the ski path took us right to the spot where we'd stepped off to go uphill earlier. We stayed low this time and retraced our tracks— and Aunt Brat's—all the way back to the bottom step of the front porch, where Aunt Brat swung the door open.

"Welcome back, girls!" she said, her face in a beautiful, natural smile. I rested, leaning on my poles, catching my breath. I tried to stop thinking everything I'd been thinking.

Guffer squeezed past Aunt Brat and bounded off the steps. He paced a circle around Raya and Sari as they unbuckled their snowshoes and shook them off their feet. He wagged his tail slightly and let out that nervous woof-woof that totally marked him as a chicken-dog. My friends took his behavior in stride, but Aunt Brat frowned.

"He's so harassing," she said apologetically. She called to the dog, but he wouldn't give it up.

"Guffer! Come!" I was firm.

He started toward me with his ears flipping down, brush tail swinging. I squatted down to receive him, only to discover that my legs were jelly. I groaned and fell back onto my butt. Guff kept coming until he had me pinned on my back with one snowshoe foot swaying in the air. There was a lot of laughing in the yard.

You might not think it possible to feel good with seventy pounds of dog stepping on your gut and stuffing a wet nose into your ear. But I did. I was his person. I rolled up to sitting and scrubbed his ruff in my hands, gave his big blond body a hug.

"So listen . . . ," Aunt Brat said. "I just assembled the ingredients for a big batch of oatmeal-raisin cookies. Anybody interested?"

My jaw must have hung. My favorite snow-day cookie!

"I love to bake." Sari rubbed her mittens together.

"And I love it when Sari bakes," said Raya.

For the first time, they were going to come inside and stay awhile. I collected my wobbly legs underneath me and climbed the porch steps. I stopped to gather an armload of firewood. Raya did the same and Sari held the door for us. Guffer pressed his way in and headed to the water bowl. We stacked the wood on the hearth.

I soaked up the scene. There was something so easy, so right, about watching my friends peel off their boots and jackets in the front hall and something so everyday about Guffer coming to inspect their empty footwear.

236

Now, Raya had her eye on the woodstove, and I almost predicted the next words out of her mouth.

"Hey, Bratches," she said, "can I clean out your ash pan?"

Aunt Brat looked a little surprised. "Oh, done this morning, thanks anyway," she said.

"How about I throw some kindling on these coals?" Raya bent down to peer into the firebox.

"You should just say yes," Sari said as she shuffled in her socks up to the kitchen table. "Raya *has* to have stuff to do."

"That's true. And if you don't tell me what I can do, I sometimes start messing with things you don't want me to touch," Raya added.

"She does," said Sari, gently.

Aunt Brat shot me a grin. "Oh. Well, sure then," she said. "It's always a good time to stoke the fire in this drafty old house."

"Also . . . ," said Sari, who was already holding up a measuring cup full of sugar and looking slightly cross-eyed as she checked the line, "Raya is avoiding having to bake. I always try to pester her into it."

"That's true too. I like to crack the eggs. Then I'm all good," said Raya.

Aunt Brat let out a short burst of a laugh. "Well," she said, "we have a lot of self-awareness in the room today.

So healthy!" I peeled the wrappers off three sticks of butter and dropped them into the bowl with the white and brown sugars.

"I'll cream!" Sari revved up the mixer.

Over the whir of the machine, I kept catching Aunt Brat's eye. I wondered if she could hear me thinking thoughts at her as she measured baking soda and salt.

I know you go to the Gerber farm. . . .

Whir-whir-whir.

It's the goats, isn't it? You're doing something . . . and it's good. . . .

Whir-whir.

If you want to tell me . . .

Raya showed up to crack the eggs. (She nudged me away from the bowl.) Sari kept the mixer running. I checked the recipe and measured out two cups of oats.

"And the raisins," Sari said above the whirring.

Ah yes, the raisins. I picked up the red-and-yellow box. I drew my thumbs across the tiny picture of the Sun-Maid with her red bonnet and basket of grapes. Ten, or maybe eleven, years had passed since I'd first declared that this was my mother on the box. It struck me: Sun-Maid raisins were not going away. I'd find my mother's likeness on the boxes again and again for years to come—

Especially on snow days, Mom. . . .

I smiled to myself.

I measured out a cup and a half, which left not one raisin in that box. Sari shut down the mixer and used a big spoon to fold the oats and raisins into the cookie dough.

I took the empty raisin box and folded all the flaps inward. I stood it up at the center of the table with support from the honey jar and the pepper mill. The Sun-Maid had a way of watching over things. I looked up and saw Sari Winkle give me a tiny nod.

Before long, the house smelled of cinnamon, sugar, and warm oats. While we waited for the first cookies, we threw together a lunch from leftovers (we were hike hungry) and heated water for tea.

Aunt Brat pulled Soonie's dog bed over beside her chair because Soonie always liked to be close. The old greyhound lowered her skinny bones down and closed her eyes. Guffer settled under the table near my feet. I massaged his skull with my sock-covered toe. He leaned in.

"So, did you like snowshoeing?" Aunt Brat asked.

"Actually, I loved it," I said. "A lot."

"And you almost didn't even try it!" Raya could not help exclaiming.

"I know. But walking on top of the snow was so cool. And climbing the hill, and working up a sweat—I loved it."

"You can use those poles and snowshoes for the rest of the winter if you want," Raya said.

"Can I really?" I imagined going out on my own—maybe taking Guffer if I could train him to go along peacefully.

"Absolutely," said Raya. She grabbed the raisin box and spun it on one finger. She set it on the table in front of her. She flicked it with her index finger and thumb and made it hop forward a few inches.

"Ohhh . . . here we go," Sari mumbled, and she was right. It turned out that this flicking must be tried again and again. The box gained height and distance each time, knocking into condiments and finally flying right up under Sari's chin, where it hit with a pop, then landed.

"Oomph!" Sari touched her chin. "Okay, Raya. Easy." She rolled her eyes. She gently slid the box back to the center of the table. Raya picked it up again.

Aunt Brat smiled behind her mug of tea. *How funny for her*, I thought, *sitting at a table with thirteen-year-olds*.

"You know what, Lyddie, if you like snowshoeing, you should try my skis," Aunt Brat said. "Add a little speed, if you dare." She pumped an eyebrow at me. "This is the place for it. One of the best things about Chelmsford is the open land."

"Oh! Oh! And just wait until you get a load of this place

during snowmelt." Raya talked fast, eyes wide. "Oh man! We get acre-wide puddles, and the river rises right across Old Fordham Road." Her enthusiasm went into her next flick on that raisin box. The Sun-Maid went spinning way up over the center of the table. Aunt Brat flinched. I put my hands over my tea mug. Sari shot up. She grabbed that box right out of the air—practically a magic trick. Raya cheered. "Aww, Sari! Awesome!" She held out her hand to take the box back, but Sari held it close to her chest.

"Not a chance, Raya! No more hockey pucking this thing around."

"What? Why?"

"Because," said Sari. "You're going to spill something or break something, and besides, Lydia wants the box." Then she turned to me and said softly, "Don't you?"

"S-sort of." I tried to say it with a shrug. How does one admit to her friends that she wants a raisin box? But I didn't have to say a word. Sari set the box close beside me.

"Aw, you should have said so!" Raya told me. "I was going for a field goal—as in, football."

"Whatever," said Sari. "In four more minutes you'll forget all about it because you'll be burning your mouth on a hot cookie."

Raya rubbed her hands together. "Can't wait."

The smell of cooling cookies brought Elloroy out of his

241

suite. He sat with us, coddling a mug of tea. He dunked his cookies without mentioning his impending death. His magnified eyes surveyed the room. "Isn't this nice?" he said. "All you astonishingly young people at our table. Hasn't happened for years." He leaned toward me. "And now, it's every day."

"When did you come here?" Sari asked. Well, there was a question.

"Born here. In the room upstairs," he said, pointing a finger to the ceiling below the room I slept in. "Kept warm in a cradle beside the chimney," he added. "Of course, I left. Went to war. Went to school. Taught school."

I was surprised by all of this and ashamed that I had never asked. I guess I was thinking that Elloroy was rather private, slipping into his own end of the house the way he did. I guess I thought he didn't want to be bothered. Not true. "But you came back," I said, and he nodded.

"My mother asked me to come home. My turn to run the farm, she said, or at least try. So I did and that went well. I always liked a little dirt under my nails."

"I love getting dirty," Raya said.

Elloroy grinned and went on. "But eventually I stopped planting. Things changed. Too hard for me alone, and too hard to find help. Last bit of business I did here was twenty-some-odd years ago. Boarded a few horses, but it dwindled and I let it." He gave a shrug. "Time to rest the land."

"And your bones," Aunt Brat added.

"Brat and Eileen help me with that part—the resting of the bones. And now Lydia too. They've got this place oiled," he said.

"I would have worked for you," Raya said. "Heck, I'll work for you now. You want to grow something again? Want to board horses?"

I thought of Eileen's herd of goats—the tragedy of that. If they hadn't been killed on the highway, the barns on this land would be full right now.

"Raya, you still have to go to school," Sari reminded her gently.

Elloroy chuckled. "It's enough for me to have you all at this table." He patted the oaken surface with his big flat hand. Aunt Brat smiled at him over her shoulder.

It was late afternoon when Aunt Brat and the dogs and I walked Raya and Sari to the bottom of Pinnacle Hill, rather than ask their moms to brave the driveway; it could be slippery. We said warm hellos. We handed waxed-paper bags full of oatmeal-raisin cookies in through the car windows. As they pulled away we waved—excessively. This was my bus stop, after all, and that's what the women of Pinnacle Hill Farm did in this spot, every weekday morning: they waved.

I felt teamed with Aunt Brat in this small, but somehow great, moment of seeing friends off. Finding friends had been one of the surprises—something I hadn't thought to think about. Then again, why would I, in the midst of my mother dying? As we climbed home with the dogs, I gave a grunt. "Aunt Brat, my legs are so sore from snowshoeing!"

"Tapped a new set of muscles, did you?" She grinned in the dusk.

"Thank you for hosting. For the cookies and all," I said.

"So much fun!" she answered.

"And hey, how great that Guffer didn't jump up and swipe a scratch into their cars, just now." I jabbed a thumb back toward the bus stop.

"He was on excellent behavior," she agreed.

Less than a minute later, the telltale knock and rattle of Eileen's truck alerted us to her arrival on the road below. Aunt Brat and I ushered each other and the dogs to one bank of the drive to let her by. Guffer wagged and hopped. I spoke to him softly and kept him close. Eileen made eye contact, then gunned the engine for the climb. Her round, smiling face was at the open driver's-side window, both hands on the wheel, as she sailed by. "Huh-haw!" she called. "No place like home!"

Aunt Brat and I laughed. Then we coughed on the

exhaust. "Oh, peew-ewy!" said Aunt Brat.

"Thank you, Eileen!" I sputtered, and giggled. I bumped shoulders with my aunt while we both fanned our noses. We waited, then loosed the dogs to let them run up to Eileen, who would without a doubt be waiting beside her truck to catch them in her arms.

40

A Place to Put a Foot

There it is, Mom . . . a beginning . . . the House of the Sun-Maid Raisin Lady.

I would not have called it art. Not yet. But I was making something. Well, altering something—namely, that raisin box. Mom's favorite crafting magazine had devoted a page in every issue to "altered art" sent in by readers. Mom used to argue with that title. She'd say, "It's not art that has been altered. It's altering something until it becomes art." (We'd altered photographs into goddess art.) Then she'd add, "Whatever it is, I love it."

I sat in my room with my back against Elloroy's bricks. I had my art box and a mix of scavenged papers fanned out before me and a glue bottle resting on its side to keep the glop near the tip. I glued a triangle of cardboard to the top of the box so that the Sun-Maid had a roof above her head. From there, I took off, closing my eyes every so often as I tried to remember the house my mother had loved.

What else was there, Mom? Give me a hint. . . .

She would have told me exactness did not matter. She'd often sat in the big picture window—really in it. So I built a square-paned frame around the Sun-Maid and glued it down. I remembered shutters on that window, so I cut a pair from striped paper. I snipped leaves and flowers from an old garden catalog and layered them so that they "grew" like a flower garden right up to the sill of the window. I broke the border with a cluster of orange flowerpots at the corner of the house. I lost one pot on a Guffer breeze when he pushed his way into my room. That gave me the idea to add a spill of potting soil. Keeping it real.

I was in such a good mood I didn't mind when the dog chose to flop down right on top of all my paper scraps. I patted him. I reached under him. I kept cutting and gluing. Every so often, I'd stop creating to scratch the dog's brow with one hand and hold the House of the Sun-Maid Raisin Lady up in the other. It was lopsided, in the very best way. But it needed something more—something unexpected. I rummaged through my buttons and charms, and the thing that found my fingers was the weathered old dog tag.

"Cici Hoover," I whispered. "She never called back." I told this to Guffer. "We didn't need her," I said. "You're a good dog. Most of the time." I rolled the tag over in my gluey fingers. "Well, Guff, if ever there was something unexpected in my life, I guess it's you. I was not a dog person," I told him, "but I fell for you." I threaded the tag onto a piece of floss and tied it to the House of the Sun-Maid Raisin Lady.

I held it up again. I liked what I had done, but even more, I loved that I had done it.

Was it finished? I wasn't sure. But I knew the crooked little house should hang with the goddesses. Risky stuff, since all my adults were home at that time. I tiptoed into the hall. Guffer followed me out. He went down and settled near the bottom of the stairs, head on his paws, eyes closed. I decided the coast was clear.

I slipped back into my room and closed the door behind me. I peeled the sheep poster and pulled my art box into the crawl as silently as I could. I fished out a pushpin and chose a spot.

So there I was, standing on my art trunk, tacking the House of the Sun-Maid Raisin Lady to a stud, when suddenly—I wasn't. I felt the box tip. There was an awful clunk and a slam as I went down. Then a sick, crunchy sound, like a house breaking. A real house. No!

Time did that weird thing where it takes a speed bump. I was on my butt with one knee bent up to my chest and my other leg somewhere below. My heart caught on slowly. Then it began to pound, pushing that river of blood through me.

Oh, Elloroy! Elloroy! Your house . . .

And then I heard his muffled voice calling from below. "She's come through! She's through!"

I'm through. I am so, so through.

I tried to gather my wits. It was a good time to have elbows, I decided. I pushed up on them. I got my hands onto two joists and tried to rise. But I was stuck.

That crunchy sound had been my foot crashing through the floor—the sound of a secret breaking wide open.

I squeezed my eyes shut and imagined my lime-green sneaker with the bright orange laces dangling down somewhere in Elloroy's suite, probably just a few feet above his head. I imagined poor Elloroy looking up at it. *I am in trouble,* I thought, and that's about the same time I heard Aunt Brat and Eileen in the upstairs hall.

"Lydia?? . . . Lydia?? . . . Dear God, are you all right? Where the heck—"

Eileen found me first. She thrust her head into the hole from my room. We made eye contact. She swore, then backed out again. "She's in the crawl space, Brat! Go pull the panel. Be careful on the joists!"

Eileen's face reappeared at the hole. I suppose I was struggling to get up, because she said, "Now just hang on. Don't move anything yet—"

"I'm okay!" I tried to say.

"Brat's coming. She's coming!"

From where?

"The bathroom!"

My last of kin came pushing through the swinging goddesses to get to me. *She is one,* I thought, even as I was concentrating to hold on to the old wooden bones of the house.

"Lydia!" she gasped. She crouched before me. "Are you all right? Let me help." She held out her arms.

"I'm okay! I am!" I said. "And I'm sorry, so sorry!"

Aunt Brat opened and closed her hands, encouraging me to grab on, just as she had the day she'd found me lying in the snow. I gave her one of my hands and then the other.

Eileen coached from the hole. "Easy now . . . gently! Gently!"

"Umm . . . we have mice . . . ," I heard myself saying as Aunt Brat pulled me up to standing. She kept hold of my hands while I yanked my foot out of the plaster.

Down below we heard Ellory say, "Oh, there. She's gone now."

I focused on Aunt Brat. "The mice . . . um . . . that's

how I found my way in," I explained—as if all of this were the fault of things with whiskers.

"Good grief," said Aunt Brat.

I mentioned the small hole behind the sheep poster. "I made that . . . um . . . bigger."

"I see," said Aunt Brat, looking at her beloved Eileen, who was still stuffed into the opening.

"I didn't know about the bathroom," I added.

"How long has this been going on?"

"A while. I'm sorry, Aunt Brat. So sorry. I—I wanted a place to keep the goddesses. . . ."

"The goddesses." She took another look around. "Yes, and they are stunning. You have been busy."

"Mom and I made them. I brought them with me. From the old house."

"Ahh . . . yes. Your box," she said. She took a few big breaths. "Well, what do you think?" she asked. "How's your foot feel? How's that leg?"

"Just scraped, I think." I drew a few ankle circles. "I'm fine." Except I wasn't fine. I was horrified.

"Well . . . ," Eileen said, leaning casually into the crawl now and propping on one elbow to look around. "Nice little private gallery here. Look at all the art, Brat. Huh-haw! I like it."

"Yes," Aunt Brat said. "What a surprise. Here, Lydia.

Come this way." She wanted us out. She held my wrist. "Stay on the joists, *please*." She led me, parting the curtain of goddesses with her elbow as we went toward a surprising block of light at the end of the crawl. We passed the copper tub piping and went through a trimmed-out opening into the bathroom. Sunlight angled in at the window and onto the honey-pine floors. Leaning against the wall was my humiliation—a simple wooden panel. Aunt Brat had pulled it right out of the wall; it was the intended access to the crawl.

I sat on the lid of the toilet like a six-year-old while they looked me over. "I'm fine," I told them. I flicked plaster dust off my shoe. I hid a few splinters that had lodged in the heel of my hand. "I'm sorry. I am so sorry."

"Sorry" was something I'd rarely had to say. Even as a little kid, I knew that being anything less than very good for my sick mom would've been heartless. Yet now I'd done a bad thing to these good people. I'd kept a huge secret; I'd broken the house they lived in.

Lydia Bratches-Kemp, you are the worst.

When Aunt Brat and Eileen were satisfied that I wasn't damaged, a couple of things happened. First, they put the bathroom panel back in place. "Otherwise," said Eileen, "it's positively arctic in here, which is, of course, the same reason we have to wait so long for hot water."

"Yes, that is most inefficient," Aunt Brat said. "I guess the blessing here, besides Lydia being all right, is that we'll finally get someone in to address it. I had no idea the insulation was so poor. Old houses are full of surprises."

The next thing we did was go into my room and drape a thick blanket over the back of a straight chair. We pushed it up against the hole I'd made.

"Temporary fix. I'll give Saundra and Nan a call," Aunt Brat said. "They're our handywomen." No one said anything about what might become of the crawl, and I did not ask.

Finally, we went downstairs to see Elloroy and let me have a walk of shame into his suite to see the place where my foot had gone through.

"There it is," said Elloroy, his old face tilted to the ceiling. (Broken plaster is not pretty.) "I'm so disappointed," he said.

I hung my head. "I'm sorry, Elloroy. Truly sorry." I was a horrible, hole-punching vandal of a girl.

"When I heard that noise," he said, "I thought, *Oh boy, oh boy, here comes the end! I'm finally going to be—*"

"Dead." Aunt Brat, Eileen, and I said it together. Our delivery seemed more muted than ever. Elloroy blinked at the three of us through his ice-cube glasses. Then he looked at me.

"But it wasn't death at all," he said. "It was your lovely green shoe."

All I could do was give him an embarrassed smile and apologize again. "Whatever it takes to make it right, I'll do it. I'll work off the repair bill. Snow shoveling. Window washing. Anything."

"Pish," he said, and that was all.

Through dinner I felt like my adults were looking at me over forkfuls of brown-rice-and-broccoli casserole. Bite after bite, I couldn't stop thinking about plaster and wood and house parts.

What must they be thinking? I wondered.

Maybe Elloroy had decided to forgive me with that "pish" of his. That little bit of relief was probably the only reason that while I was feeling sorry about what I'd done, I was also feeling sorry that I'd lost the goddess gallery. I was sure that a broken floor *and* ceiling meant I'd be evicted from the crawl.

41

A Not-So-Small Repair

Saundra and Nan, the handywomen, came that weekend. After they'd been into the crawl and out again, we all gathered in my room—even Elloroy. He sat on the edge of the bed, smiling.

I stood out of the way and listened.

"First thing," Saundra said, "we recommend wrapping all the pipes. Then out with the old insulation and in with new."

"Okay. That," said Elloroy. "I want that."

"We have to demouse it. We do that the nicey-nice way, so we'll lend you our traps starting tonight. You'll have to check them each morning. It'll take a few rounds."

"There's never just one mouse," Nan added.

(I knew this to be true.)

"Now, we suggest tearing down this wall," Saundra said, patting the one I'd made the hole in. "Push it back a couple of feet and expose the corner of the chimney in this room."

"It means you gain a nook or a niche," said Nan.

"Nice place for hanging art, perhaps?" Aunt Brat mused.

"Yes," Eileen interjected. "Because art has got to have a place."

"The niche," Elloroy said. "I want that."

Aunt Brat turned her shoulders toward me. "Do you like that idea?"

"As long as it's all okay with Elloroy," I said.

"How soon can you start?" Aunt Brat asked. "I'm concerned about all this cold air."

"If you're ready, we can start today, close up the cold spot, patch the ceiling, and finish everything in a few days," said Saundra. She looked at Nan, who nodded in agreement. "But remember you'll be relocating mice for several weeks."

Elloroy slapped his knee. "Well, youth and beauty, you're on mouse duty," he said, and I figured that was fair.

They got right to it. Saundra donned gloves, a paper suit, and a shower cap. She immediately began rolling up and bagging the old insulation.

Saundra would not let me into the crawl. But she cut each goddess down with care and handed them out to me. She rescued the House of the Sun-Maid Raisin Lady before it went out with a heap of insulation. "Nice little housie," she said. "You're an artist!"

A niche was going to be nice for the room. But—and I wouldn't have ever said so to my adults—I wasn't sure I wanted to hang the goddesses in the open. For the time being, I would store them back in the box they'd traveled here in. I pulled it out from under the bed and lifted the lid. There on the bottom sat the sad-looking plastic sack of greeting cards from my never-present father, including that newest orange one that had come right here to Pinnacle Hill.

I never told Aunt Brat about it, and now I felt a weight settling back on my shoulders. I'd had mixed feelings about being caught for what I'd done to the crawl space. Oddly, I was relieved. Aunt Brat had said it: keeping secrets from the people you live with doesn't feel right.

But the orange envelope was different. I hadn't hidden it from her—not exactly. Yet I knew Aunt Brat would want to know that Kemp had sent it here. Was not telling her the same thing as keeping a secret? Or was it choosing not to share? Was there a difference? What about Aunt Brat's secret? Something was going on with those little pygmy goats, and Eileen, my aunt's partner in all things—most things—didn't know. But there could be a good reason. I knew that. In the last two years I'd heard my mother lie to my aunt on the phone; she told her all was well, when it wasn't.

Mom hadn't wanted anyone else calling the shots. Now that I knew my aunt, I had to say, I think she might have taken charge.

I turned to the goddesses, all spread out on my bed. One by one, I picked them up and layered them into the box on top of the bag of envelopes.

Packing them up again, Mom . . . at least for now. . . .

I whispered her a promise: "I'll find them a place."

42

The Moving of Mice

I did not like taking the mice away from the house—their home. But I liked our method better than some of the horrible ways that humans deal with the tiny creatures. For the last three days we'd found one mouse in each of two traps. Today, day four, was no exception.

"Oh, Lid-jah!" Eileen exclaimed. (She'd recently given me the new nickname.) I was walking toward the front door, an occupied mousetrap in each gloved hand. "What's that? Two more? And all for the love of a dollop of peanut butter?" I set the traps into an old canvas tote.

"Yep," I said, "poor little things." Then, as I did every morning now before the bus, and as the sun was rising, I stepped into Moss's old boots. Then I went out and buckled into Raya's snowshoes. I leashed Guffer and we hiked into the woods to release the mice.

I was proud of the dog; he'd gotten used to the scary snowshoes. He didn't bolt—much—and, so far, he hadn't pulled me over. Then again, I had the advantage of walking on top of the snow, while he sank in on four legs. That sometimes made him yip. He'd learned he had an easier go if he walked behind me and stepped in my tracks.

I stopped just before the little trickle of a stream and tied Guffer to a tree—just while I went to empty the traps. (I didn't want him to pounce on a mouse.) "Stay," I said, "I'll be quick."

Guffer didn't love this part of the woods; this was the section that eventually backed up to the Capperow farm, where the sound of the green wheelie machine often sawed through the peace and quiet—especially to a pair of sensitive dog's ears. I came this way on these mouse mornings only because of the stream.

Elloroy had said mice were less likely to come back if you carried them across water. I wondered if a stream this skinny counted. But it was the closest one to the house and all I had time for on school days.

I hopped over the stream, not so easy in the snowshoes. I landed and the metal mousetraps clinked against each other inside the tote. I winced. Poor mice. I apologized for the turbulence, though it was the least of things to be sorry about. Some of the mice would become prey. Some might survive in the woods, and others might come back to Pinnacle Hill Farm.

"I would if I were you," I told the day's first mouse. I released the pin on the trapdoor. The mouse shot out like it'd been fired from a cannon. The next one clung to the sides of the trap. "Go, little buddy. Go!" I coaxed.

Meanwhile, Guffer watched. He sat in the snow tipping his head left and right, as if to ask, What is that, Lydia? Can I have it?

Finally, the little clingster dropped out of the trap and scurried off across the snow. I put the empty traps in the tote and gathered up my walking poles. I hopped the stream and went stomp-stomping back to Guffer. Before I reached him I noticed that he looked strange. His head was low and he craned his neck left, then right, as if he were trying to see around me. I heard the low rumble in his throat. His sharp bark pierced the air. Next thing I knew he was rearing up like a pony, his blond chest high and his ears forward. He barked again and pulled his leash into a straight line behind him.

"Guff! Easy, easy!" I took a few running steps to meet him. I dropped my poles and grabbed the leash. "It's okay!" I told him. I turned and looked into the woods. Then I saw—and heard—how wrong I was.

Coming straight toward us was the bright green four-wheeler. I crouched and held my dog. The low buzz of the engine grew louder. The view grew clearer. I could see the Capperow uncle riding high with an ugly scowl plastered on his face. He stopped on the other side of the stream, no more than twenty feet away.

The man said not one word. He just sat staring at me. He revved that monstrous engine. I clung to Guffer. The dog twisted and turned with fright.

Moss Capperow's uncle raised his arm and made a swipe through the air as if to say, Go on! Get out!

I did not move.

He made the same motion again with more force—he even stood up off his seat. He leaned at me. He sneered. *Git!*

But how could I *git* when I had this scared dog in my arms? I stayed low and held on to Guff. I didn't dare take my eyes off the Capperow uncle. He stared right back at me, waiting.

If I could make it look like I was leaving, maybe he'd be satisfied. I reached for a walking pole, and dragged it close to me. Capperow shifted on his seat.

He used the sound of the machine to give me a final scolding. Then he cut a tight turn and circled away. The four-wheeler leapt, spitting out snow behind it. The awful noise faded to a whine in the distance.

Guffer stopped straining in my arms. I stood and steadied my knees. I covered my nose against the stinky fumes Capperow had left in the otherwise perfect air. I scanned the woods. His tires had chewed through the snow and torn up the damp earth, leaving raw, muddy trails. We were well away from his field, even farther from his barns. He had no business here.

Suddenly, I knew. This was about Guffer.

He thinks he can keep us out of these woods. . . .

A sweaty chill made me shiver. I untied Guffer from the tree and we hustled home.

Inside, I stood in the front hall and kicked off the old boots. Everyone was in morning bustle mode, but I had business. "Question for you all," I said, and that got everyone's attention. "I pointed hard with my whole arm and asked, "Heading thataway, whose land is it? Where's the property line?"

My women looked at each other and blinked. Then they both looked at Elloroy. "Rock wall," he said. "Edge of the woods. Somewhat toppled last time I saw it."

I set my hands on my hips. "Oh really?"

"What's wrong, Lyddie?" Aunt Brat asked. She was checking the clock. It was a university day.

"That scumbucket Mr. Mick Capperow is what's

wrong!" My adults stared at me, eyes wide. "He just rode right onto your property, Elloroy. And he sat there churning up the engine on that ugly, stupid, green four-wheeled thing and he did it just to scare Guffer." I wiped a bit of spit off my lips.

"What did he say to you?" Aunt Brat wanted to know.

"Nothing! He said nothing!"

"Power play," said Eileen. "It's creepy. Unacceptable." She gave Aunt Brat a sideways glance.

"I don't understand it," Aunt Brat said. "Does anyone here think Guffer has been roaming over to the Capperows'?"

"No!" I said. "Especially not in the deep snow. And besides, I kind of know Moss, and he would've told me if Guffer was causing trouble there."

Elloroy shook his head. "Sounds like Capperow's the one creeping over to our place, not the other way around. Who's the bad dog now?" he said.

"Huh-haw!" said Eileen.

But I didn't want them to make jokes. Elloroy brushed my arm. "I don't blame you for feeling shook up. I'm sorry about it," he said. "You going to be okay, youth and beauty?"

"I'll be fine," I said, "but today, you can call me youth and fury!"

43

Goddess Spill

The niche was done. It was beautiful, with its exposed brick and new drywall and a couple of coats of creamy-white paint. The room smelled new. The bricks radiated warmth.

But I missed the crawl—or maybe I missed the goddesses. I slid the box out from under my bed. Guffer plunked down and rested his great yellow side against it as if I'd put it there for him. He watched, sleepily, as I took two goddesses and held them up in the niche. In truth, it was a fine place for them, and Aunt Brat and Eileen had given me proper picture-hanging hooks. The lengths of braided yarns were still attached to each goddess. But I, who had been so willing to make that one very large hole, had so far resisted driving even the tiniest nail into the new walls. I sighed. Did I want to hang them in the open?

I pulled a few more collages out. I laid them one atop the next with the yarn hangers all off to one side. I checked with Guffer. "What would you do with them? Besides chew—"

His sharp bark pierced the room—and me.

"Whoa! Guffer! Startle me to my bones, why don't you."

He continued to rumble. Then he dove right over me. His legs kicked out behind him and thumped the box. I grabbed for the dog, but I missed. He bolted, toenails scratching, feet slipping on the hardwood floor. He came to a sliding halt inside my bedroom door. His hairs stood on end. He barked into the hallway. Turned out he had two good reasons.

Raya Delatorre and Sari Winkle stood just a few feet away—in our upstairs hall. I scrambled to my feet. How had I not heard them on the stairs? Who had let them in? And up? And oh!—the goddesses! I glanced behind me. The box was on its side, probably back-kicked by a big yellow dog.

Goddess spill!

I tried to be wide—block their view.

"Oh, hi! Hey, you guys!" I said. I sounded ridiculously chirpy, cheery—and loud. Meanwhile, Guffer continued to bark. I hooked two fingers around the dog's collar.

"Guffer, sit. Leave it!" I said. I tugged him back. He kept barking. "Guffer!"

Raya might have said hi. Sari too. Who could hear?

"I think he's just startled! Because you're upstairs!" I tried to be heard. I saw Sari lean toward Raya's ear. Both of them crossed their arms over their chests and looked up. Ha! They'd remembered!

Guffer stared at them. *How long before he gives up?* I thought. *Can I sweep these goddesses under the bed before my friends look down again?* I scooted myself backward a little, dragging Guffer with me.

Finally he quieted down. Engine on idle. I let go of the collar. He turned away from Raya and Sari, who were still standing at my doorway, chins turned high. Guffer checked Raya and Sari one more time. Then he circled—full turn—and lowered himself onto the floor with a grunt.

"Good boy," I praised him.

"It worked!" Sari breathed.

"Sure did," said Raya. They both relaxed

"Atta boy, Guffer. See, it's just us," Sari cooed.

"No, no. Keep ignoring him," I warned. "At least for now."

That was going to be easy. They were both already looking past the dog and past me. I turned and looked behind me. Goddesses everywhere.

267

Great. . . . Say hello to my paper friends.

"Oh . . . wow. . . ." Sari made her way closer. She slid to her knees for a better look.

"Yeah. Wow," Raya echoed. She eased past Guffer. She knelt next to Sari and kept her hands tucked close to her belly. *Raya, not touching,* I thought.

"Oh. Mess," I said. They ignored that, and I had little choice but to join them at this unexpected viewing.

"Oh . . . Lydia. What are these? Did you *make* them?" Sari asked.

"Y-yes." I felt an unpleasant heat in my face. What to do next? But then I just said it. "My mom and I made them. I brought them here with me."

"Whoa! Wowza . . . ," Raya said.

Sari let out another long breath. "I can't believe you have these. I can't believe *I* get to see them."

Me neither, I thought.

"Do you know how cool these are? No, no, 'cool' isn't even the word. I don't think I know the word." Sari looked up at me. "And I'm not sure what they are . . . except beautiful . . . women!" Her eyebrows went up. "I *love* them."

She slid her hands gently underneath a goddess and lifted it up. She looked closely at the surface. "So it's a collage. An old photograph . . . and paint," she said. "And papers, and some fabric—oh look, and lace." Then Sari Winkle read my mother's handwriting. "The Goddess of Gratitude." She glanced back at the art on the floor. "So, are they all goddesses?"

I gave a tiny nod.

Then Raya began to read in that husky voice of hers. "Goddess of the New Moon right here, and the Goddess of the Third Heart—wow. The Goddess for Winter's End—that's cool," she said.

"They were my mother's idea," I said. "She was very creative and full of heart." I spoke slowly. "Ironic, because her own heart was freakishly weak." I pressed my hand against my chest.

I guess I am going to tell them. . . .

"Her illness brought a lot of pain to our family— troubles. And when there were troubles Mom would try to move us both through them by creating the goddesses. The Goddess of the Third Heart is from when she got passed up for transplant for the third time."

My friends were motionless.

"And when there were good things, well, she thought we needed goddesses for that too." I felt the most unexpected laugh come up inside me. "We did this to cope and to keep hope. Have some fun. And celebrate."

"And make art," Sari added. She shuffled gently

through the goddesses. "Neat materials. . . ." She gave me a smile.

"Always on the cheap," I said. "Salvaged, scavenged, or found—papers, cloth, stuff from flea markets. Some ephemera—"

"Efema-who?" said Raya. She pushed back her eggplant-colored bangs.

"Ephemera," I said. I laughed and thought about how to describe it. "It's common stuff that had a use, and usually, it'd be thrown away afterward. But then for some reason, people collected it. Saved it. So mostly printed paper things, like postcards, stamps, or soap labels."

"You mean if you really loved the picture on a food package or something?" Sari was catching on.

"Yeah. Things like raisin boxes," I said. I started to laugh—and almost cry too. I leaned forward, tapped a finger on the House of the Sun-Maid Raisin Lady, which had spilled out with the goddesses. "You could just think of it as turning junk into art. Recycling—"

"Oh! The raisin box! Look what you did! Now I get it!" Raya said.

"Goddesses. . . ." Sari swallowed. "We should probably all be making goddesses." She sounded wistful—like precious time had already been lost, which made me smile.

"Hmm," said Raya. "Come to think of it, there have been a few times I could've used a goddess."

"Really?" I asked. "For what? I mean, if you made a goddess . . ." Despite the fact that all of mine were spilled across the floor, it seemed like too personal a question to ask. But Sari Winkle dug in.

"For my first goddess, I'd have to go global," she said. She gave a little nod. "Like, maybe I'd make . . . hmm . . . a Goddess for the Good of the Earth. Or the Goddess to Reverse Climate Change. Something like that."

"Me too," said Raya. "A Clean River Goddess. Something like that."

My own head swirled with images.

"But for myself"—Sari tilted her head—"I'd make the Goddess of Figuring Out Your Love Life."

Raya faked a cough. "Do you *have* a love life?" she asked. "'Cause if you do, that's news to me."

"I don't have a love life," said Sari. "But I think about it." She gave a shrug and lowered her eyelids. "I kind of want one."

"For real? Right now?" Raya asked.

"I'm probably not ready for the whole falling-in-love part," Sari admitted.

"Yeah, do ya think?"

"But I want to kiss . . . somebody," said Sari. She hesitated. "And I think I want to kiss a girl just as much as I want to kiss a guy."

I was suddenly thinking of . . . someone. . . .

"Okay," said Raya. "That's cool. But not me, please. Just so you know."

"If I wanted to kiss you, I would have already asked," Sari said. One side of her mouth curled toward her friend. "It's funny, isn't it? How I know that much, yet the rest is so . . ." She stopped and shook her head.

"Mystifying?" I offered.

"Perfect word," said Sari. "See, part of it is I'm not sure if men can be as . . . hmm . . . warm as women are. Like, for your whole lives together." She shrugged. "But maybe some can be, and maybe it's wrong for me to say that."

"But you can say it to us," I said gently. "I've wondered too."

"Hmm. I guess it'll depend on who I fall in love with, and who falls in love with me."

My eyes started to fill. I thought of my mother, and of the morning Kemp and his broken soul walked out. I pressed the sleeve of Mom's sweater to my nose.

"Well, I know that, for me, it's guys," Raya said. "I just know it is. And the mystifying part for me is that sometimes I *feel* like a guy myself." She shifted a little, but she went on. "And sometimes I wonder if other people think I'm kind of guy-ish. Because I know more guys than girls who like to do the stuff I like to do. And I'm not being sexist. I'm going by the numbers. And by what I've seen.

Like, the wood shop? One of my fave places? It's almost *all* guys. Down at the river, fishing? Same thing. Doesn't mean girls don't fish. I'm a girl. I fish. But I don't see a lot of girls fishing; I see a lot of guys fishing. And maybe that's just here where we live. I don't know, because I haven't lived anywhere else." She thought for a second. "But when I think about being married someday—when I picture it—I see my husband as kind of like my bro, because we're going to do stuff together. All those things I just said." She pushed her lower lip out and thought. Then she said, "So yeah. For me, it's guys. And you know what? Good thing we don't have to figure this all out this afternoon."

The three of us laughed. Guffer got up and came over to us, head tilting. He tucked his nose right into Raya's armpit for a sniff. "Whoa! Whoa!" she said. "What is this?"

"Ha! He likes deodorant," I explained. "And shampoo." Guffer gave Raya a huge push and a snort and knocked her over. Then he walked right across all the lovely goddesses.

"No! No!" Sari leaned down and spread her arms over them. She giggled and called out, "Save the goddesses! Save them! Help! Help!"

We fell apart laughing, the three of us. We patted Guffer and coaxed him off the art. Then we scooped the goddesses off the floor and onto my bed.

"You know, Lydia . . . ," Sari said. She began to spread the goddesses out, looking at each one. "I don't know the order, but I bet you do. You have a whole story here." She stopped to fix her large blue eyes on me. "They're a memoir, Lydia. They are."

44

By the Woodpile

First, I heard a lot of barking. Then I heard Aunt Brat. "Wood delivery!" she called up the stairs. "Lydia? We can't keep Jaycinda waiting."

"Coming!" I hollered back. I ran down the stairs, stepped into the cruddy brown boots, and stuffed my arms into my jacket. Eileen was already out on the porch watching Jaycinda back her pickup truck toward the house. Jaycinda's little dog, Jaxy, yapped in the back window of the truck. Guffer answered with deep, chesty woofs.

Eileen made hand circles encouraging Jaycinda backward. "Yep, yep. Snug it right in. . . . Little more . . . little more . . . Halt!" She held both palms out.

They dropped the tailgate. We put on our work gloves and became an ant farm of wood-carrying women. Guffer and Jaxy ran zoomie circles nearby. As long as Jaxy stayed, Guff stayed too. Soonie stood out of harm's way on the porch and kept her fawn eyes on Aunt Brat.

This was my first wood delivery. I liked stacking the logs, fitting them against the outside wall of the house under the overhang of the flattish roof. The ends of the logs formed a mesmerizing pattern of pie wedges and circles with radiating cracks. But there was a pace to keep. The stack climbed higher. Aunt Brat and Eileen and Jaycinda grunted and chatted as we thunked more logs into place.

"Looks good and dry," said Aunt Brat.

"I don't bring green wood," Jacinda said. "Promise you that. This was cut and split eight or nine months back. Moisture content below ten percent."

"I vouch," said Eileen. "The last cord burned clean and hot."

I kept a smile to myself during all this talk about firewood, which is not to say I wasn't interested. I learned that oak was the most abundant firewood in our part of the country. So there you go. I felt like a knowledgeable countrywoman.

Guffer took a break from the chasing game to check out all the new smells that had arrived on Jaycinda's truck tires. He added a sprinkle. Jaycinda laughed. "Guess I'll be wheeling his résumé all over town today."

"Lot of wood deliveries?" Aunt Brat asked.

"You said it. Everyone is taking a look at their stack and deciding they need more. Overwhelming! I can only get so many in during the week. Depends what time I can finish up the mail route. And whether it snows."

"Put the wood on the mail truck, then," Eileen quipped.

Jaycinda, the Goddess of Deliveries, I thought. I watched her balance a few more logs atop the pile. When she turned we happened to look right at each other.

"Well, I guess we know what you're good at, Lydia," she said.

"What's that?" I asked. I brushed wood confetti off my sleeves.

"Hard work." Jaycinda grinned at me.

"True! Ever since she arrived," Aunt Brat said with a little nod. She brushed a mitten across her brow. "We have never gotten this job done this quickly. I'm grateful. Not my favorite chore," she confessed.

I raised my arms, elbows crooked, to suggest that I had biceps under my jacket. "The mighty!" I said. "Maybe this is my year for growing muscles." We laughed.

"You just had a birthday, didn't you?" Jaycinda asked.

I shrugged. "Not really. November," I said. I was thinking it was a funny question. I was also thinking that I'd had the last birthday I'd ever have with Mom. I felt the wash of sadness—it had been catching me so randomly ever since she'd died. Then just as suddenly, I was able to think: *No, I'm okay. Right now, I am okay. I'm on top of the great gray threat.*

I saw Jaycinda scrunch her brow. "Sorry. I thought I'd seen a festive sort of envelope, addressed to you."

Aunt Brat stopped still. Our eyes caught for a split second. I took a ragged little swallow. Eileen looked at me too. She whistled a few notes of a non-song, which must be very hard to do when your face is stricken and your cheeks are paralyzed.

Jaycinda's tone changed, like she meant to back off, but she couldn't. "Well . . . I shouldn't have said anything, it's just that real greeting cards stand out amid all the circulars and credit card offers. Makes a mail carrier feel good to deliver something personal now and then."

Oh! Could she please stop talking? Aren't there any more logs to stack?

Finally she shrugged. "Happy Birthday anyway!"

I have to hand it to Aunt Brat; she waited. She waited until Jaycinda rolled away, until we were back inside and out of our boots and gloves. She waited until after lunch. In fact, she waited until *I* brought it up.

"Aunt Brat," I said, "before this becomes a thing, I want to tell you about the *festive* piece of mail."

She gave me a bit of eye to indicate that she was listening.

"And Eileen, you too, of course. Okay. So. My father—you remember him, right? Kemp?"

"Yes, I knew Kemp," said Aunt Brat. "Though not well." She tried to keep her tone even—almost like she was bored.

"Not me." Eileen gave her head a little shake. "I didn't know him. Never met him." She pressed her chin forward, looking peeved. "But I'd have a strong opinion about any person who leaves their—"

"Eileen!" Aunt Brat interrupted. "Lydia, go ahead," she said.

I told them how he'd sent cards for all these years and how I could tell that it upset Mom, even though she'd never say so. "It made me wish the cards wouldn't come," I said. "I rarely opened them. I know that's weird. But it would've felt like betraying her. I don't know if you can understand."

"We can." They said it almost exactly together.

"And he sends money," I said, "or at least he did, but I don't use it. A few weeks back, there was an orange envelope in the mail. That's what Jaycinda was talking about, and yes, it's from him. I haven't opened it. I probably won't."

"But Lydia, wh—"

"And I know you want to know why I didn't tell you about it, and the answer is, I don't know." I took a second to think. "But it wasn't a secret, and I wasn't trying to deceive you. I did the same thing with that card that I've done with every other one. I stashed it away." Ugh. I could only hope that made sense to them.

"But Lydia, this is different. Your life has changed. A lot. Your mom dying, and this move. We didn't expect to hear from him."

"Neither did I!" I said. "I'll give you the card! You can read it. I don't care!"

"So, you didn't open this card?" Her voice was very gentle.

"No," I repeated. "Are you going to make me?"

"No. Never," said Aunt Brat.

"No, never," Eileen echoed.

"I'm just wondering what's on his mind," Aunt Brat said. She drew a breath in and let it go slowly.

"The few cards I did open over the years said almost nothing."

"Okay. But let me say something, Lydia. If ever you want to reach out to Kemp"—I let my body sag, I rolled my eyes, but Aunt Brat waited me out—"and just see what he's all about, I'd rather help with that than have you sneak around about it. Please. *Please?*" I was already nodding yes, making the promise. "Because he is your father, and—"

"Yeah, but he's the one who chose to turn that into nothing but biology," I said.

A faint smile crossed Aunt Brat's lips. "That sounds like something Holly would say," she said, and the smile grew broader.

"She did say it."

"Huh-haw," said Eileen.

"But Aunt Brat, and you too, Eileen, I was not trying to hide that piece of mail from you." I waited a second, then added something that was a surprise even to me. "I was keeping it unimportant. Just like all his cards."

Oh, my gosh, Mom. I just put it into words. . . .

45

Wrong Thing, Right Reason

Aunt Brat wanted to see where I had most recently encountered Moss Capperow's uncle. On a Sunday morning in the middle of March, she skied and I snowshoed out to the tiny stream. I carried the two mousetraps in the tote. Aunt Brat had shouldered her backpack. It wasn't unusual for her to take it on her ski outings. I did note that something was rattling around inside of it.

We'd left the dogs at home. That was Aunt Brat's idea. "In case we do encounter the Tormentor Capperow, or if we want to journey afar today."

"Afar, did you say? Boston by sundown?" I teased, and she laughed.

For now, she followed me, using her fat skis the same

way one walks on snowshoes. I wondered how I'd keep up with her if we did go *afar*. She could glide; I couldn't. But I had become surprisingly swift on the snowshoes, and I figured I'd race her if I had to.

"This is the place," I said when we reached the tiny stream. I hopped across it and pointed with one pole into the woods. "See the gouges?" I said. "Those are from the four-wheeler."

"It's a bit sickening," she said. "And this *is* Elloroy's land."

Aunt Brat watched me release the first mouse. We gave it kudos for heading into a hollowed tree stump. But the second mouse skittered out of its trap and over the back of my hand.

I let out an "Eeep!" Then an "Ayi-yi-yi!" I jumped backward. I tripped on the snowshoes and fell on my rear. I looked at Aunt Brat. We made the same face at each other: mouths and eyes wide open in surprise. Then we burst out laughing. The mouse was gone.

"Come on!" she called when she could talk again. "Get up! Let's hike!"

"Ha! Easy for you to say," I said. As I came back across the stream, she reached to take the tote from me. She rolled it up, traps and all, and tucked it into her own backpack.

"Now you're less encumbered," she said. "Try to keep up!" Off she went, bending into each glide of her skis. I stabbed my poles into the snow and chased her.

I know that she slowed down for me. I'd catch up every hundred yards or so, only to fall behind again. I sweated. My nose dripped. But Raya and Sari had taught me the useful art of shooting snot rockets, and I did what I had to do when I had to do it.

We began to climb, and that's when I knew I'd been on the other side of this hill before.

We crested and started down, both of us sidestepping. Soon, we were just a few feet from the place where I'd asked my friends to turn back a few weeks ago. Both Aunt Brat and I knew this set of tracks. She said nothing, but she chose to rest here. We stood catching our breath. I looked down on the Gerber farm—the view in miniature.

"Shall we?" Aunt Brat said.

"Shall we what?" I asked. "Go down?" I continued to breathe.

She nodded. "I want to check on them."

"On the Gerbers?"

Aunt Brat gave me a soft smile. "No, Lyddie. The goats."

We looked at each other.

"I know you know," she said. Then, almost as if we'd planned it, we switched our gazes down the snowy slope to the farm again. The shiny obsidian creek had become a wider line through the snow.

"Well, you did come home with hay on your socks," I said. "And you did make a path. . . ."

"Hmm," Aunt Brat hummed.

"Why have you kept them a secret?" I asked. "I mean, what about Eileen? She wanted them."

"I did it *for* Eileen," she said. She sighed. "Oh, Lyddie. If it had been anything but goats that turned up at the Feed that day . . ." She shook her head in a confounded sort of way. "I could neither bring them home, nor leave them to be rescued by someone else—because they were goats. I wanted them for Eileen. I knew we could give them a home—the perfect home. But given the horrible shape they were in, and after what Eileen went through with her herd, I just had to know that this little pair had a fighting chance. I needed to know they were going to survive."

"Yes," I said, though it came out no louder than a breath. She was right, I thought. "And? Do you know now? Are they going to be okay?"

My aunt nodded and smiled. Her eyes pooled with hopeful tears. "Weeks of touch and go. But they've done well," she said, a high little song of triumph in her voice. "They will need special care, and prostheses, and we can do that."

"So, when?" I asked. "When will you tell Eileen?"

"Soon," she said. "I'm sorry, Lydia. It is unfair of me to ask—and secrets are a burden—but I need us to hang on just a little longer."

I opened my eyes wide at her. "Aunt Brat . . ."

"I want to get them through one last course of antibiotics. I want them to be one week stronger, a little closer to ready for their prostheses. Eileen will be so good at helping them through that next stage."

"Right," I said. "Okay, Aunt Brat." Nothing she was saying seemed wrong or untrue. But I could not help worrying about how Eileen was going to take this news once Brat broke it to her.

46

A Bag Full of Stones

Aunt Brat glided, and I chased her, down the hill to the Gerber farm.

We cleaned the stall together, filling a wheelbarrow with old bedding and laying down new. The goats stood and stumbled on their little pink casts, then lay curled against each other. Their weird hyphen-pupil eyes seemed eerily wise and maybe grateful.

"Enchanting, aren't they?" Aunt Brat said. She stopped midpass with the hay rake in her hands.

"I wonder . . . ," I said, but then didn't finish.

"What, what?" my aunt pressed me.

"I wonder . . . if they had both their ears—in full, you know—would they use them the way a dog does?"

"Hmm. In an expressive way?" She sounded wistful. "I don't know the answer." Aunt Brat took up her raking again.

How hard she must have worked at this, I thought. She'd given them medications, she'd mucked stalls. Perhaps she'd changed dressings and dealt with blood and puss—I did not know. It could not have been easy in the first weeks to look into the eyes of two injured creatures and hope that they could understand that you were there to help. At least Aunt Brat had had Gwen and Florry for all those things—and to shoulder some of the secrecy.

But Aunt Brat was alone in having kept this from her partner in love and life. The coming home and not saying . . . well, that had to be like carrying a bag full of stones.

Okay, Lydia Bratches-Kemp . . . you carry that bag with her now.

I grabbed the handles of the wheelbarrow, lifted, and pushed forward. I hoped with all my heart that Eileen would feel Aunt Brat's love when she found out about this.

I met Florry Gerber at the end of the barn. She swung the wide half door open for me and I wheeled the load out to the compost heap.

"Hey," I said. "How are you? How are your Belgian Hares today?" I asked. I struggled as I tipped the wheelbarrow up to empty it.

Florry didn't answer me, except for her blooming grin. She followed me back down the center of the barn. I let myself back into the goats' stall with Aunt Brat. Florry climbed up and stood with her feet hooked under the bottom board and her chin on the top one, looking in.

"Yore the onliest few what took 'em." She said this to my aunt. "Onliest one what could pay for those."

Aunt Brat, who was giving one of the goats a rubdown—checking for fleas or scabs or other trouble, perhaps—nodded. "I couldn't have done it without you and your mom."

I watched Florry absorb the compliment. Her face began to glow.

Minutes later, Gwen Gerber came out to the barn with a thermos tucked under one arm and the handles of four mugs hooked on her thumbs. She seemed unfazed to see me with my aunt. Florry started pulling on that thermos. Gwen chuckled and let her daughter have it.

"How goes the caprine infirmary, Bratches?" She bent to set the mugs on the top of a wooden crate.

"They both seem well," Aunt Brat answered, and again I heard that hopeful lilt. She pulled a bottle of pills out of her backpack. The two women discussed the next part of treatment for their patients.

Meanwhile, Florry had twisted the lid off the thermos.

She began to pour, her cheeks rigid with concentration. She filled each mug without a spill. Threads of steam rose and released the scent of chocolate.

"Ah . . . cocoa," I said. I was thirsty and tired from chasing Aunt Brat. Cocoa was going to hit the spot.

Florry slowly turned to me with one mug pressed between her hands. "Not too hot. Muthas furst," she said. She pushed the mug at me and opened her eyes wide. "Take it. You give it to your mutha. Furst." I cupped my hands under the mug. I turned toward Aunt Brat.

"Hey, Florry," said Gwen. "Remember what I said? Bratches is Lydia's aunt," she explained. Florry blinked.

"Yee-ah. But she's the onliest few what can be hur mutha," said Florry. I saw Gwen cock her head and close one eye, as if thinking how else she might say it.

But Aunt Brat spoke up. "That is a stunning and lovely thought," she said. She was smiling at me ever so softly. I stretched toward her with the mug. She took it, closing her hands over my hands.

"Well," I said, "you are my last of kin."

47

A Big Reveal

Aunt Brat took her last sip of red wine. She held it in her cheek. I caught her looking at me through the thin wall of the glass. She swallowed and cleared her throat. "I wondered if I could take a minute to say something," she said. "I have a bit of a confession to make."

I saw Eileen halt. She turned to look at Brat. We set down our forks—as if that were required. Meanwhile, Elloroy raised his head to tune in. He pushed his lower jaw forward. Then he set his fork down too.

Aunt Brat looked at me again. She dipped her chin ever so slightly. She turned to face Eileen.

"I have something to tell you all, and Eileen, especially you, since you were the inspiration." Aunt Brat paused and Eileen sat up straight with a curious grin on her face. "Y-you remember the unfortunate little goats?" Aunt Brat said. "The ones that were left at the Feed—"

"Bratches!" Eileen winced. "Of course we remember. But why would you go bringing that up now? Here at our table, and all these weeks later. . . ."

"Because, I have them," Brat said.

"You *have* them?" Eileen drew her chin back so that it doubled up.

"Oh boy," whispered Elloroy. (I may have been the only one to hear.) His great, magnified eyeballs seemed larger and more meandering than ever.

"What does that mean, Brat?"

"I took them in," Aunt Brat said clearly. "With help from the good women at the Gerber farm—"

"What? Why would you . . . For how long?" Eileen's face twisted up like she'd been fed a lemon. I started picking the ruffled edge of Mom's sweater.

"Since . . . since it happened," Aunt Brat said.

"That was weeks ago," Eileen said.

"A couple of months."

I grunted. Why would she say it like that? Elloroy seemed to agree. His mouth hung open and he huffed a breath.

"And you didn't tell me? Why? Why the hell couldn't

I know? Huh, Bratches?" Eileen fixed a stare on my aunt, who sighed heavily.

"Eileen, I was devastated right along with you after what happened to your herd." Brat's voice began to catch. "Then seeing those poor damaged creatures—"

"Damaged? They were abused, Bratches! That's abuse, what happened there! Let's call these things by the right name." Eileen indignantly balled both fists on the table. "As for my herd, that was slaughter. Murder."

"Yes. And I know that it broke your heart all over again when the little goats turned up at the Feed. I felt that with you."

"So if you were going to do something, why not bring them here, like I wanted?" Eileen demanded.

"They were too close to death." Aunt Brat said it plainly. "I was worried about you. You would have been devastated if they didn't survive." She cleared her throat. "So yes, I took them—for you—but I also kept them from you. And I know that sounds ludicrous. . . ."

In the next silent second I glanced at Elloroy. He sat tracing the edge of his plate with one hand and the foot of his wineglass with the other.

"Well, damn it!" Eileen shouted. She slapped her hand on the edge of the table. That made Guffer leap onto his feet. He burbled out a halfhearted woof, then began to pace. If Eileen noticed him, she ignored him. "And Barley?" she went on. "All he ever told me was that he'd heard they were coming along okay in spite of everything. He knew it was you, didn't he?"

"Yes. But please don't blame him. I made the decisions. I asked for secrecy."

Well, Eileen lost it. Not loudly. Not with words. She just lost it. She got up from the table. Guffer trotted over to her, dog-certain that Eileen would head outdoors—and that's what she did. Guffer led. There was a flash of plaid flannel, and bang! Out the door.

Aunt Brat and Elloroy and I sat in silence. My heart thudded. I thought we might hear Eileen's truck start up. When it didn't I figured she was out in the paddock pacing about with Guffer. Maybe staring off to the south with him.

Soonie came tapping over on her long toenails to stand beside Aunt Brat, who put her hand on the dog's head. Finally, Elloroy leaned over to Brat and said, "Thank you for not making me complicit." She nodded and might have flicked a tear away with her knuckle. Elloroy excused himself and went into his suite.

"I'll clear," I said, and I began stacking plates.

"Thanks, Lyddie."

"Sure. And Aunt Brat, I just want to say, I get it. I get all of it," I said. "And I know things are not so good tonight. But it's going to get better. I really believe that."

I couldn't stand the sound of my own chirping anymore, so I turned the kitchen faucet on full blast and scrubbed the heck out of those dishes.

48

The Lump in the Couch

I was worried about my women. For two days, Eileen sulked. She had good reason. In the mornings, she'd be on the couch in an angry-looking twist of blankets and I would know that she'd slept there. She took her coffee out on the cold porch and sat under a blanket sipping it, rather than be at the table with us. Later, she'd walk off toward the barns before work. I'd see her leaning with her back against the outside wall while she stared at her feet. But the worst part was, she barely spoke to Aunt Brat. Everything felt heavy and a little broken.

On the third morning, I took Eileen's coffee mug to her before she'd gotten off the couch. "For you," I chirped. I set the mug on the side table. Then I sat on Eileen. Well, on the edge of her. She grunted.

"I'm sorry," I said.

"Then get off me!"

"No. Not sorry I'm sitting on you. I'm doing that on purpose." I let go a long, loud sigh, tried to make myself heavier.

"Then what are you sorry about?" she said, looking pitiful.

"I knew, too. About the goats—"

"Oh, hell, no, no, no!" Eileen turned and pushed her face into the couch cushion. "I can't stand it if everybody knew—everybody except me!" she yelled into the upholstery.

"There is no everybody, and I didn't know the whole time. I found out by accident." I nudged her. "Come on, Eileen. I know you're mad. But look at the positive."

"Humph," said the couch. "What's the positive?"

"Those goats are doing well and they have a home because of you."

"*Not* because of me."

"It *is* because of you. Aunt Brat cared because she is a good human. But she also cared because you cared."

"That's sideways, is what it is. What you're saying is, it's *sort of* because of me," she said.

"Okay, sideways and sort of, if that makes you feel better," I said. "But come on. Come on, Eileen." I pushed at the heap of blankets and the woman underneath them. I set my elbow on her hip.

"Don't!" she said, and she made a funny snorting sound.

"Why?" I asked. I dug my elbow into her. I jiggled it.

"Tickles," she said, squirming. "And don't go getting any ideas."

I jumped to my feet. I held my hands up like claws and wiggled my fingers at her.

"Nope!" she said. "Nope!" She burrowed again. Guffer came bounding over with his curious face on. He shoved his nose into the blanket. "Lydia! Stop!"

"Not me!" I laughed.

Eileen popped her head out to look. Guffer jumped back and barked. "Oh, Guff," she said. "It's okay, boy." She held out her hand and he opened his mouth over it to give a soft chew. Then he slapped a big paw up onto the couch, just missing Eileen's nose. Eileen took hold of his foot, and darned if she didn't put it right in her mouth. She gave it a gentle bite. The dog pulled back, but then he jumped right up on the couch—all fours—on Eileen. "Help! He's standing on me! Lyd-jah!"

"Hey," I said, and I started to walk away. "Don't like it? Guess you better get up."

49

Coming Around Again

I cupped my hands around my mouth megaphone style and hollered from the front porch, "Eileen! Supper's ready!"

She'd been in the small barn all afternoon. Now dark was falling and the little square window of the barn glowed with cheddar-yellow light. She hollered something back at me, but it was all bubbles.

I jumped off the porch and jogged closer. "Eileen!" I shouted again. "Come to supper!"

She stepped out under the pan lamp at the doorway where I could see her. "Go on and start without me!" She flapped one hand at me. The handle of the push broom was in her other fist.

"Aren't you hungry?" I asked. I dropped my shoulders. I hoped she'd see me looking sad and slumpy and come inside.

"Nope," she said. She slipped back into the barn and closed the door.

I accepted defeat. I turned to go back to the house. But I realized something: all that couch misery of the past few days was gone from Eileen's face. Whatever she was up to, she was enjoying it.

Inside, I reported to Aunt Brat. "Eileen says we should start without her. She'll come along when she's ready." Small lie. But I figured Aunt Brat deserved a little hope.

Elloroy rattled into his chair and Aunt Brat brought a pot of beans. She slipped a small plate with a slab of ham in front of him. "Ah!" he said. "Can't knock me off the top of the food chain. Not until the day I'm—"

"Dead." Brat and I said it together.

"Right," said Elloroy. "Where is the cantankerous Eileen this evening?"

"In the small barn," I said.

"Still? She's been there all day. Is she going to stay all night too?" Elloroy chuckled. "Free up the sofa?" he added. Aunt Brat gave him a tired smile.

We were nearly done eating when Eileen came into the kitchen. She went straight to the sink. She soaped up her hands. Wisps of hay stuck to her plaid flannel back and in the cuff of her pants legs. In fact, she looked like she had a nest built around each ankle.

"Eileen, where have you been all afternoon?" Aunt Brat asked. Of course, she already knew the answer.

"Barn," Eileen said. She did not turn around or raise her voice over the running water—probably on purpose. I could tell neither Aunt Brat nor Elloroy had heard.

"Barn," I translated.

Eileen shut off the water. While she dried her hands, she added, "And it's ready. Thanks to me."

"Ready?" Aunt Brat asked.

Eileen did a half turn from the sink to show us all a scrunched face. "For our goats," she said. She arched her eyebrows and thrust her jaw forward. "Not like we need to shelter our animals on someone else's farm," she added bluntly. "I'll bring a truckload of hay bales home tomorrow. You tell me when, and we'll move them in."

Yes! Eileen is back!

I was just about dying, trying to keep a smile to myself.

She sat down to supper. She pulled her chair underneath her and let the legs land hard. She rubbed her hands together and picked up her fork. "Pass the applesauce, please," she said, giving a finger point at the bowl in front of me. I lifted it in her direction. She served herself. "And the beans. Please." She pointed in front of Aunt Brat and kept her eyes on the pot as it came to her. Elloroy pushed her the plate of brown bread.

We all watched Eileen. She looked anywhere that wasn't at us. She gave a sigh as she tucked a forkful of supper into her cheek. She savored. She swallowed. Finally, she looked at my aunt, lifted her chin, and said, "What are you staring at?"

I looked down into my plate. If ever there was a right time to become fascinated with a puddle of baked beans, this was it. But I heard Brat answer plainly.

She said, "Someone I love."

56

The Goats of Pinnacle Hill

According to my upbringing, March was the month of the Chaste Moon. "We must bless our garden and prepare for planting," Mom used to say with a wry grin. If she'd been well, she would've had a magnificent flowerbed. Instead, the postage-stamp yard in Rochester had always been banked with dirty snow come March. Come April, it would turn into a scratchy patch of crabgrass. Still, Mom had insisted that it was our garden. Every March, she'd stood at the glass storm door and had given the yard a little bow. "There. It's blessed," she'd said.

The Chaste Moon is a signal to prepare yourself for change. In our hemisphere, that meant that weather. Springtime. For us, the women on Pinnacle Hill, the greatest change this March was making ready for two new adoptees.

The night before the goats arrived, Aunt Brat and Eileen sat shoulder to shoulder at the table after supper. They reviewed a "brief history of goat notes," as my aunt called it. I had to laugh; leave it to Aunt Brat to come up with something textbookish. They discussed antibiotics, probiotics, sweet feed, and—ugh—goat diarrhea.

Listening in, I learned that a first set of molds had already been taken for the prostheses. As the stumps changed, they'd have to be done again.

"Oh, boy," Eileen said, rolling her eyes. "Ka-ching."

"Yes," Aunt Brat said. "A challenge for the budget. But we'll manage."

I worried about their money. There'd been the unexpected cost of me, and now these goats. There was money from the sale of the house in Rochester, but Aunt Brat had said it was for my future education and we should all consider it "unspendable" until then. I tried not to be expensive. Then again, there had been that renovation to the upstairs, due entirely to yours truly.

Other expenses that had to do with the house had come up at the dinner table from time to time. Elloroy would often close those conversations out by saying, "That can come out of my piece." But he was staying goat-neutral, much like he'd stayed Guffer-neutral. Budgeting for the animals was up to the women.

They talked on. "Now, remember, the goats cannot go outside yet," Aunt Brat reminded Eileen. "No stumps in the snow." (The thought made me cringe.) "No cold and no wet."

"Brat, you already told me that," Eileen said. She pushed back in her chair just a hitch. "And I already know anyway. I *know* goats."

"Of course you do," Aunt Brat apologized. "It's just that all these notes from the vet have formed little mantras in my mind all these weeks. This is how I've kept it together."

"Well, now you've got me," Eileen said.

All in all, I thought my aunt seemed relieved to be turning most of the care of the goats over to Eileen. After all, she had a stack of student papers to read. "I've never been this far behind." She'd said it more than once recently. "Then again, I've probably never been so fit either," she quipped.

"Ski, ski, ski," said Eileen in a sassy sort of way. But she set her hand on my aunt's forearm and added, "Don't worry, Brat. You'll catch up over spring break. I'll pick up on chores."

Silently, I celebrated the way Eileen had managed to stop being mad at Aunt Brat. The temporary crack in my sense of home was healing over. My women were a team.

They named the goats Gigi and Effie. That was Eileen's idea. "Gigi for the G in Gwen, and Effie for the F in Florry," she said. "If it hadn't been for the Gerbers, well, who knows?"

The first Saturday of spring, the Gerber women came to help move the goats into their new digs in the small barn. It was bittersweet for Gwen and Florry; they had become quite attached to the pair. Florry wept. Gwen put an arm around her daughter and pulled her close. "Hey, hey. I know it's hard. But they'll be right here, and we'll come see them often," she promised.

"When they get the feet on," Florry said. She rubbed her eyes.

Gwen jostled her girl. "Oh, you bet we're coming back for that."

So Florry kissed Gigi and Effie goodbye. She cupped her hand around the place where each ear should have been and whispered something that only she and the goats would ever know.

Later, we brought the dogs into the barn. I feared trouble, not from Soonie, but from Guffer. But both dogs seemed to understand that the goats were ours—all of ours. There was no charging or chasing or barking, but Guffer was very curious. He paced about with his head bobbing and nose working overtime. Eventually, he settled at the barn door, chin on his folded paw. He looked handsome as a lion and somehow pleased that he had something to guard.

"Not bad for a chicken-dog," I pointed out, and my women agreed. But it was Eileen who was the real guardian of the goats. She crawled out of bed and into her plaid jacket several times a night to check on them.

I begged Aunt Brat and Eileen to let me invite Raya and Sari to see the goats on Sunday.

"As long as it's just the two and things are quiet, I say fine," Eileen said.

But on Sunday morning, I watched at the front window as Raya and Sari came up the hill with half of my eighth-grade class in tow.

"Uh-oh. Sorry," I muttered.

Aunt Brat looked up from grading papers. "What?" She looked outside, then simply said, "Oh . . ."

"It looks like the news got away from me." There was Charlotte, and Axel, and Gilly. "Oh, and Moss Capperow," I said out loud.

"Capperow? What?" Eileen looked alarmed.

"You mean Capperow the boy," Aunt Brat clarified. "Right?"

"Yes," I said. "Six kids in total." I grimace-grinned.

"Well, this is a big reveal for this small town," Aunt Brat

said. She focused back on her paper grading. "It'll be fine. . . ."

"Take them in a few at a time so the goatsy-girls don't get overwhelmed," Eileen said.

But I felt shy about corraling my classmates. Even as I swung out the front door with Guffer at my heels, I didn't know what I'd say. Guff was excited to see so many people coming into his yard—and not in a 100 percent good-dog way. There was barking and jumping and slinking. Raya and Sari instantly showed everyone the invisible-dog trick.

"Chins up and arms across your chests!" Sari called.

"Until he retreats," Raya added.

I explained that we were still keeping things calm for the goats, and every head nodded and every voice lowered to a whisper. These friends were better versed on the care of goats than I. Charlotte had come bearing gifts—four fleece goat jackets. "So you can use two and launder two," she explained. Axel brought a bottle of caprine vitamins.

Soon the seven of us were sitting on the floor in the small barn with our backs against the hay bales. My classmates took turns stroking and cuddling Gigi and Effie, who fell asleep against the warmth of human bodies.

Everyone felt curious—if upset—about the stumps and earflaps. "Did they ever find out who did this to them?" Axel asked. But as far as I knew, that was a still a mystery.

Everyone watched the sleeping goats except me; I

watched Moss Capperow. I couldn't help it. I liked the tallness of him—even sitting on the floor of a barn he seemed tall. *How funny*, I thought. I liked his large nose, which I could see in profile as he gazed out, smiling his usual Moss smile at something—or maybe nothing—near the barn door.

"Wow, Lydia." I watched the whisper come off his lips. "He's so great," Moss said.

"Uh . . . oh, no," I told him gently, "both goats are females."

"Not the goats," Moss said. He turned to look at me—tall Moss, with his greenish-gold eyes. "Your dog," he said, and he gave a nod to Guffer, who was resting placidly in a patch of sunlight at the door, guard hairs glowing in tiny wisps of silver white.

51

The Glue

At school, word about the goats went around quickly, and because Chelmsford was Chelmsford, anywhere from one to three kids hopped off the bus at my stop that first week. They'd follow me up the hill to spend time in the small barn gazing at the goats. Everyone wanted to watch those goats heal; they wanted the animals to take food from their hands. I could see how good that felt.

I was happy to swing open the barn door for them. I invited them into the house for snacks afterward. (Elloroy loved to shuffle out of his suite to sit down for tea "with the young people.")

But mostly, I felt like the pygmy goats were Aunt Brat and Eileen's project. I helped when they asked. But maybe

310

it was enough that I'd become a dog person. There was something else: creatures in need were part of their glue as a couple, I decided. (I didn't miss that that meant that *I* was glue too.) Or perhaps I just made all of that up. I didn't know much about couples. But I had been observing.

It'd been twelve weeks since Aunt Brat had first driven me up Pinnacle Hill in her boxy car. Sometimes I'd stand stock-still while time and space floated around me. I'd try to remember what I had been doing before. Where was my other place? Then I'd look at Guffer—giving my shoe a chew or heading into the kitchen to pick the trash—and I'd think, *You too, Guff.* We'd arrived the same week; we'd both had our lives changed.

Our visitors were good for Guffer. He became less mistrustful. Sometimes he seemed glad to see them. I loved it when Moss Capperow thought to bring him a dead soccer ball. We all made a game of kicking it around the soggy enclosure while Guff bunny hopped in for a steal, then trotted away with the ball clamped in his kisser. People said Guffer was gorgeous, and he was.

"He's done well since you rescued him," Moss kept telling me, and I knew he was right.

In April, new snow fell but melted quickly. I missed snowshoeing. But I took the poles and went rock hopping and puddle jumping. Guffer trotted along behind me on his bendy legs. I found myself breaking into a run, poles flicking at my sides.

I'm running into April, Mom!

Cold rains flooded my little mouse-crossing stream into a wide, ankle-deep divide. That was fine. We'd gone two weeks without a mouse in either trap, and I had no wish for a meeting with the Capperow uncle on his four-wheeler. Guffer and I stayed out of that patch of the woods. But there were plenty of evenings, right around suppertime, that I knew Moss's uncle was out there. Guffer would hear him from inside the house—dog ears standing at attention. He'd leap to his feet and pace and rumble at the back window.

I imagined myself braver than I was. I daydreamed about coming face-to-face with the man on the green machine again, and this time, I would not be speechless. I'd tell him to stay away from my yellow dog.

52

At the Top of the Stairs and Down

I was the first one into the kitchen that morning. Above me I could hear hurried footfalls, the kind that tell you that your adults are running late and probably can't find their overalls or their snowflake socks.

I put the kettle on and started the dog food. Something was missing: Guffer. I glanced up the stairs and there he was with his mournful face on. I thought nothing of it. That face was just a part of his charm.

"Guffer! Come! I'm making your breakfast," I called. The kibble hit the pans. The sound would bring him running. I sloshed the warm water around in both bowls to coat the kibble. I set them on the counter to soak.

I looked again, and Guffer was still up at the top of the stairs. Same look on his face, except he seemed to be tipping his chin up slightly. Staying upstairs? Especially once his breakfast was made? That was not normal.

"Guffer?"

He shifted his hinds under him and made a mewing sound.

"Guffer, come."

A few more seconds passed. Something was really wrong. Suddenly, the unmistakable smell of dog poop filled the old house.

"Oh! Hey, Guff? What's going on up there?" I went to the bottom of the stairs. He looked away from me. Then awkwardly, hesitatingly, he reached and put a paw onto the first step. He started down, looking all kinds of wrong: front end dragging the hind end, the hind end looking like dead weight. His back legs made a terrible sound as they hit each step. *Kudda-thunk, ka-thunk-thunk.* He was picking up speed—slipping and falling down the stairs.

I sprang forward. I took the stairs two at a time and met him halfway. "Aunt Brat! Eileen!" I screamed. I caught the big dog by his shoulders. I couldn't stop him, but I slowed him down. I supported him—me going backward—until we reached the floor. He tried to stand, but his hind legs slipped out from under him. Brat and Eileen appeared at the top of the stairs.

"Oh, pew! What happened here?" Brat said.

"Watch out. I think it's poop," I said.

"Oh, it is! Ew. It's here at the top of the stairs," Eileen confirmed. "What on earth? He hasn't done that in weeks."

"I know," I said. I tried to sound steady. They weren't quite getting this, and I hated to break it to them—or to myself—that this was bad, bad, bad. "H-he's having trouble," I said. "He just slipped all the way down the stairs. I had to help him."

I stood behind Guffer and lifted him by his hips. I got his legs under him—enough to prop him up. But when I let go he swayed. Then collapsed. He cried and craned his head and shoulders toward the door. As stressed as he was, he wanted to go out.

"Something's really wrong," I called. My voice was breaking now. "He can't walk. He can't even stand!"

Eileen swore. She came rushing down the stairs, one strap and buckle of her overalls swinging. "He wants to go out," I said. She grabbed a towel, looped it under Guffer's loins, and used it as a hoist. She helped him to the door, and I followed, all the while watching his useless hind legs tap the floor. Even his toes bent under the wrong way.

Aunt Brat called, "I'll be right down!" I heard her hurrying back and forth to the bathroom, running water and flushing the toilet. She had to be cleaning up a colossal mess at the top of the stairs. By the time she made it down to the kitchen, with Soonie right behind her, Eileen was bringing Guffer back in through the door.

I'd been standing, frozen, with my hands clamped together, pressing my knuckles into my bottom lip. "Is he back on his feet?" I asked. But I could see that he wasn't. Eileen was still using the towel to carry him—like he was a dog suitcase.

She shook her head as she let him down to a sitting position. "He peed," she said. "But we've got big trouble. He's in pain. And he's lost control of his hinds." She gave my aunt a look that sank my heart.

"Then what? You think it's his spine?" Aunt Brat's voice quavered.

"That'd be my guess." Eileen was solemn. Aunt Brat stared at the dog. Soonie approached and sniffed Guffer from head to toe. She stayed close to him, blinking her eyes.

"Well, do you think he got hurt? I mean an incident? An accident? Lyddie? Did you see anything?"

I tried to think. "He was fine last night. Came up the stairs."

"I looked him over, felt his bones," Eileen said. "Not a lump or a scratch on him. It's just . . . I don't know. It's weird."

"Oh, Guffer," I whispered. I got to my knees beside him. I touched him ever so gently. He rested his chin on my shoulder for no more than a second. He made a shrill yip as he pivoted in place. He turned his back to all of us. I looked at his pale pointed ears and round head, the golden ruff that turned lighter down his shoulders like a perfect shawl. Something was terribly wrong inside his handsome dog body.

"This is no trip to the local vet, Brat," Eileen said. "He's got to go to the hospital."

"Yes, I'm afraid so," said Aunt Brat. She came and knelt in front of Guffer and held his chin in her hand. "Our poor guy," she whispered. He lifted his chin away. He mewed again. "Aww, I'm so sorry, boy. So sorry."

"I sure don't like this," Eileen said. She bit her quivering lip. I flashed on the day the little goats had been dumped at the feedstore and felt the same sort of gravity in all my ribs. I wanted to comfort Eileen. But I thought if I did anything—if I touched her—we'd both crumble. Guffer did not want to be touched either, so I put my arm around Soonie, warm old set of bones that she was. I strummed her velvet coat. She shivered.

"Okay. Okay then." Aunt Brat stood up. She kept her voice steady. "I'm going to call ahead so they'll be expecting us." She jammed on her glasses and picked up her phone and headed to the window to get the best signal. She looked back at me over the glasses. "Lydia, are you all right?" she asked. I nodded. She nodded back. "That was a very good catch there on the stairs," she said, poking numbers into the phone. "He's a big dog." She leaned against the window glass, phone to her ear. "Yes, hello . . ."

I couldn't bear to listen as she described his symptoms, and I don't think Eileen could either. She lined up our shoes, and coats, and Aunt Brat's purse, all at the door. Then she went to tell Elloroy that he'd be home alone with Soonie for at least the morning.

I cuddled Guff's big blond face. I tucked my fingers into his ruff and let my forehead touch his. I needed to take in the woolly smell of him, to touch the curly chin whiskers. He accepted, but without one drop of enthusiasm. An ache grew inside my chest. *This poor, strange, difficult dog,* I thought. *He has to be all right. He just has to be.*

"I wish you could tell me what's wrong," I whispered to him. "We'll find out, though. We'll get you fixed up. I promise we will."

Don't make that promise . . . you don't know!

Our big yellow dog looked like a broken marionette. *How,* I wondered, *how will he ever be all right again?*

53

The Worrying Room

In a flurry of conversation I learned that the animal hospital was near the university. "Well, at least I know how to get there," Aunt Brat said. She took a worried breath inward. "Oh, Eileen, do you think you can take the day off—"

"Of course I can!" Eileen stood tall. "Did you think I'd leave you alone with this? Not a chance! We'll go together. The three of us."

Aunt Brat's shoulders dropped. "But Lydia has school—"

"Oh no, she doesn't." Eileen gestured all over the room, but mostly at the dog and me where we huddled. "You think she's going to sit in a chair learning lessons this morning, Brat? Really?"

"Please," I said. "Let me come. I'll help. I need to be with him." My jaw ached. I almost said the awful thing I was thinking: *What if they have to put him down?*

"Of course you should come." Aunt Brat conceded. "I don't know what I was thinking."

It took all three of us to get Guffer into the boxy car. We lifted and hoisted. He sat next to me on the back seat. He was pitiful, with his head hanging and his yellow felt-like ears so low.

Aunt Brat took the car slowly over the country bumps, then pressed the speed limit on the smooth highway. I kept my arms around Guffer the entire way. Cold, nervous sweat formed in my pits, and I shivered.

Everything was awful.

We lifted the poor dog, slung in his carrying towel, through the big glass doors to the animal hospital. A biting, antiseptic smell hit my nose—so much worse for Guffer, I thought. He tried to turn and leave, eyes wide with fear. He whimpered. We coaxed.

Reception calmly logged him in as "Guffer Bratches." It sounded so adorable it made my eyes flood. I hid my face in my sweater sleeve.

They sat us down in the waiting room. They might as well have called it the worrying room, because that's what we did for the next twenty-five minutes. I sat on the cold

320

linoleum beside Guff. I wondered, was it good that the attendants at the animal hospital did not seem as alarmed by our flop-legged dog as we were? Hope fluttered in my chest but went still again with my next thought: *They're letting us sit here like this because they can already tell how hopeless it is. . . .*

Finally, a young woman wearing a candy-pink smock came. She had a megaphone voice and the kind of forced cheerfulness about her that makes everything worse. "Okay, Guffer!" she screeched. "We're so sorry this happened to you. This way! This way!"

Ugh! I wanted to stuff my fingers in my ears. She chattered at us all the way into an examination room. There, we waited some more until the veterinary surgeon finally came in. Guff cried through the exam. We winced and we worried.

"I can't be sure without images, but this looks like some sort of anomaly of the spine," the vet said. "Your dog has little feeling in his hindquarters." He said something about an interruption in the neuropathway. "The only way to find out is X-rays and an MRI."

When Aunt Brat asked about the cost, he said that finding out what was wrong would run in the thousands.

I heard Aunt Brat slowly fill her lungs.

The room swam.

The vet went on. "Depending on what we see, you could be looking at a surgery. It's expensive," he said with a tick of his tongue.

"Doesn't matter," Eileen declared. "We're committed to him. He's a special one." She took a hard swallow. Aunt Brat nodded in agreement, though her face looked gray.

"Okay," said Aunt Brat. She sounded just as blunt as the doctor now. "Images. How soon?"

"The earliest we can get him into the tube is first thing tomorrow morning," the doctor said. "Then I'll give you a call and tell you what we're dealing with."

"He has to stay the night?" I asked.

"Yes. We will make him comfortable and sleepy," the surgeon promised.

I felt about half a percent better. I planted a long kiss on the cap of Guffer's head between his ears. I breathed in the woolly smell of him. I cannot explain how it hurt to turn and leave him there. Outside, I marched to the car, with my women right on my heels.

"Well. That was no picnic," Aunt Brat said. She wrapped her fingers on the steering wheel and took a cleansing breath.

"Damn straight," Eileen agreed. She rested her head against the passenger's-side window.

I sat on my half of the back seat, reached over, and

swept together all the pale Guffer hairs he'd shed onto the black leather. I rolled them in my fingers, spun them into a short little piece of blond yarn.

"Well, I feel like he's in good hands," Aunt Brat said as we sat waiting at the first stoplight on our way home. I closed my eyes and felt the vibrating of the car. "The surgeon has a great reputation," she added.

"Yep. Got a good feeling about the staff at that place too," said Eileen.

I grunted. Not on purpose. "I just hope that person in the pink smock won't *yammer* at Guff the whole time," I said. "She's too loud. He'll hate that."

"True." Aunt Brat and Eileen said it exactly together, and if that weren't enough, they did it again. "She did yammer." There was a pause. And a snort. They looked at each other and burst out laughing, and so did I. Then I cried without making a sound the whole way home.

54

Dog Cash

Aunt Brat didn't make me go to school at all that Friday. From the second we arrived back home I felt it: we had too much space and too much quiet without our big yellow dog to wreak us some havoc. We were empty.

I called Soonie up onto the couch beside me. She jumped up, then stood with four feet poking into the cushions before falling into a restful curl—on me. I curled up too and let the dog settle on my hip. I wrapped my arm around her knobby-boned back. She was warm as a radiator; her rhythmic breath sounded like steam running through her.

I worried and I stewed. What if Guffer's trouble was something unfixable? Or too expensive for Aunt Brat and

Eileen—on top of the cost of the goats? What if they *could not* say yes—even if they want to? I thought I should tell them: I'd rather have Guffer than a college education. They could spend my nest egg. I didn't care.

We don't know what's wrong yet. We won't know until morning.

Ugh! It's a warped-up, messed-up thing to not be able to do anything but wonder what's coming.

We wait and see. . . .

My mother had said those words more times than I could count. I realized that she'd never once said, All we can do is wait and see. She'd haul out a sheet of watercolor paper and click open her box of paints, and create something.

And what are you going to do with these next long hours—huh, Lydia Bratches-Kemp?

For the time being, I burrowed. It wasn't even noon, but I was drifting toward sleep, helped along by the warmth of Soonie. I reached out to my mom before I was all the way out.

It is April . . . the Seed Moon . . . time to plant seeds of desire. . . .

I desire my dog to be well. . . .

Surround yourself in light and flowers. . . .

My eyes are closed. . . .

Decorate eggs to bring joy. . . .
It's going to take more than a few eggs to bring me joy. . . .
Sing in the rain. . . .
It's not . . . raining. . . .

When I woke Aunt Brat and Eileen and Elloroy were in the kitchen making lunch. "What'll you have, Lyd-jah?" Eileen called to me, and I forced one eye open.

"Hmm. Nothing for me, thanks," I said. I hoped they would not protest. I had dreamed myself up some thoughts—or pictures—or something. I slid myself out from under the sleepy greyhound, hugged my long sweater close against the lost warmth of the couch and the dog. I climbed the stairs. Midway, I remembered: *This is where I caught Guffer this morning—exactly here—on this stair.* I wanted him home so much.

In my room, I knelt beside the art box. I wanted the wax pencils—all the yellows, creams, and golds. I dug them out and held them in a bundle. *And now a blank sheet of paper,* I thought. That was in the other box with the homeless goddesses. I popped the lid off. The very first thing that caught my eye was the plastic sack of cards from my father—

Wait! Money! . . . We need money!

I tore right into that orange envelope, the one that Jay-cinda had brought through the snow.

A pair of hundred-dollar bills slipped into my lap when I opened the card. "Whoa," I whispered.

For the first time in my life I had a reason for wanting this money. So why did I even start to read the card?

Kemp had straight-up tall handwriting.

Dear Lydia,
I can't imagine a harder time for you. I'm so sorry Mom is gone. I'd like to see you. Could we do that, please? I'm willing to—

"No!" I snarled. I sent the card flying across the room—or tried. Greeting cards are hard to throw. It opened up, caught air, and landed not far enough away. I swore. Who sends a festive-colored card when a mother dies, anyway? And why does he get to say *Mom* like that? "Ugh!"

It is the worst feeling when you look for your dog, thinking you will bury your face in his coat for comfort—but he's not there.

I pressed my eyes into my knees. I thought about how scared Guffer must be, and lonely, and wondering. . . .

Guff, are you okay? Are you comfortable and sleepy?

I thought about his quirky walk—the bunny hopping—and his weak hind legs. Was whatever had happened this morning part of that? Was something always wrong inside but we missed it? I thought about how I'd failed to understand the dog in the beginning—and the awful days when I'd really not wanted him—

But I love you now. I do. I cannot bear it if I lose you. . . .

I lifted my face and blinked. Then I used the scissors and cut away the top edge of every envelope. I picked the bills from inside each card—no reading. Kemp had sent larger bills as I gotten older—and yes, it was all cash, through the mail. Risky. He must have been trying to make it easy for me to use the money. But I hadn't spent a cent.

I had seven years' worth of bills in my lap. I counted it up. I had just short of two thousand dollars. I could hardly get down the stairs fast enough to turn it over to Aunt Brat.

She balked when she saw the cash. "Wow," she said. "It's a lot, isn't it?"

"Enough to make a difference," I said.

"Right . . . but I can't see us accepting your money, Lyddie." Aunt Brat shook her head. "Eileen and I will figure this out."

"But you've already spent so much. If he needs a big operation . . . Please?" I said. "I don't want it for anything else. It's never felt right to use it."

"Hmm. Because of the way Kemp walked out," Aunt Brat said. She stared off, looking rather tired. "Bad money." She exhaled.

"Yes. Bad money. And Guffer is sort of a bad dog—the

best bad dog ever." My voice cracked. "I didn't want him." I said the horrible words. "But now . . ."

"He's grown on you." She smiled softly.

I nodded, face beginning to crumple. I was one kind gesture away from a full-out cry.

Aunt Brat stepped up and closed her hands around my hands. She drew the bills away from me, saying, "Okay. We'll use it. It's a fine thing to do with this money."

She was about to fold me into a hug. But I slipped away, and of all the crazy things, I went outside. No coat. No shoes. I stood on the porch and sucked in an enormous breath of chilly April air. I swept a little handful of wet snow off the railing and held it against my eyes.

"I want the dog back," I whispered to absolutely no one. "I want him back!" I took another minute just looking out to the south the way Guffer so often had.

Well. Thank goodness for firewood. I filled my arms and went back inside. I piled the wood on the hearth.

"Hey, are you okay?" Aunt Brat asked. "If you're not, I don't blame you. I'm not so okay myself."

"Hard day," I said, because it was. "I'm just going to go back up . . ." I suddenly remembered my gold and yellow pencils.

"What about something to eat?" she coaxed, but I think she could already tell I would say no thanks. "Well, here. I'm having afternoon coffee since I missed out this morning. I made you some, too. Milk and honey, just the way you like it." My aunt held out a mug.

Morning seemed a long time ago. I wasn't hungry, but I could use the coffee. "Thank you," I said. I cupped the mug, breathed in the steam.

"Go ahead. Take it upstairs," said Aunt Brat. I loved her for that.

I swept the cards and envelopes off my bedroom floor and packed them back into their plastic bag. I shoved the lot under my bed.

I looked at the chimney wall where the new niche had been built. I moved my art box into the bottom of the space—a perfect fit. I brought over all the cream and yellow-gold pencils and a blank sheet of paper. I sat with my back against the warm bricks, my coffee mug by my side. I used the top of the art box like a lap desk. I started drawing yellow dogs.

55

When a Dog Is Gone from Home

I woke to a hand gently shaking my shoulder. Aunt Brat was settling on the edge of my bed, with her phone in her hand. She mouthed the word "sorry," but she smiled and pointed to the phone.

I sat right up. I blinked. It was Saturday morning. Aunt Brat had the surgeon on the phone! And unless I was terribly wrong, she looked happy! She put him on speaker. I listened.

"So his images show a ruptured disk, and actually, that's good news."

Really?

"He can have surgery. It's a long recovery, but I expect he'll do well."

Oh yes . . . yes . . . yessss. . . .

I squeezed my aunt's arm. She showed me her tightly crossed fingers. "So, when you say he'll do well, what is the success rate? What may we expect?" Aunt Brat wanted to know.

"It's very good. Ninety-five percent of my surgeries are one hundred percent successful."

"What will he be like afterward?" I couldn't help piping up.

"It's a significant period of rehabilitation. You have to severely limit his activity for six to eight weeks," he emphasized. "It's a lot of healing. He'll need around-the-clock attention." Aunt Brat and I nodded at each other. We had this. "Eventually," said the surgeon, "he'll be good as new."

I fell over sideways and pressed my face into Aunt Brat's old sleeping bag. "Good as new! Guffer!" I muffled my own squeal.

When I looked up, Aunt Brat was grinning.

"Can we come see him?" I blurted at the phone.

"I'm sorry? What? Oh, can you see him? No time for that today. We'll be going into surgery within an hour. Maybe sooner."

"All right, then. It's a go," Aunt Brat said.

Wow. Our big broken dog was going to have an operation. I climbed out of bed and went to stand in the niche.

I leaned on the still-warm brick and looked at yesterday's yellow dog drawings. My eye landed on one sketch: the dog sitting with his back to the viewer, his head and nose in profile as if catching a breeze.

Behind me, Aunt Brat was wrapping up the call.

They're going to open up his beautiful back, I thought. I cringed. That was going to haunt me all day long. *Worth the worry,* I told myself.

Aunt Brat stood next to me now. We looked at my drawings together. "A grouping of Guffers," she said. "Beautifully rendered, I might add. You've captured him."

"Thanks," I said. "It felt good. Well, as good as anything felt yesterday. I guess I was drawing my wishes. Aunt Brat, I'm still worried about him."

"Oh, I'm with you on that. We'll have to stay busy. So you get dressed. Then let's go down for coffee, and some breakfast for you," she said firmly. That was fine. I was suddenly hungry.

Down in the kitchen Elloroy sat with his mug and his reader. I came up behind him and wrapped him with one arm. "Hello, youth and beauty," he said. "Heard you got some good news."

"Yes!" I said. I topped his coffee, then poured my own with the milk and honey. He smiled at Aunt Brat and me as we stood at the kitchen window sending Eileen messages, then laughing at the happy faces she sent back to us. If I knew Eileen, she was dancing a crooked jig across the floorboards at the Feed. Huh-haw!

Guffer . . . in surgery. . . .

I held some little part of my breath most of the day. I pushed away a thousand little pinpricks of fear.

Well, Chelmsford was Chelmsford, and somebody who'd been to the Feed early in the morning must have seen Eileen dancing that jig. That person must have asked her why. Before you could say "big yellow dog," word had gotten around that the one on Pinnacle Hill was down for the count. That's why Raya and Sari knew to come with hugs and muffins (with raisins) and their own genuine concerns about the dog who had so often harassed them. Sari brought cream-colored wool and circular needles. She got me knitting again.

Not long after, Gwen and Florry Gerber joined us. So we were six women around the table buttering muffins, sipping from mugs, and even laughing.

Then Elloroy came out of his suite to say the most surprising thing I could possibly hear. He said, "House full of goddesses today, I see."

56

When the Call Comes

By late Saturday afternoon, I was pacing. Still no call from the animal hospital. Every time the slightest sound pinged, I bothered Aunt Brat. "Was that your phone? Did you leave it close enough to the window? Is it charged?"

She answered in the gentlest way. "No, yes, and yes." She was anxious for news too. Both of us began to envy Eileen her busy Saturday at the Feed.

Even Elloroy looked up from his reading several times to ask, "What do we know about the big yellow dog?"

"Not enough." I sighed. I worried that something had gone wrong. My mother had been bumped from the transplant list all those years ago. How much did I trust medicine of any kind? It'd been hours. Guffer's surgery must have become complicated—

Stop telling yourself bad things, Lydia!

Then Aunt Brat's phone rang. I scooped it up and checked the screen. "It's them!" I cried. I nearly threw that phone into her hands. Then I held my breath.

"Hello?"

"Speaker! Speaker!" I whispered at her. She fumbled. I pulled at the phone and hit the button for her. Elloroy turned in his chair to listen.

". . . did very well. He's going to be just fine. . . ."

Elloroy's mouth dropped into an old turtle smile. I landed myself flat on my back on the floor, arms wide, with the gray-green sweater laid out underneath me like my own private sea to float on. I gazed at the ceiling, my chest rising and falling. Oh, it is an amazing thing when joy rides on your breath in both directions.

Above me, Aunt Brat put her hand to her chest. She bent forward and spoke into her phone. "Ha! Oh! Thank you! We are so relieved!"

The surgeon explained that they'd be keeping Guffer over several nights. "Maybe as long as a week."

"A week?" I sat up and mouthed the words to Aunt Brat. She nodded, as if begging me to be patient.

"We want to keep him very still—sedated—while the

wound knits. First days are crucial. He's been through a lot," the surgeon cautioned.

"Well, can we come see him?" I blurted.

"We ask families to give it some time. We don't want him to get excited, and we don't want him to feel depressed when you leave him again. So please sit tight, and just try to keep sight of what's best for your dog."

I resented that. I would have little else in this world in my sights. Didn't he know that?

Still, I listened while the surgeon told us how to prepare for Guffer's care. Aunt Brat scribbled notes.

"Before you know it," the surgeon said, "he'll be home again."

For that entire week, whenever I wasn't at school pretending that I could concentrate, I prepared for the dog's homecoming. I recruited my adults. We moved living room furniture to set up an area where Guff would be confined but would not have to be in the crate that he dreaded so much. The coffee table would be his gate. Eileen brought home a foam pad mattress that Guffer would be able to get up and down on easily. We put it right beside the couch so that one of us could always spend the night beside him. We agreed to alternate on that duty, but I was already planning to cover all shifts. How could I not?

April vacation was coming in perfect time for Guffer's return. I'd have nine days off, Eileen would take the next week off. Aunt Brat's last day of regular classes for the semester was at the end of that week. We were covered for the first part of Guffer's rehab. We'd figure out the rest.

57

The Tale of Little Goats

On Tuesday afternoon our handywomen, Saundra and Nan, who had built the niche in my room, came to construct a ramp for Guffer. It'd be a long while before he could do stairs again.

I watched them at their sawhorses from the window as they expertly cut notches in two long boards. They fit them over the porch steps and topped them with a sheet of plywood. Soon they were finishing the job, tacking down a strip of carpet for traction.

A small utility van pulled up beside the carpenters. By now, I knew who was likely to stop at Pinnacle Hill. But I did not know this vehicle. "Someone's here," I said. I watched a woman with gray-brown curls hop out. Her

339

dark green barn coat flapped open. Eileen nudged me over so she could see out too.

"Oh, that's the farm vet," Eileen said. "Doc Marin."

"That's unexpected." Aunt Brat stood up. She tidied her stack of papers on the table. "She must be here to visit the baby girls."

"Barn party!" Eileen said.

We grabbed our jackets and tested Guffer's new ramp on our way. Aunt Brat and Eileen called hellos to Doc Marin. Soon, the four of us stood in the goat barn together.

This was the vet who'd helped Aunt Brat with the goats in the very beginning. Eileen thanked her—no trace of hurt feelings.

Doc Marin looked Gigi and Effie over, admired the healed ears and the new ski-boot prostheses. The goats showed off how well they'd adapted by hopping along the clean barn boards and up onto the fat tree stumps Eileen had gotten from Jaycinda. "They look healthy. They're gaining muscle," Doc Marin noted. She laughed because goat antics just naturally make people laugh. But her real reason for being there was that she had a story to tell us.

She'd gone out on a call to check a few animals that'd been left behind after a foreclosure on a property. "It's about a thirty-minute drive from here," she said. "The

340

owners lacked husbandry experience. The place was too much for them. Sad state of decay all around."

"And the animals?" Eileen asked.

"Surprisingly, no serious heath issues. I reached out to a rescue group and they'll all be homed this week. But while I was tending to the animals," Doc Marin said, "a neighbor stopped over. I had the feeling she wanted to talk, and finally, she did. She mentioned that there had been twin pygmy goats born there earlier in the winter."

"Oh my goodness," Aunt Brat said. She pressed her hand to her collarbones.

"Huh," said Eileen.

"Of course, that rang a bell," said Doc Marin. "The neighbor told me that both babies showed serious frostbite early on—ears and hind feet."

"Frostbite," Eileen echoed.

"The neighbor had the feeling the owners couldn't afford to call a vet. She offered to help but the owners declined, and seemed ashamed. She pushed them, but they shouted her off their property. This neighbor hadn't seen the goats again."

"And this was when?" Eileen ventured.

The vet gave a nod. "Well, I'd bet my last nickel the goats from that farm are the same ones you found abandoned at the Feed. These babies, here," she said. She gave

Effie a rub on the head with her knuckles. The goat leaned closer for more.

I closed my eyes for a few seconds. I remembered those raw but clean cuts. "But wait," I said. "Is that what frostbite looks like?"

"Very good question," said Doc Marin. "No. What you'd see first is swelling. That's from liquid in the cells freezing and rupturing the walls."

That is the science. . . .

"The damage is permanent. The tissue starts to fall off. It can even snap."

I shuddered. Aunt Brat hunched her shoulders uncomfortably. But Eileen was nodding and holding her gaze on Gigi and Effie. She understood. She knew goats. "Well, it can happen. Shouldn't. But it can," she said.

"Yes, little newborns are especially vulnerable. They need the warmth of the barn," Doc Marin said. "But the hind feet on these animals had been clean-cut, right at the pastern joint, as you know. The ears, too, looked sliced, not snapped, which is why I didn't initially think of frostbite. In retrospect, I should have. We'd had a cold spell—you might remember. As dreadful as it sounds, I think these people tried to amputate."

"Oh, dear God—they should *not* have!" Aunt Brat looked ready to empty her stomach. I felt a wave of

342

light-headedness. Eileen sighed sadly.

Doc Marin told us, "They probably thought removing the bad tissue was the best treatment. Misguided, to be sure. I'm surprised these goats didn't bleed out. Once the wounds got infected the people probably just didn't know what to do. My guess is they dropped these animals at the Feed in desperation. So . . . I think we have the answer to the mystery."

"Well . . ." Eileen gave her head a shake and a scratch. "Misguided isn't quite the same thing as cruel," she said. "But nothing changes what happens from here. We keep the goats and we protect them from harm. For all their days," she added.

Later, her words came back to me:

Protection from harm . . . for all their days. . . .

That's what it is to be at Pinnacle Hill Farm, I thought. Guffer would be home soon where we could protect him—though not soon enough for me.

58

Coming to an Understanding

The week stretched long. But things were looking very good for a Thursday homecoming for the Guff. I talked about it all day long at school—I couldn't help myself. The good thing was, my eighth-grade class and I were outdoors most of the afternoon. This was the long-planned-for field trip to the state reserve to release the fingerling trout we'd raised in the school's tank.

I was never so glad to be wearing Moss Capperow's boots as when my feet sank into the soft earth at the edge of the Bigelow River. Sari Winkle pulled me back gently, while the water slurped over my toes. Raya, Moss, and Axel wore high waders and stepped right into the easy current. They settled the buckets full of young fish into the water and waited for the temperatures to equalize. I liked that care was taken not to shock the fingerlings.

When all was in balance, my friends slowly tilted the buckets. Our trout slipped into their new home and swam.

"Wow," I breathed, and Sari hugged my arm as we watched them go.

"Good luck in the new place, tiny finger fish," I whispered.

Sari Winkle leaned on me and giggled. I daydreamed of all the things that go home and find home and survive in new places.

We ate bag lunches beside the river. There were whispers—a secret in the air—something about all of us coming back here to the two picnic tables, the carpet of ferns, and the lichen-covered boulders. "For Springerle," they said—or that's what I thought. I wrinkled my nose at Raya and Sari.

"Springerle? Like the cookies with the pretty pictures stamped on them?" They put their fingers to their lips to hush me. They hid smiles and glanced at our teachers. In low voices my friends filled me in.

"Yes and no," Sari whispered. "Same word. Springerle means 'little jumping horses' in German."

"Yeah." Raya leaned close. "And that's sort of what we

do. We jump our fences and run loose. Just for one night. One of our eighth-grade ancestors must have made it up. It's a big Chelmsford tradition."

"You run away?" I blurted.

"Shh . . . shh . . . yes. Our whole class. We come here. We stay out all night beside the Bigelow."

"Happens in June," Sari told me, eyes sparkling. "Plan for it, Lydia."

"Right . . . ," I said. Already, I knew I'd be the Chelmsford tradition breaker; I'd be the only eighth grader staying home. But there seemed no point in saying so now.

The bus rocked us back to school. I closed my eyes. My dog was coming home tonight. Everything was perfect.

I sprinted up Pinnacle Hill that afternoon. Our plan was to go straight to the veterinary hospital to reclaim Guffer. But Aunt Brat had news—itchy, scratchy news.

"I'm just off the phone with the hospital. Guffer's stomach is funky," Aunt Brat explained. "It's just some diarrhea but they want one more day to get it under control."

"And for that, we can't have him yet?" I was crushed.

"Well, we could risk it, but—"

"Oh, let's go get him, then!"

"I knew she'd say that," said Elloroy. He raised a long finger.

"Well, of course," Eileen said. She pushed at Elloroy's hand. "That's her dog! Don't make it worse by stating the obvious," she scolded him.

"I didn't. You did," he said. "You said it's her dog, and that's obvious."

"Oh, all right, hush!" Eileen said.

Oh, both of you hush! . . .

"Lyddie, I know you're disappointed," Aunt Brat told me. "But it's just one more night."

I nearly burst into tears. I knew it was babyish, but I felt outnumbered. "Oh come on!" I protested. "You barely blinked when I put a hole in the wall upstairs and crashed through the ceiling. But a dog with a little diarrhea turns you shy? It's not like he's never pooped in here before," I said. I pouted. Then I accidentally puffed out several laughs. Then we all laughed. I suppose that was good for us. But I had to cover my face because some crying was getting mixed in there.

At suppertime, Eileen sent grumpy-me to the pantry shelf for a box of bow tie pasta. At the back window, I heard it—the faint buzzing. I cupped my hands against the glass, set my face close, trying to see out.

Moss Capperow's uncle was in Elloroy's woods, I was sure. If I'd had to guess, he was out near the little stream where I'd set the mice free all winter. I stared. Suddenly, a horizontal beam of light cut through the trees—or, did it? I lost it so quickly. But the long, low light flashed again. It shrank, then spread wide, as if completing a turn. And all the while, there was that buzzing. I drew a breath inward.

"What's the matter, Lydia?" Aunt Brat asked. She came up behind me.

"It's Capperow. The uncle," I said. I turned to face her.

"Capperow? What about him?" Eileen asked. She came around from the stove.

"He's out there on his four-wheeler. In the woods. Right now," I said. "He can't do that anymore." I stepped around my women. I made a beeline for the door.

"What?"

"Guffer will hear him. He'll get upset. He'll bolt up and hurt himself!" I thrust my arms into my jacket.

"Wait. Lydia!"

"I'm going out there," I said. "I'm going to tell this to him straight."

I threw open the door.

"Flashlights!" Eileen cried. She pulled out the kitchen drawer with such a bang it made me turn. She raised two flashlights—one in each fist.

She and Aunt Brat rushed to catch up to me. Eileen grabbed her plaid and Aunt Brat her gray wool. Out the door we went and around to the back of the house. I dashed forward and led them into the woods.

What a sight we must have been—three women running with our jackets flapping, boots half-tied. We ran through the woods toward the flooded stream. I waved my phone light overhead—because why not, and what else? Not like I had a plan.

I reached the water and splashed forward. Cold and wet seeped in at the soles of Moss Capperow's old brown boots. The headlights of the four-wheeler shone against the trees. The motor revved. I held up both hands—one with the light from my phone, the other, the bare flesh of my palm. I called out, *"Halt!"*

The lights dimmed. The four-wheeler sat humming on the far side of the overfull stream. Aunt Brat and Eileen came up behind me. Both held flashlight beams on the Capperow uncle.

"Cut it!" I yelled, meaning the engine. I made a slice with one hand across my throat. Oh, I was *not* used to this—telling an adult what to do. But I thought of Guffer, and I held my ground.

"Please turn that off!" Aunt Brat hollered politely from behind my shoulder.

"Shut her down!" Eileen reinforced.

Capperow did as he was asked. The woods fell silent.

He stood squinting into the beams of light that my women held on him.

"You know Elloroy Harper?" I said. "He owns this land—the land you're on right now." The man was still. But I was sure he could hear me. "Y-you say this is about the dog. But the truth is, the dog hasn't been any real trouble to you." Moss would've told me.

"Can't take the chance," the uncle said. "The dog doesn't like this machine. So I'm fine with letting him know it's here. He stays away."

"But you're coming onto Elloroy's land to do it," Eileen said.

"Yes! Makes you a bigger menace than the dog!" Aunt Brat called.

"The dog is down—seriously down," I called. "And it's going to be a long time before he's better."

Capperow grunted again. "What happened to him?"

"Lumbar disk eruption," Aunt Brat called.

Eileen snorted. Under her breath she said, "Really, Brat? So formal?" She raised her voice. "He had back surgery. He's got weeks of rehab. He'll be no trouble to you—not that he ever was." She stuck her chin forward.

"We have to keep him still. That machine of yours terrifies him. He hears it from inside our house." I jabbed my lit phone back toward home.

Capperow's chin lifted. He seemed to be listening.

"We'd like to hear you tell us that you understand," Aunt Brat said. "And that you'll keep behind the wall. Off Elloroy's property."

"Yeah," said Eileen. "Hear what we say, now. Because last thing he wants to do is string a chain to keep you out."

"But he will if he has to!" I said. "So that's the real question. Does he have to? It's up to you, Mr. Capperow." I was breathless now.

He looked down at his feet. He pulled off his hat and slowly ran his hand over his flattened-down hair. He turned away, but he raised his hat into the air. A surrender? He climbed onto his four-wheeler. He cranked it up and spun away from us. We watched him bumping through the woods, over the rock wall and back to his own pasture. Gone.

"Yes!" I shouted. I picked up my sodden foot and stamped it back down into the water. We cheered. We fell together, celebrating, our shoulders and elbows bumping, flashlight beams swinging like swords.

"Here's to Lyd-jah!" Eileen howled. "Huh-haw!"

"Yes! For her fearlessness in taking on the malevolent green machine and its ignoble rider!" Aunt Brat said. She waved her flashlight overhead.

"One for the Guff!" I called. "Woo-hoot!"

351

We three linked arms and plodded back toward the trail, relieved and still reveling. I held my women up; they held me up.

These are my goddesses, Mom! They won't let me down! I will never fall down! . . .

59

When a Dog Comes Home

On Friday morning, the three of us sat in the uncomfortable chairs at the veterinary hospital. Eileen cleared her throat and grumbled. "This sure is an old lesson," she said.

"What's that?" asked Aunt Brat.

"They don't call waiting rooms 'waiting rooms' for nothing."

"Oh that," said Aunt Brat. "Yes."

I sighed and raised my legs out in front of me. I knocked the toes of my good lime-green sneaker-boots together. The hem of my sweater coat was ringed in dried mud from the night before. Aunt Brat saw it too. She gave me a side-eye.

"Could be time . . . ," was all she said. For sure, this wasn't the first time she'd had the thought that my sweater needed a good washing.

"Hmm," I said with a shrug. "I'd have to take it off."

She smiled the wry smile.

Eileen fidgeted in her chair. "Where's our dog?"

Finally, we were called into the tiny examination room—and finally, our big yellow dog was helped in. My breath caught at the sight of him draped over a bright blue sling at his belly. There was a long patch shaved into his deep, deep fur. A zigzag of black stitches, maybe seven inches long, showed through a clear bandage.

"Guffer," I whispered.

I thought I might never see you again. . . .

The attendant let him down to a sitting pose and I crouched low to be with him. At first, our dog didn't seem to recognize us. His golden-brown eyes bugged out, whites exposed. He gazed around the room but didn't focus.

"Guffer? Hey, buddy."

"He is still very sedated," the attendant explained.

So I knelt beside him, and I talked to him. Slowly, he seemed to come around. He mewed. He edged closer to me. Our foreheads touched. He let out a few sleepy, dog-talk sounds—a moan, a little yowl, then something more like braying. Then one single long howl, as I'd never heard from him before.

Aunt Brat and Eileen and I laughed in sympathy; we almost cried. He acknowledged us then, even wagged his tail just a little while all three of us found a place on him that we could pat.

"I know," I said. "It's been so long. But we're going home, Guff. Do you remember home?"

They showed us his gait—and let me say, it was awkward. His hinds buckled, and he listed to his left while he swung his right hind foot wide. His toes caught and turned under every other step. He didn't seem to feel that.

Was this really success? I think we all wondered. But the surgeon insisted all signs were positive. He'd get better and better.

One thing was clear: Guffer had always wanted to charge forward, and he still wanted to. We decided that was a good sign.

With our instructions in hand, we hoisted him into the car. He sat on the back seat with his big fur body leaning into my side—and didn't I love that?

Eileen read our instructions out loud while Aunt Brat drove. "Do not let the patient run," Eileen said. "Keep him leashed at all times. Use the sling to help him get outdoors to void. Enjoy some fresh air with your pet—oh, I like that idea," she said. "Ahh, keep to the medication schedule. It says he'll sleep a lot in the coming days, and that'll be good for him. That's going to be a different sort of Guffer," Eileen said.

That turned out to be true.

All through my April break I kept watch over him. Old Soonie sat with us like a devoted granny-dog nanny. I cuddled her while Guffer slept—and he did sleep, for hours at a time. Whenever he woke, I helped him outside and down the new ramp. There was a bit of art to lifting him in the sling and then whipping it out from under his belly so he didn't sprinkle it with pee. Business done, I'd let him wobble-walk several yards before I turned him back. I opened a lawn chair in the yard and I sat with him balanced between my knees where he could face south while the mid-April breeze blew across his nose.

Friends came to visit, no more than two at a time so as not to overexcite Guffer, though he often slept through arrivals. (Different dog, for sure.) Raya and Sari admired the way I was all camped out on the couch with Aunt Brat's sleeping bag right beside Guffer's new floor mat.

"Are you dying of boredom?" Raya asked. "Because let me tell you, I'm not a good nurse. I'd be going crazy." Then she quickly added, "But if you do need someone to cover, you know I would do that."

"Same here," said Sari.

I thanked them. "I really want to be here with him."

I'm sure they thought it seemed like long hours to keep beside a mostly sleeping dog. But I had a project to work on. I brought all the goddesses down to the couch, and like Sari Winkle had suggested weeks before, I was putting them in order and starting that memoir.

Sitting with the dog reminded me of the days I'd sat propped at the edge of my mother's bed. I didn't tell that to anyone. Guff was a dog, after all; someone might not understand. But I knew my own truth about it. I also knew I was looking at a different outcome this time. This vigil was joyful, and that opened the door for me to visit Mom again with the help of the goddesses. I started by jotting down the smallest of memories. Our story grew from there. Soon the passages I was writing began to feel like letters to my mom.

I wrote and wrote and wrote.

60

Blountville Calling

All seemed well. I'd grown up knowing the freeing feeling that comes when worry lifts and moves off for a while. So it was with a mom whose health made her dip, then rally. Guffer was recovering; these were rally days.

One day, Aunt Brat, Eileen, and Elloroy were all downstairs covering Guffer while I showered. I was in my room, rubbing my hair dry, when my phone buzzed. The number didn't look familiar. *One of* those *calls,* I thought. But then I saw the origin: Blountville, Tennessee.

Blountville?... Tennessee?... Wait... why do I know this?

I accepted the call. "Hello?"

"Yeah. Cici Hoover here. You called me." It sounded like an accusation.

"Oh my gosh," I said. "Right. . . ."

"About a dog?"

The old tag—I'd taken it off Guffer's old collar . . . how many weeks ago?

"Oh, yes. Uh . . . but we—"

"I know the one. The blond shepherd. With a mix of something else in there." Cici Hoover coughed dryly into the phone. "I handpicked that pup off a farm. Damn pretty dog, that one."

I started to smile. *Handsome Guffer. . . .*

"Even if he was dumb as stump."

Oh . . . unkind. . . .

She laughed a wheezy laugh before she went on. "But I figured I could either sell him or use him to make more like him."

"Make more? You mean breed—"

"People have always gone for purebreds," said Cici Hoover. "But they'll pay for good-looking mutts too. Designer dogs are the new market. All I needed was to find a female just as pretty."

I began to feel uneasy—no, worse than uneasy. What was Cici Hoover's story? I had to keep listening.

"But then I'd see him out front where we kept him tied up, and I started seeing something not so right. He had bad hind legs. There's a thing called dysplasia. In the hips.

I got a good eye for troubles. Could see it, especially when the kids rode by him on the dirt bikes."

Machines . . . with wheels. . . .

"God, they used to tease that one. He was a big coward." Cici stopped to laugh. "He'd skitter away till his line jerked. That dog looked like he'd just as soon hang himself." She laughed again, then coughed a gross cough.

I covered my mouth with my hand.

Poor Guffer . . . and he'd been just a pup. . . .

This was his dark past unspooling. I knew it.

"Got so he could work right out of his collar. Got loose all the damn time. The kids had to go chasing after him and drag him home again." I heard a huff-puffing sound. Cici Hoover was smoking a cigarette. "Ended up crating him most of the time. And pretty soon, I look at them legs and think, *Naw, not worth breeding. Good for nothing.* And every day I'm feeding him, it's costing me. So I listed him. Got someone interested—and then I get busted! The police come for me, and some group comes for the dogs. Humph. Calling itself a rescue. It was robbery. They took all my dogs. All the pregnant ones—three about to whelp. Cost me thousands. And then they made me sign some surrender papers. They said it'd go better for me that way. Liars! I had to do time anyway."

"Time?"

"Yeah—jail! They hit me with this count, then that count. Animal cruelty. There were twenty-seven dogs here. By the time it got all added up I had four years to serve. Got it reduced to time served plus a hundred and forty days." She let fly a few choice swear words. "I missed your call while I was locked up."

I swallowed hard. Cici Hoover was silent except for her huff-puffing on her cigarette. Long seconds, those were.

"You still there?" she said.

"I am," I said. I pulled my fingers through my damp hair. I shivered. "The dog . . . he had a weak disk in his back. It ruptured, and—"

"Huh? His back, you say? See. Knew there was something, and it can get passed on, ya know. In the genetics."

I closed my eyes. "Yes," I said. "Well, he's had an operation. He's doing well. He's got some fears," I said. "But he's a good, sweet pet. And, if you care at all, Ms. Hoover, I can tell you this: He is loved."

"Oh yeah?" she said. "Well, before you get all attached, you should know, I'm planning on getting them all back."

"What?"

"My dogs. My business. If I was a baker, they wouldn't take away my ovens, would they?" Her voice was louder now. "Just cuz I go to prison for a while. Get what I'm saying? Breeding dogs is not illegal. I want my dogs back. Every one of them—"

I killed the call. I threw the phone on my bed. Then I grabbed it up again. I blocked her number—fingers shaking.

Oh . . . Lydia! . . . What did you do? . . .

Seconds later I was down the stairs and standing in the kitchen having the fit of all fits while I held the phone in my trembling hands.

"Th-there was a name. On his tag. Back when we got him." I was frantic to explain. Three mouths hung open. All eyes were wide—especially Elloroy's circling behind his lenses. I started to babble again.

Aunt Brat reached to cup my hands in hers. She peeled my phone out of my fingers and handed it off to Eileen. My aunt held me. I slowed down. I told them everything that Cici Hoover had said.

"Sounds like an illegal puppy mill," Eileen said.

"Those are dreadful," said Elloroy.

"They did the right thing taking those dogs off her property," Aunt Brat said.

"You're not kidding," I said. "Cici Hoover comes off like a dirtbag even from the way she tells it!" My jaw quivered. "To think I called her to see if she could help us. I thought she could tell us why Guffer was so difficult and scared and spooky. I'm sorry," I told them, "but it wasn't a secret. There wasn't anything to tell since she never called back. Not until now. She says she's going to get all her dogs back. She means Guffer!" I looked over at our long yellow dog, lying on his side, his black lips slack with sleep. I don't think I could have loved him or wanted to protect him more than right then.

"Lydia, it's all right," Aunt Brat said. "This woman is *not* going to come for Guff."

"Yeah. She's bluffing," Elloroy added. He flapped a large paddle hand.

Meanwhile, Eileen looked up the last call to my phone.

"I already blocked her," I said.

"Good work," Eileen said. She put the number into her own phone.

"You're not going to call her, are you?"

"Nope. But I'm going to report her. The rescue group will want to know. They'll tell the authorities."

"As a precaution, yes," said Aunt Brat, "because she threatened—"

"Bluffed," mumbled Elloroy.

"—and I am sorry that happened," Aunt Brat finished her sentence. "But I promise you, I am not worried about this."

"Me neither," said Eileen.

"Well, I am!" I could not keep the squeak out of my voice. "What if she means it? What if she tries to take him? What if Elloroy is here, all alone, when she comes? She could take the dog—"

"Over my dead body!" It was the loudest thing I'd ever heard Elloroy say. He pressed the heels of his long flat hands against the edge of the table until his elbows straightened and his old bones cracked. He spoke again, much more quietly. "Nobody takes the dog. Not as long as I'm still breathing."

61

A Handful of Dirt

Elloroy had an appointment with his doctor. Aunt Brat and Eileen both wanted to go with him.

"Elloroy, are you all right?" I asked.

"Routine visit," he said. "They just like to have a look at me. See if they can figure out why I'm robust when I ought to be—"

"Dead," we said.

So I was alone with the dogs that afternoon, still playing nurse to Guffer. I'd just gotten him settled on his sleeping mat after a trip outdoors. Soonie had curled up onto the couch. Her long nose tucked into the cushion, she was ready for a good nap too. Outside the window a big SUV was rolling up. I knew all the cars and vans and pickups that ever came climbing up Pinnacle Hill. But I didn't know this one, and neither would the other great watcher of arrivals: Guffer.

He would want to greet, bark, jump, and be slinky. It was one of our big worries while he was recovering. But right now his eyes were closed and he was breathing steadily. So I slipped back outside to intercept our visitor.

The car had stopped in front of the house. The low afternoon sun blanked out the windshield. I squinted. We had ourselves a stranger on Pinnacle Hill. Who could this be? Suddenly, I felt like a lightning bolt had speared me.

It was Cici Hoover.

Had to be. She'd said she was coming and now she was here. No bluffing. I was alone. My heart throbbed against my ribs.

No way, I thought. *No way will I let her touch a single blond whisker on my dog.*

Over my dead body. . . .

I squatted down and grabbed up a handful of dirt. I made myself tall.

The car door opened. I watched Cici extend one leg out. Long khaki pants. Not what I expected somehow. A head and shoulders emerged behind the open car door. She stepped into view. Cici Hoover was—

Wait . . . this is a man. . . .

He was tall and thin. Reddish-brown hair and beard. He was looking right at me. He took a few steps forward.

"Lydia?"

"Yes."

No! . . . Don't answer! . . .

"Wow. It's really you?" His voice was warm as a cup of cocoa. A soft smile pressed his beard into folds up both cheeks. I squeezed my handful of dirt and stone. He came forward, head on a tilt. He said, "S-sorry. I know this is a surprise. Do you know who I am?"

I did.

"You're Kemp," I said. "Aren't you?"

Without "Bratches" attached to the beginning, his name didn't sound so much like my own. Amazing that I should be thinking about that while my long-gone father came closer.

"Gosh," he said. He closed his eyes and opened them again—wider. He shook his head. "I can't believe it's you."

"Well, I'm not really me," I said. "Not the same me as . . ." I waited. What should I say? "You don't really know this me."

He dropped his chin. He nodded. "I guess that's fair," he said.

"Well. Seven years," I said with a shrug. "More than

367

half my life. Why would I be the same—" I stopped. He should be talking. He was the one who'd come here—and shouldn't have.

"I expect you to be hurt. I know I failed. I'm ashamed of it. Ashamed of leaving you and your mom."

"She's gone," I said. "But you know that."

"Yes," he said. "I was sorry. She lived a long time consid—"

"Not really," I said, though I knew what he meant. "That's why I live here now." I swept my fist backward to point out the farm. A few grains of dirt escaped through my fingers. "I'm here with her sister. My aunt Brat. Well, I'm home alone right now, but . . ."

Don't tell him that. . . .

"Everyone will be back soon. In a few minutes," I lied. "The whole family," I added. "W-was there something you wanted?"

Oh, why ask him that? . . .

"I wanted this," he said. "To see you. Check on you."

"Why? I mean, why find me now?"

"Lydia, I've always known where you were. But then I heard that your mom had passed—"

"*Died*," I said. "Passing is for the salt and the pepper."

And the peas, if you like them. . . .

He breathed a laugh—a sad and gentle one. "Right.

That sounds like Holly. Sounds like your mom. When I heard, I sent a card to you at the old address."

She died . . . and you sent a card. . . .

"But it came back." He scrunched his brow. "You must have been up and out of there quickly."

"Yes. Aunt Brat came for me. Immediately," I said. "We didn't leave a forwarding address form. Not for me." I avoided his eyes.

"Right," he said flatly. "Well, I saw that the place had been sold. It took a while for me to find you. I had to make sure you weren't alone—"

"I'm not. Like I said, Aunt Brat stepped up—along with her family. There is Eileen and Elloroy." It felt good to say their names—like a blanket around my shoulders. "Also, I have friends here now and—" The truthfulness of everything I was saying struck me. "The thing I don't have is Mom. I miss her. I miss being her daughter. . . ."

I stopped myself yet again. Why was I sharing this with him? "But it's all been getting better," I said. That was true too. I shrugged. "Turns out I'm pretty strong," I told him.

"Yes," he said slowly. "And I'm sorry . . . sorry that I'm probably not the parent you got that from. Holly's—your mom's health issues, they broke me."

"I know," I said. I dropped my little ball of dirt and scuffed it into the gravel with one foot. "So, what about you, anyway?" I asked. (If we covered that, then maybe he could be on his way.)

Kemp told me how much better he'd done. Like, since leaving Mom and me, though of course he didn't say it like that. He had started a computer service business. He had six employees now, four vans. He'd married. They had two girls, six and eight years old.

"You have an eight-year-old?" The words slipped across my lips.

"Yeah," he said, and then again, "Yeah."

Math . . . it can make your blood boil. . . .

"You traveled a long way to come here," I said.

He shrugged. "Not so long."

"Well, maybe I don't mean the miles." I tried to think what Mom might say, because she was nicer than I was— kinder. "But your soul," I said, "what a journey that must have been."

He fixed his gaze on me. "It's been bittersweet," he said. "I mean to be better than I am." He blinked. I thought his eyes twinkled then, at me, or *for* me. But what did I know of the looks that Kemp gave?

I wanted him to get back in his car now and drive away. I asked myself, *Is that right? Should I be more interested in him?*

I looked at Kemp. I saw a sorry man. A father. But not mine, except for biology. But he was also a human being, reaching out. That had to be Mom, swimming through my mind and telling me to be human back to him—if I could.

"Hey. Do you remember the raisin boxes?" I asked.

He laughed and nodded. "I think about that all the time," he said. "You liked those better than toys."

"Because I thought that was Mom's picture on every box."

"You were a good daughter to her, Lydia."

"That was easy," I said. I waited, thinking about the morning he'd left—how it'd seemed to me that all my Sun-Maids were watching him go. Did he remember that? Maybe I should not have mentioned them. I gave a little cough. "Well, I have responsibilities." I poked my thumb back behind me. "We have a dog, and he's been through a lot recently. He needs me."

"I understand," he said. "And you know where I am if you need me. For anything." He was looking at me intently. "Same address. For years now."

I knew that he meant I could get his address off the envelopes. I think we both knew that I wouldn't.

I didn't answer. I couldn't even make my head nod. I turned and walked to the door and went inside. I stood back from the window and watched. He got back in his car and fiddled with his phone, maybe set his maps. Then he was gone—just like he had been for seven years.

I felt still inside. I knew why: it was because the best

thing about Kemp showing up was that he wasn't Cici Hoover.

If she'd come here thinking she could take Guffer away, I would have flung my fistful of dirt at her. I'd have kicked her in the shins. I would've screamed at the top of my lungs from Pinnacle Hill.

But it was only Kemp, I thought. *Only Kemp.*

I got down onto the floor close beside Guffer and tucked my nose into the golden fur at the back of his neck. "Oh, Guff," I said, though he was out cold. "It is so complicated to be a human. . . ."

His eye opened slightly in his sleep. The inner lid stretched over the inside corner, the way they sometimes do. I laid my hand over the shaved patch and the scar on his back. How amazing; he'd been *opened*. The not-right part inside of him had been fixed. So many of us needed something fixed. "But it isn't always possible," I whispered. I was careful not to send a ticklish breath into his ear. I lay on my back, looking up at the ceiling, my side snugged up against the dog.

"So glad," I whispered. "Glad you're here. Glad I'm here."

62

Remembering the Nugget

As soon as Aunt Brat, Eileen, and Elloroy got home I told them.

"You'll never believe it. Kemp was here."

"What?" said Eileen.

"Who?" said Elloroy.

Aunt Brat turned to face me. "Kemp? Really? Whoa! Did you know he was coming?"

"No! Aunt Brat! I would never keep that from you."

"Good to know," she said. She sounded like she was trying hard to be chill. "So, what was the nature of his visit?"

"Really, Brat? The nature?" said Eileen. She bobbled her head.

"He said all he wanted was to check on me. He knew about Mom. He told me he has a wife and kids, and a good job and a good life."

"Pfft! Barf!" Eileen coughed. Elloroy patted her on the back and wanted to know if she was all right.

We ended up laughing about that, which was good. We started making dinner together, and talk of Kemp got lost in a yeasty batch of pizza dough and toppings.

But later Aunt Brat sat on the couch with me. We'd been doing this—Eileen too—because all of us wanted to sit near Guffer and Soonie. The goddess memoir was pretty public now. I often sat with a collage across my lap while I wrote. My adults and I had talked about Mom more and more.

"So, about Kemp's visit," my aunt said, "you seem all right. Are you?"

"I think I am," I said. "Isn't that weird?"

"Not necessarily. But if you feel there's anything to sort out, I'm here."

"Thanks, Aunt Brat. But I think I get it," I said. "It would've been hard for me if I thought I needed him. But I don't, and I know that in my bones." I drew my fingers over the surface of a collage; I traced the head of the goddess. "I can't remember exactly what she said, but Mom left me some little—I don't know—a nugget?" I smiled at

374

Aunt Brat. She nodded back. "It was about me not having to take care of his soul. Ever. You know? She said even if I love him again someday, I shouldn't feel like I need to try to fix whatever that thing was that let him leave us.

"Oh, my goodness. Your mom—my little sister—was something else," Aunt Brat said, and she dabbed at her eyes. "That is a very useful nugget."

63

The Letter I Didn't Know I'd Write

I kept working on the goddesses. I kept writing and putting thoughts out there, like sending love letters to Mom.

Well, what a twist, and what a surprise, when one day in May, the blank page in front of me turned into a letter to Kemp. Ever since his visit, I'd been having little "dialogue moments" with him inside my head. There were some things I might have said, if I'd been prepared for that reunion, but other things I could know to say only because of it happening just the way it had.

I wrote: "Dear Kemp."

Then I struck through it because I wasn't sure he was dear. I started again.

~~Dear Kemp,~~

Hello Kemp,

~~I'm sorry if~~ I might have seemed very rude the day you came to Chelmsford. ~~I apologize for~~ I won't apologize. I'll just say that I was afraid. Not OF you but ABOUT you, if that makes sense. I wasn't sure what you wanted. Maybe I still don't know why you came.

There is something I want to tell you. You might ~~remember~~ not know about the goddesses. They are art pieces. Mom made them ~~sometimes~~ with me. I kept them all, and now they hold our story. Memories. They've also helped me sort out ~~all the feelings~~ life.

There is a Goddess of Gratitude. She's a hard worker. I was looking at her after you left. I realized I have two things ~~that I should~~ to thank you for. First, thank you for the money you sent over the last seven years. ~~I had weird feelings I hadn't used it and~~ I admit that I didn't open all of most of your cards. Not when they came. I didn't know how to use your money. I could not understand what kind of gift it was, so I couldn't spend it. But then one of our dogs here needed an expensive operation. It's a dog that I love ~~in a deep and wild way that I also don't understand~~. That's when I knew what the money was for. The operation worked. He is doing well. I'm grateful. To you.

377

The second thing isn't simple to explain but I'll try. When you showed up here I suddenly felt like there was something I could lose. That something is belonging. I saw you and I felt ~~in a whole new way~~, how much I belong here with ~~Mom's sister~~ Aunt Brat and her people. They are my people now too.

The way I see it, I still have seven or eight years to become an adult. I hope I get to go to college ~~before I'm done~~. But what I am saying is that this is the place and these are the people who ~~will grow~~ are growing me now, and they are the ones I see myself coming home to even after I'm grown. Thank you for coming here so that I would know that. Thank you for making me sure. ~~I didn't even know myself how much~~

~~Sincerely~~

~~Wishing you the best~~

~~Regards,~~

Love,

Lydia

I wrote the whole thing over, clean. I read it back to myself—but only once. I took the letter down the hill, walking slowly, while my yellow dog limped along close by my side. I shut the letter into the box and patted the door with my hand. "Take it away, Jaycinda," I whispered.

64

Chelmsford, Night to Morning

June is the time of the Dyad Moon.

. . . two parts . . . like mother and child . . .

I, Lydia Bratches-Kemp, did a terrible thing to my aunt.

I wrote:

> Don't worry!
> At the Bigelow River with friends.
> See you in the morning.
> I love you.

I'm sure I was the only eighth grader to leave a note. But I had to; my adults were inexperienced.

I slipped out of my bedroom window and crossed to the edge of the flattish roof. There, I dangled myself down until my feet met Moss Capperow's shoulders. He grabbed my hands and I jumped to the ground. You might have thought we'd practiced. But we hadn't.

I walked beside Moss under the early June moon.

At Soldier's Chimney we met Raya and Sari, who squeezed my arm. (She always did.) "Lydia! You made it!" she cried. "We weren't sure you'd come. . . ."

But here I am. . . .

Our class gathered—not a single one missing. Then we—the little jumping horses of Chelmsford—hiked along the night-quiet road to the Bigelow River and to the very spot where we'd sent the fingerling trout home.

I spent the night in the forest with my friends.

We sat shoulder to shoulder around a campfire, roasting marshmallows or just holding sticks to the flames until they caught.

They told stories. (I listened.) We hummed and sang, then laughed at our singing. All night long these twelve watched out for one another—and for me. I'd seen it all semester.

In the middle of the night, Moss and I went hunting for firewood. We headed up a trail that wound above our little camp.

"Good thing we've got the moonlight," I said, reaching down for a twig. Smiling, of course, Moss agreed.

We hit the jackpot—a fallen limb with lots of dry branches. We set to cracking them into pieces under our feet. We began to gather it up. I reached for a stick; Moss chose the same one. His fingers curled around mine. I looked into his face—so impossibly close—

I could kiss you, Moss Capperow. . . .

At sunrise, we hiked out to the road—heavy feet carrying tired bodies. I didn't expect to see the cluster of parents waiting with their steaming coffee mugs, and I didn't expect to see Aunt Brat. But there she was, talking with the other parents. She caught me with her narrowed eyes.

"Good morning," she said.

"Morning," I echoed. She scooped an arm over my shoulder. I hugged her waist. We bumped hips on the way to the car.

"How did you know where to come?" I asked.

"Another parent took pity and tipped me off."

"Oh . . . and did you see my note?" I asked.

"Yes. Thank you."

"Welcome," I said.

"You're not off the hook," she promised.

The boxy car jiggled us up to Pinnacle Hill, and when

I walked in the door everything I loved the most was waiting for me.

"Why, Lyd-jah!" cried Eileen. "Love those twigs in your hair." She wrapped me in a hug, then passed me to Elloroy. Soonie stood by, blinking, and Guffer—my Guffer—wove through my legs and wagged so hard he tottered. Then he lifted his chin and sang me a long, long dog-song.

"So?" said Eileen. "What did we do all night by the big Bigelow?"

"Hmm . . ." I yawned. I felt giggly and goofy. "Well, we built a campfire, toasted marshmallows. We sang, really badly, and I kissed a boy."

"You what?" Aunt Brat's eyes popped open.

"Not very well." I shrugged. "But then he kissed me back. And he was better at it."

"Huh-haw!" said Eileen.

Elloroy's jaw dropped into his old turtle grin. He chuckled.

"Wait, wait!" cried Aunt Brat. "There was kissing?"

"Yeah," I said. "I'm surprised, too. . . ." I headed for the stairs.

Up in the hall I hesitated—stood smoothing my hands down Mom's long sweater.

January to June . . . it was time. . . .

I shuffled into the bathroom, pulled back the curtain on the tub. I ran the cold water with a capful of shampoo. I slid the sweater off my shoulders and laid it into the water. I sank it and swished it. A thin cloud of gray floated into the suds. I left the sweater to soak.

In my room, I collapsed on the bed. I closed my eyes, but Aunt Brat swept in—not done with me yet.

"I'm so tired," I groaned.

"I'm not surprised." She set her hands on her hips, attempted a scowl. "Happens to those who stay up all night."

"I'm sorry," I said.

"You should be. Not a lot of fun, finding your bed empty," she said.

"But you knew. You said someone told you."

"Yes, Raya's mom called." Aunt Brat's voice softened. "I just didn't think you'd go."

"Yah. . . ." A yawn got away from me. "Me either."

Aunt Brat sat down on the bed beside me. She pulled her legs up under her long skirt and tucked her fist below her chin. Suddenly, her eyes were shining, and she grinned. "I'm kind of glad you went," she whispered.

"Aunt Brat. . . ." I laughed such a tired laugh.

"So . . . there was a little romance, huh?"

"Yeah . . . but that's over. Because we're so small.

Chelmsford, I mean. Our class can't have a couple. That would leave the others out."

"Oh . . . I see. Well, was it fun? Being out all night?"

I started giggling. "Aunt Brat, you're doing this wrong."

"Am I?"

"You're supposed to stay mad. Just a little longer."

"Oh. I suppose there should be consequences for an unsanctioned overnight escapade."

"Yeah . . . you have to ground me. For a week, I think. Raya's mom can tell you. . . ." I sighed a sleepy sigh.

"Hmm. A town-wide grounding is it, then?"

"Every eighth grader," I said. I rubbed my eyes. "Because we all went. Together."

"That's rather sweet, isn't it?" Then she sighed. "Oh, but high school's coming. Lydia, please don't make it too awful for me, will you?"

"Hmm . . . ," I said. "I can't promise."

"Lydia!"

"Hey, it'll all be new for me, too," I mumbled. My eyelids felt like weights now. I let go a yawn that nearly split my jaw. "It was good of you to take me in, Aunt Brat."

"I wanted to, Lyddie. With all that I am."

"I believe you," I said. "But I know that I changed everything. You *all* got me. Eileen got me. Elloroy got me. Even the dogs got me."

"And nobody flinched," she said. "They came right on board. Do you want to know what Eileen said to me the night you arrived?"

I nodded. I fought to stay awake.

"We were out by the car, getting the last of your boxes . . ."

And I was out on the flattish roof. . . .

". . . and Eileen said she knew now what people meant when they told stories about bringing home their new babies, and how they instantly felt like a family. Eileen told me, 'I love her already.'"

"I love her back," I said. "And I love you. And Elloroy too. I love home. . . ."

I felt the old sleeping bag being pulled up around my shoulders.

I heard a whisper—a voice so much like Mom's. "Sweet dreams, Lyddie. . . ."

Sweet dreams, goddesses. . . .

Acknowledgments

Katherine Tegen, my wise editor, thank you for your faith and patience while I slow cook my stories, and thanks to my tireless publishing family at Katherine Tegen Books and HarperCollins Children's Books for the hours of love and support you've poured into our books. I am grateful to you all every, every, every day!

Miriam Altshuler, my agent, thanks for shining the way you always do—positive and full of good ideas—and thanks to everyone at DeFiore and Company.

Doe Boyle, Leslie Bulion, Mary-Kelly Busch, Lorraine Belby Jay, Kay Kudlinski, Judy Theise, and Nancy Elizabeth Wallace, thank you with all my heart for helping me sort the gems from the junk on project after project. You are a group of gosh-darn goddesses, you are!

Ali Benjamin, Molly Burnham, Jackie Davies, Lita Judge, and Grace Lin, thanks for your open hearts and sage advice; I cherish our circle.

Speaking of circles, thank you to the kidlit community for all sorts of kindness and bolstering. This is not all of you by any stretch, but most recently, I'm grateful to Kirby Larson, Barbara O'Connor, Cammie McGovern, Corey Ann Haydu, Tricia Springstubb, Padma Venkatraman, Gary Schmidt, and Lynda Mullaly Hunt for their kind words, and to Rob Buyea who sings my praises everywhere he goes. I feel honored to know you.

Kimberly Newton Fusco, thank you for sharing in the writer's journey with me. It means everything to me knowing that you will meet me somewhere in time again and again.

Thank you, Nichole Cousins, for so willingly accepting our request for a reader, and for your graceful response to this work.

Julie McLaughlin, first impressions are crucial! Thank you for creating the gorgeous cover art that so aptly portrays the mood of this story.

Sandi Shelton, my very heart thanks you for the many times you have lifted it up with your love, friendship, and good cheer. (Wish we'd thought to count up all the hours of plotting we have done in your car—world record!) Love you.

Nancy Hall, darn, I miss you! Our long, long friendship survives the miles that separate us now, and your quips (which I've been stealing for years) remain ever-fresh in my ear. Sending you love.

Jan and Mark, Elly and Dan, love you guys. Thank you for your friendship over these many happy years, and for contributing to this book in a way that could only have come from your incredible family.

Members of my family, you seem to pour more support my way with each book! Jonathan, I have always felt you cheering for me and loving me. Sam and Kristy, Marley and Ian, I couldn't do this work without you to inspire me and offer "tips on how to be hip." Mom and Dad (my favorite octogenarians), my siblings, cousins and aunts and uncles, nieces, nephews, and in-laws, thank you for your genuine interest in this little thing I do. You all amaze me with your love.

My very special thanks to the staff and students at Eastford Elementary School, especially to the graduating eighth grade class of 2019 and Denise Chambers, for opening their hearts to me.

Thank you, readers! Of this book! And past books!

And even if you just gave one of my books a try! I am so grateful! Special thanks to all the librarians, teachers, parents, and others who make it their work to set just the right books into young people's hands. You are awesome.

Lots of love and extra treats go to my beloved dogs who are vital to my writing life: Broomis (the big yellow dog), Atticus, Lola, and Luna. (RIP, my old Soonie girl.)

Finally, to every human who has ever helped an animal in need or given one a loving home, thank you for taking that chance. This story is woven with the threads of your good deeds. I think you know the rewards.

Turn the page to start reading

Aurora

The Letters

When our letters from the school come, we sit together on the deck at the A-frame to read them. Actually, I'll be doing all the reading.

Frenchie sits, spine straight, his freckled face tilted up. He works his fingers along the strap of the needlepoint purse he carries. In his other hand he holds his envelope. He squints and blinks at the breaks of the sun coming through the pines.

"Any birds up there?" I ask.

He doesn't answer. He never does. Not with words. But he arches his back a little.

"I saw your pine warbler early this morning," I tell him. The mention of birds is my best shot at getting his

1

attention. But it doesn't always work. It's possible I will never figure out why. But that's okay by me.

I tear into the envelope addressed to me: Aurora Pauline Petrequin.

I shake the folds out of my letter as fast as I can. "Come on, Frenchie. Open yours too!" I say. He might not get how important these letters are. But I know, our entire sixth-grade destinies are typed inside.

"Okay . . . we're about to find out who our next teacher is," I tell him. I drum the soles of my sneakers on the deck boards.

"Can you feel that? That's suspense," I say. "Here we go!" I take a huge breath and hold it while I scan the page. It takes forever to zero in, but then . . .

"Ms. Beccia!" I shout. "Yes! We're in Ms. Beccia's class! Whew!" I fan myself with my letter, then go limp where I sit. Here's what I know: Ms. Beccia is brand-new. This is a small town and the only other sixth-grade teacher is Mrs. Hillsbeck. She's been around forever, and she's *spoken to me* on the playground during recess a good number of times. Her reasons for that have all been *unreasonable*: dangerous climbing on the climber, running too close to others, handling dirt, clogging the drinking fountain with a pebble and turning it into a sprinkler, which everyone loved. Except Mrs. Hillsbeck. She got soaked trying to make it stop. She got angry too. That's some pretty bad history. There was a better place for me to spend sixth grade.

2

"Ms. Beccia. Yes!" I sit upright again and turn toward Frenchie. "Can I open yours now?" He is holding his envelope so lightly it's easy to take it from him.

I pick the paper triangle open. No need to drum my feet. The suspense is over. His letter will look like mine, right down to the Ms. Beccia part. "It's so great getting the new teacher," I say. "I love a fresh start."

I unfold the page, which is addressed to Nathan French Livernois. Makes me snort because nobody ever calls him Nathan. I clear my throat.

"Okay." I work my way down the page. What I see makes me quiet. (I am not a quiet girl.) I reread it. I look at Frenchie. He's still staring up into the branches.

"What the heck?" I whisper. I let the letter fall into my lap. Then I yell, "What the heck! How's that going to work?" I jump to my feet and run in through the open door of the A-frame calling, "Mom! Pop! Gracia! There's a mess-up of all mess-ups here! Frenchie and I got put in different classes!"

Aurora

The First Time We Met Jewell Laramie
and I Tried to Play Softball

Mom and Pop are as surprised as I am about Frenchie being in one sixth-grade classroom and me being in the other. Pop even called the school to make sure the assignments are right. (They are.) They all tell me it will work out fine. Frenchie and I will still take the bus together. We'll see each other at lunch and on the playground.

Mom says things like: "Remember, Aurora, there was a time before Frenchie lived here and you survived just fine."

I say things like: "Yeah! That was three years ago! I'm not used to that anymore! And what about Frenchie? Can we agree that there is a little bit more to this than just two

4

friends getting separated? Can we?"

I remember the summer before Frenchie and Gracia came. That was the year I tried playing softball, which I only did because the coach came to our house to recruit me. And it was a chance to play *something* with other kids. I already knew I had a darn-good throwing arm. That comes from me being a rock hound.

I don't have much of a collection. Yet. I am particular. I'm searching for tourmaline. Parts of Maine offer great gem hunting. I'd give up sour pickles for a month to go digging for minerals over in Oxford or Androscoggin. That's where the old mica mines are, and the really cool pegmatites. Those are veins of igneous rock, and that's where you find the good stuff like beryl, topaz, *and* tourmaline.

Around home, I pick up rocks all the time. They're mostly granite, and I have collected enough of that. I throw them far as I can so I don't refind them. Why let a rock disappoint you twice? Pop says the lack of tourmaline in our part of Maine (fact) could be my ticket to the majors (joke). He says my arm gets stronger every time I *don't* find a piece of the good stuff, which is, so far, all the time. I like choosing targets. Mostly boulders so I don't hurt the trees—or anything else. Underhand, overhand, I've got good aim, and I can put enough speed on a rock to make it zing.

Our town has a girls' softball league, and Coach Jewell

Laramie wants every girl in town to play. That's why she came to see me. She thought we were new here because the A-frame was newly finished. The door was open because of the stinky new paint smell, and because Mom and Pop were bringing in the kitchen cupboards that day. Jewell called hello. Then she walked right in and thunked a hunk of something frozen all wrapped in plastic on our kitchen table.

"Hey, neighbors! I'm Jewell Laramie." She tipped her cap, which looked to be trapping a pouf of pale golden hair.

"I'm Aurora. Aurora Pauline Petrequin," I told her.

"Ah! Just the girl I'm looking for," said Jewell.

That was an even bigger surprise than seeing her sweep into our new house. I waited while Mom and Pop introduced themselves—Rene and Ed—and pronounced our last name twice over.

"Brought you folks some dinner!" Jewell nodded toward the hunk in the bag. "Venison tenderloin," she added.

"Oh, we don't eat that," I said. "That's deer meat. Deer are mammals. We don't eat mammals."

Jewell looked at Mom and Pop. "Oh. Tells it like it is, does she?" She cocked her head in my direction.

"She does," said Mom, and Pop nodded.

"If it makes you feel any different, there was no suffering. I took this deer during bow season. Had a clean, double-lung shot. The only shot I'll take."

Clean, double-lung shot.

How can that *not* cause suffering? I looked at the package on our table and thought about pointing out that it was dead.

"We appreciate the gesture," Pop said.

"Doesn't offend me," Jewell said, "and I hope I haven't offended you."

"You haven't, and we don't mean to be ungracious," Pop explained.

"But we still don't eat that," I repeated. "Oh. That sounds ungracious, doesn't it?"

"A little bit," Mom said.

I looked at Jewell. "I blurt things. I do that a lot," I told her.

"Nothing wrong with honesty. I like it," Jewell said. "Tell me, what do you eat?"

"We say feather, fin, and flora," Pop told her. "Local dairy and a little seafood."

"Yut, yut . . ." (Some Mainers will say *yut* instead of *yes*.) Jewell Laramie nodded like she was really paying attention. So when she started to tell us all about her girls' softball league, I listened to her. She practically begged me to come play.

"All levels are welcome, and U-eight is all about learning the game and having a good time," she said. "Think about it, Aurora. I bet there's an athlete in you." She picked up her frozen deer meat, held it under her arm, and gave it a pat. "You folks should know . . . hunters are a fact of life in Maine."

"Acknowledged," said Pop. "We aren't new to Maine."

"Yeah, I've been here all my life," I said.

"And I've been here half of mine," Pop added.

"And about a third for me," Mom said. "We're not even new to town. Just new to this spot."

"Yeah, we moved out of our house on the bay, and now we rent it out to folks from away," I said. (If you are from away, it means you don't live in Maine; you are a visitor.) "And maybe you saw that little house right next door here?" I pointed. "We're going to rent that one out too."

"Gotcha," said Jewell, and she put up her thumb, which had one of those purple nails on it. Like she'd whacked it with a hammer or pinched it in a wood splitter, probably months before. There's something about a purple thumb like that—always makes me like the person who's got it. Enough to go try playing ball.

But, sheeshy-sheesh! That game is full of rules, and you stand around that diamond for hours and nothing happens. Ugh. Then if someone finally does hit a ball and you decide to run across the diamond to stop it, your own teammate by the name of Darleen Dombroski could decide to *cry* because you got in her way on the play. And stepped on her ankle. And gave it an accidental grinding. Never mind you made a perfect throw to first base and

8

got the hitter out—*which I did*. That night Darleen got her mother to call my mother. (Darleen's mother has been calling my mother since we were in kindergarten.) This time, Mrs. Dombroski told Mom that there are *positions* in softball, and that maybe she could help her daughter (me) understand that so no one else would get hurt.

Well, Coach Jewell tried playing me everywhere. Not like a punishment. She tries everyone everywhere. She rotated me to the outfield, where there was *less than nothing* to do—except handstands. I pulled my glove off and kicked my feet into the air. I tried cartwheels next, and I figured out the cool trick of pulling up grass on the way over. Then throwing it like confetti.

Coach Jewell leaned out of the dugout, calling, "Aurora! Aurora P.! No gymnastics out there! Be ready! A hit could come your way."

"Yeah, I won't hold my breath about that," I called back. "I could take a nap out here." I faked a yawn, but it turned into a real one—noisy too. Some of my teammates giggled. They snorted and covered their faces with their gloves. "I could grow a year older waiting out here . . . am I nine yet? Am I ten?"

But before the game was over, my teammates, who were also my classmates at school, started to whisper that I was "not funny" and "so annoying." They were tired of me, and I was tired of softball.

Jewell Laramie came to the house the next day.

She brought us a brook trout. She set it down and said, "Feather, fin, and flora, correct? Well, here's some *fin*!" Then she showed me how the game of softball works by putting all our mugs and the salt and pepper shakers on the table in a diamond. She said *teamwork* at least five times. I propped my chin on the table and tried not to interrupt.

Finally, I said, "Coach, I know all that." Because I did. "But it takes way too long for something to happen. I can't stand it. I need more to do!"

Jewell looked me over a second. She nodded and said something nice about me and my raw talent. Mom gave Jewell a bag of apricot muffins. Muffins for brook trout. Like, all good. We're friends. But my days on the softball diamond were done.

I didn't miss it. Plenty of rocks to inspect and throw, and that's what I did pretty much all summer long. On my own. I didn't have my little brother, Cedar, yet, and I was the only kid living on our road. But that was about to change.

More from award-winning author
LESLIE CONNOR

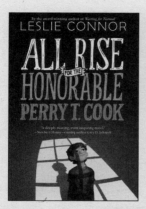

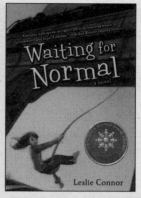

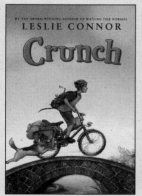